CELESTE

ALSO BY:

Jenn LeBlanc

THE RAKE
AND THE RECLUSE
(BOOK ONE IN THE LORDS OF TIME SERIES)

THE DUKE
AND THE BARON
(BOOK TWO IN THE LORDS OF TIME SERIES)

THE DUKE
AND THE DOMINA
(BOOK THREE IN THE LORDS OF TIME SERIES)

THE SPARE
AND THE HEIR
(BOOK FIVE IN THE LORDS OF TIME SERIES)

Jenn LeBlanc

THE TROUBLE WITH GRACE

BOOK FOUR IN THE LORDS OF TIME SERIES

Dedication

GRACE

my thanks :

RHONDA STAPLETON :
EDITING

JOYCE LAMB :
EDITING

PRODUCTION :

KATI RODRIGUEZ :
ASSISTANT OF ALL THE THINGS
POKÉ WRANGLER

SHELLY DAS :
ASSISTANT ARTISTIC DIRECTOR
SWAG COACH

KIMBERLY DISTEL :
MAKE UP / HAIR
H20 WRANGLER

PRODUCTION INSPIRATION :
BRITNEY

credits:

CELESTE MORAVIA AGATHE ALAIN
Kaleila Jordan
& Kris Branch

QUINTIN JOSEPH WYNTOR
Patrick Rash

THORNE MAGNUS CALDER
MARQUESS OF CANFORD
Steven Dehler

WITH SPECIAL GUEST
LULU DUCHESS OF WARRICK
Shelly Das

*These illustrations are meant to be
a work unto themselves.*

They aren't meant to depict the scenes with perfect accuracy in setting, costuming or design. They're meant to accompany the text and evoke the emotions of the scenes in the same way the words do.

More of a companion than a direct visual translation.

Certainly you will notice discrepancies between the scene and details in the images, but that's the nature of creation, some things don't work visually when they do work with words.

Thank you for understanding and I hope you enjoy this illustrated version of Celeste.

Hugs n' smooches,

Jenn

Epigraph:

LEARN TO...BE WHAT YOU ARE,
AND LEARN TO RESIGN
WITH A GOOD GRACE
ALL THAT YOU ARE NOT.

~Henri Frederic Amiel

PROLOGUE

What I remember from that day I don't actually remember, because I'm not a reliable witness to my own history. I have been, and continue to be, treated for a mental illness that never existed.

Or perhaps it did.

It depends upon how I feel in any given moment. Some days I fight reality, and some days I don't. Some days I believe in my memories, other days I believe in theirs.

What I remember from before that day is the warmth of a mother. Something I haven't felt since, and don't expect to ever feel again. I feel the loss of that like a weight upon my shoulders.

What I remember from that day is pain, because I was hurt. I don't remember how. I only know I was chasing…something.

What I remember from that day is heartbreak, because I lost everything I knew to be true.

What I remember from that day is waking up in the arms of the stranger who became my father. Or perhaps he already was, and I did deserve to be locked away.

Regardless, what I remember from that day…are the two boys who came to my aid. One dark, one light.

An angel and a devil.

What I remember from that day is a name…And no matter how I fight that memory, the name never fades. It has taken up residence in my soul and is whispered with every beat of my heart.

Quinn.

Calder

Calder worked the room as best he could in his current mood. He watched as his cousins Warrick and Roxleigh—both large, dark, and brooding—spoke. Their wives tittered in the corner, or whatever it was wives did in ballroom corners. He had to admit these wives didn't seem much like the wives of society at large, so tittering was probably beneath them.

Calder had always known that the women of his family, Trumbull women, were different—and this fact included the women who married in. Though he didn't carry the name, his mother was absolutely a Trumbull to the core, and so would be his own wife. Should he ever find her. Should he ever wish to. Should he ever deign to try…and he should wish to try. For his family, for his titles, for his queen and country.

But for himself? There was only one person he'd ever wanted, and that person—*no*, he chided himself. Calder halted the consideration before his mind wandered entirely too far. *Not tonight.*

"Rox," he said as he approached his cousin. The heir of the heir, his cousin carried his grandfather's title and the family name on his broad shoulders.

"Calder." Roxleigh took his hand and shook it.

"Gray," Calder said to Warrick and shook his hand as well. "Things are well?" he asked as he cut a glance to Gray's new wife, Lulu, across the room. She was stunning. Bright auburn hair, not quite red, strong vivid eyes that held more knowledge than anyone could possibly know, and enough power to handle his cousin Gray, the darkest of them all.

"As can be," he replied, and Calder nodded.

When he heard the calm strains of a waltz begin, Calder closed his eyes and edged himself away from the group and into the shadows, watching as the only person he truly wanted took the hand of another and went to the floor.

They held each other as was proper, swinging through the corners—her dainty hands on his powerful shoulders, his strong arms encasing her delicate frame, her sweet smile beaming up at his much larger and more serious countenance…but the hand between her shoulder blades fisted instead of spreading along the edge of her spine, and Calder saw how his knees stiffened when she accidentally swayed a bit too close to him, and he wondered at that. Considered it, even.

Calder turned his attention to her, the Lady Alain. Her long, dark hair; her simple, perfect, trained touch; those brilliant, forest-green eyes that caught the light from the chandeliers and shared it. She was stunning, just what any man would want in a mistress, some a wife—even with her circumstance. She would make a good Trumbull wife, that one. She was stronger than most in countenance and will. She was also opinionated—*God forbid*—and smart, though she hid those things quite well, as was proper. This sweet, lovely, intelligent woman who should marry his cousin. Who *could* marry his cousin. Who would most likely marry his cousin Quinn.

Quinn had danced with other women. Quinn had done much more than that with other women. But it was this woman who crawled under Calder's skin like a cat attempting to snuggle with its claws at the ready. At least, that was how he perceived it. It was unwelcome to him this want to watch her, to migrate toward her, to figure her out. He didn't like it, not a whit.

Calder realized—rather suddenly—that he had a problem. He didn't want to admit it, but his blood rushed as he thought about Quinn, and it refused to slow. He'd hoped that time and distance would soften the feelings he had, but they hadn't. If anything, they made his feelings more powerful, his want more potent.

Calder looked back to her, swaying through the corners in his arms. He wanted everything *she* had. He wanted to taste her mouth, hoping…*hoping* it would taste of him. He wanted to drown in the scent of her, the feel of her, the taste of her, if only to discover what it was about her that Quinn seemed to want, perhaps not so very much, but at least some. Calder wanted to kiss

the back of her hand, knowing it had only just grasped those shoulders he wanted to grasp for himself. Though he imagined putting marks on them while doing something perhaps not so very gentlemanly.

He closed his eyes and rubbed his temples. He had to get out of here. He wanted Quinn, but even more, he wanted *her* to stop touching him. He wanted to take her and keep her like a bug under a glass. Maybe, just maybe, if he had her, he could figure out what it was he needed to do to get Quinn away from her and back to him. If he had her the way a husband would have a wife. If he had her the way Quinn would have her. And should they marry, Quinn *would* have her.

Calder felt his blood rise, his breathing heavy in his lungs, his fingers sensitive from want of touch, his senses heightened from want of discovery. Perhaps that was it. Maybe, just possibly, if he got to know *her* better, he could figure out what it was that Quinn wanted in her so very much, and he could prove once and for all that *he, too*, could give Quinn those things.

But of course he couldn't. There were quite a few things that Calder could never give Quinn. A legitimate heir, for one—and that worked both ways, even though Calder had a younger brother he would happily abdicate to.

Calder had to sidestep when Warrick nudged his shoulder, stumbling then catching himself on the wall to his left as he steadied his breath and his nerves.

"What's got you tonight?" Warrick asked as he inspected him.

Now he was the bug, and he didn't particularly care for it. Calder shook his head, straightening and pulling the edges of his sleeves down, the front of his coat, checking the knot at his throat. "Nothing, just…nothing," he said as he stared at the ground, wishing he'd left sooner. Wishing he was away from here and the hell he'd just put himself into.

"I can't pretend to know the extent of what it is you continue to run from, Calder, but at some point you will have to stop and face it."

That thought made Calder shudder, but he was much too exhausted. He glanced at the dance floor, then turned back to Warrick. "And how is your lovely wife?" Calder asked as he tried to sway the conversation to a safer place.

Warrick cocked his head and his gaze went through Calder as if to assess his next move, and Calder knew he was considering whether to cut him open with words and leave him writhing on the floor at his feet, as only Warrick could. But Warrick's recent marriage had made him softer—impossibly, somehow—and he and his wife were just starting to find their way together as a married couple. Which meant Warrick was preoccupied, and Calder was all the more thankful for that small blessing. Considering the marriage had been contracted for Warrick's eldest brother, now dead, when the bride was but a child, the two of them had much to manage. Truthfully, though, their arranged marriage was the least of their considerations since Lulu wasn't exactly the woman anyone had expected for him to marry.

Warrick's gaze shuttered as though the thought of destroying Calder had never crossed his mind. "Lulu is well. She would like it if you would visit. I think she appreciates your..." He paused to consider, and Calder looked up at him then, thinking he was jesting, only to find Warrick in deep thought. "Humor," he said slowly.

"Was that thought truly so difficult?" Calder asked him.

"Yes."

Calder laughed at that. His cousin was a man of very few words, which meant he was meticulous and specific when he used them.

"What more of her father?" Calder asked.

"You know more of him than we do."

Calder stopped at that. He'd said *we*. Warrick was a *we*. Even Warrick and all of his terrifying proclivities was somehow a *we*. And here Calder was, with no hope of a *we* in his future. "I only meant to ask if he'd come around again since last I was there."

"Actually," Roxleigh cut in, "Warrick and I were just talking about Lulu's father. Warrick mentioned you were there the last time Exeter called on her."

"I was," Calder said. "He wasn't very genial. Point of fact, I don't believe he cares for me terribly," Calder said with a half-hearted grin. Warrick almost smiled. Almost laughed. Almost...but not quite, and almost, for Warrick, was very nearly triumphant. "I believe there may be more girls under contract with him and his people," Calder said.

Roxleigh shook his head, and Calder saw the fire in his eyes as he glanced over to his own Francine. She'd been purchased for marriage with the help of that group of men, but back then none of the cousins was aware it was a group with any sort of structure. That discovery had been accidental.

They'd thought it just a single man and his two friends wishing for things they shouldn't wish for, girls raised in controlled environments, bred for the purpose of marriage as perfectly chaste and virginal brides. Much too chaste, as it happened.

"More girls." Roxleigh's muscles tensed infinitely. It would have been truly unnoticeable to the general crowd, but Warrick obviously noticed and so did Calder.

"Unfortunately, yes, but this is different. These girls aren't being prepared for marriage. My hope is that we can intercept them and return them to their families." Calder said.

"You believe them to be stealing girls now? The families are not complicit?" Roxleigh asked.

"Not since they started trawling in India. With everything else happening there, the focus has shifted from proper wives to…well, to things that shouldn't be discussed in ballrooms," Calder said.

The arrangements were horrific, and Rox had spent the last few years attempting to cease them—which included finding out more about these men, most of whom were peers. The main obstacle, as Calder saw it, was that Her Royal Highness wasn't keen to draw attention to the worst of them while her Diamond Jubilee was approaching. Calder believed the inaction to be rather shortsighted and selfish—not that he would say so. It just meant he had to find a way around that small, black-clad obstacle.

"So do you think they'll bring this mess to England, or will we be able to do something about it before they leave India?" Rox asked.

"I'm yet unsure. I will undoubtedly need to return to India, but not quite yet. I would like to have some more names to follow before I go," Calder said. "In the meantime, you need to watch Exeter. I don't want him trying to complete that scheme with Lulu."

"We've stopped him at most turns, and my hope is he abandoned that scheme," Warrick said.

"I sincerely doubt this," Calder said. "He's just working on a new angle, one which may also bring Lulu down with it. After all, he doesn't seem to have much regard for her beyond the status token she holds."

"What should I do?" Warrick asked.

"Not a damn thing. You take care of Lulu. I'll see to him. As I was saying before, I believe their machinations are back in full swing, regardless of the plot to destroy you and your title," Calder said. Unfortunately, Calder did know the man better than both Warrick and his bride, and Calder didn't care for him. Calder hated this business, but dealing with Exeter would keep his mind from his own miserable situation.

Lulu and Francine made their way around the room to them, two finished confections in a bowl of sugar. He admired them regardless his own inclination. Francine was stunning for more than her dark hair and pale skin. Her smile alone could stop any man in his tracks—it had stopped him.

She and Lulu both wore watered silk and velvet gowns that pinched the waist and bloomed the backside as if they hid a gentleman somewhere beneath there. He bussed their cheeks and the backs of their hands in greeting.

"Gray," was all Lulu said, and Warrick turned to her, his jaw tense.

"We're off," he said as he took Lulu's hand to his arm. Without another word of farewell, he pulled her through the crowd toward the entry. Calder watched after them. His initial concerns for the marriage had waned once he met Lulu and saw how much she'd changed Warrick. Well, his initial concerns had been for Warrick's marriage to Cecilia, but Cecilia wasn't here and Lulu was. That was a stroke of pure luck, or fate, or kismet, or some sort of odd word for perfection and timing.

Francine smiled after them. "They'll be all right," she said quietly, probably noting Calder's own concern. Calder already knew they would be, eventually. He knew how they suited better than most, even Francine. Nobody knew Warrick the way Calder did, except perhaps Lulu.

He nodded. "And you? How are you?" he asked, and Francine smiled that amazing smile, the one that stopped the ballroom and all of its occupants in their tracks with its sheer brilliance and truth. "Good God, you're too happy for my liking," he said.

"I won't apologize," she said quietly.

"Nor would I expect it of you," he replied with a smile.

"May I share a secret with you?" she said as she took his arm and leaned into him, forcing his feet toward the doors to the gardens.

"Of course you may."

"We may have a new Viscount Pembroke," she whispered at his collar.

Calder stopped at that, rattling off Roxleigh's many titles in his head to be sure he had the correct idea. Duke of Roxleigh, Earl of Kelso and Sussex, Viscount Devon, and—he smiled when he came to the last—Pembroke. Calder turned back toward the room of guests to find Roxleigh's gaze bearing down on them. Rox had that viciously possessive look about him that Calder hadn't seen since…he truly had to consider it for a moment, but he hadn't seen it since Francine had been kidnapped by Hepplewort years ago—and he knew then it was true. They were to be parents, Francine and Roxleigh, and it was a beautiful thing. He knew how much Francine wanted someone of her own blood, and Rox, of course, had always wanted sons. Though Calder thought perhaps he should have a few daughters just to ruffle his feathers and his ferocity. Knowing Francine and Rox were starting the next generation filled Calder with a sort of pride in family.

"Well, one thing this family could absolutely use is another baby, a small pink thing for my mother and aunts to goo over so I might be left alone for a time."

Francine laughed, and Calder wasn't sure how the whole of the ballroom didn't just stop and stare at her every time her mouth dropped open. For a woman, she was terrifyingly mesmerizing—and that laugh. God love him, if she hadn't already been in the family, he would have seen to it that she would be somehow.

"Well," he said, "congratulations to you and the monster you've created."

"Are you speaking of the babe or the father?" she asked with a grin, but Calder merely shrugged. Francine laughed again, and Calder was certain the lights of the house pulsed.

He heard a deep, throaty sound behind him and turned. "Speak of the *monster* and he shall appear. Apologies, Roxleigh, did we leave your sight?" he asked.

Roxleigh grunted and took Francine's hand.

"You've regressed to that terrifying recluse nobody wanted anything to do with. Next you'll be pulling her across the floor by the hair," Calder said, and Francine laughed yet again, this time stifling it with her petite, gloved hand.

"He has become a touch possessive again. Use your words, dear. This is just your cousin, *and he knows*," she whispered to Roxleigh dramatically.

Rox's eyes widened, and his gaze shifted to Calder. "Me. A father," was all Rox said, with a note of fascinated wonder.

Calder laughed. "Yes, *you*, and I congratulate you as I did your lovely wife, but you may want to work on the demeanor before the poppet arrives, or you'll frighten the poor thing. Can't have that now, can we?" Calder asked.

Rox smiled and nodded. "Yes, just, I want to be sure she's safe, you know?" he said as he pulled Francine into his side and gazed down at her, his face open and loving as he wondered at her.

Calder nodded because he did know. He remembered when Francine had been kidnapped. He remembered helping Roxleigh's brother, Peregrine, rescue his wife, Lilly, from that same man, and it was that memory that had him determined to stop all the men involved. Calder couldn't imagine loving someone so terribly, only to lose them. To know where they were and not be able to touch them, to take them home and hold them, to love them however they wished to be loved.

"Hello, Devil." That voice. It was low and gravelly and rough and raked through his senses and…perhaps he did know what it was like to love someone so terribly and not be able to touch them.

"Hello, Quintin!" Francine said happily as she embraced him.

"I asked you to stop calling me that, Quinn," Calder said quietly, referring to his childhood moniker. He looked to his gloves, which suddenly seemed much too tight.

"Yes, well, it still seems to suit," Quinn replied as he released Francine and shook Roxleigh's hand.

"Where is Lady Alain?" Calder asked, looking past him and back into the ballroom.

"She's off powdering something or some such. Who knows, really, what women do out of the sight of men?" He paused for what seemed forever, his gaze attempting to meet Calder's and not give way. "You should ask her to dance."

Calder's head swung toward Quinn in astonishment. *I could not have heard that correctly. Why would he…is he teasing? Taunting? What purpose does Quinn have in suggesting this? Why would he—*

"She's a lovely dancer," he said as though he knew Calder's mind had run loose. "And I know you aren't much for marriage at the moment, even as your mother would like to see you attempting to woo a lady. I also happen to know Celeste wouldn't mind you using her to quell talk of you *not* dancing. Unlike the other girls who may expect something from you, she won't," Quinn finished quietly.

What? *Why?* Why would Quinn push a woman at him? Calder was so angry, the entirety of his body froze. He felt a feminine hand on his elbow, and he jerked away quickly before catching himself, because he was suddenly just so *tense*.

Francine inspected him. "Are you quite well?" she asked. "You've gone a bit pale."

Calder swung his head again back toward the ballroom. Lady Alain was still here, probably hiding in some shadow somewhere to avoid the ire of society. He could do it. He could ask her to dance—take her to the floor and smell her hair, hold her spine with his fingertips as though to feel the warmth of her skin where Quinn had only just held her. He could listen to her breathe the way she would have breathed against Quinn, felt those hands clutch his shoulders as they had only recently clutched Quinn's shoulders. He could…he could…crush her like a bug under his shoe. Make a scene of her right in the center of this ballroom.

"Calder?" Francine said, reaching out but not touching him this time.

He darted his gaze to Quinn, but couldn't read anything in those deep-green eyes of his. "I—am not…" He dropped his gaze. "No, I'm not feeling quite myself. If you'll forgive me, I'm for home." He needed to get out of here and walk this off. He bussed Francine's cheeks, shook Roxleigh's hand, and nodded toward Quinn without meeting his eyes, and left.

Quinn

uinn watched Calder go, shoving his way through the ballroom in such a way that even though he parted the crowd rather roughly, nobody seemed to notice. Or perhaps they did, but as they looked back in question, there was nothing to be found. Amazing how he could do that, be seen and yet unseen. Be loud and brash, yet fly completely blind and quiet like an owl in the night. In the next moment, he was gone, and Quinn wished he could go with him. When he turned back, Roxleigh and Francine were examining him.

"I remember a time when you and Quinn were inseparable," Rox said quietly, matter-of-factly, questioningly.

o do I," Quinn said. He gazed back toward the doors, searching for any sort of evidence that Calder had ever been here. A small gap in the crowd, a female fixing her rumpled bustle—anything—but there wasn't anything. He was gone and had left no evidence in his wake, save the emptiness in Quinn's chest.

"Quinn?" Francine asked.

Damn, he needed to pay attention, not stare after Calder like a sick puppy.

"Apologies, Francine. You were saying?" he said with what he thought to be a genial smile. He watched as her eyes darted in the direction Calder had taken, then back to him, and his shoulders ached from the sudden anxiety. He tried to shake it off.

"I was only just saying that you are to have a new cousin soon," she said, a bit less enthusiastically than that sort of pronouncement usually carried.

"Truly?" he said as excitedly as he could muster. He turned to Rox to demand confirmation and received naught but the twitch of his mouth. "Ah, lovely, this is simply lovely. Congratulations," he said as he wrapped one arm around her back and pulled her closer to kiss her cheek. She smiled then, and all his tension fled. She was magical like that. "Certainly all the aunts are on high alert for the impending celebrations?" he asked, trying to keep the subject on this new, lighter trajectory.

Roxleigh shook his head stiffly, and his eyes narrowed at Quinn. "Don't you think it. I do not want my home invaded just yet. If word gets out, I'll know exactly who to flay, so don't you dare, for one moment, consider telling anyone." Roxleigh bit the words out, and his ferocity forced Quinn back a step as he remembered exactly why he'd never been as close to Rox as some of his other cousins. His powerful presence tended to send Quinn into heart palpitations, and he was forced to concentrate in order to calm himself. As for Warrick, he never went anywhere near him.

"No, Your Grace," he said respectfully, and yet not. "I wouldn't dare. I leave that joy to you to spread." He looked down to find Francine twisting Roxleigh's thumb as she stared up at him.

"Stop being so vicious to your family," she said.

Roxleigh shied in compliance. "Yes, dearest, yes. I am remiss, Quintin. What I meant to say was please leave that joy to us to share with the family at large," Roxleigh said with a forced grin.

Quinn nodded and laughed uncomfortably, then turned back to the room to see Lady Alain making her way toward him. She shouldn't be searching him out so often, even if he did want her to, for some reason. He hadn't ever felt that distinct pull toward a woman, and he'd wanted nothing more than to spend time with her since he met her. Well, no…there was one thing he wanted more, one someone he wanted more—Calder—and he would forever be in the back of Quinn's mind even if something came of him and Celeste. For now, he needed her to understand that people would comment on them being seen so much together, because he was sure she didn't want to be noticed in that way.

He gave a short bow and kissed the back of her hand once again and turned her to Rox and Francine. "Might I present you the Lady Alain?" he asked.

"Of course," Francine said sweetly. Quinn noticed how Francine watched him, instead of her.

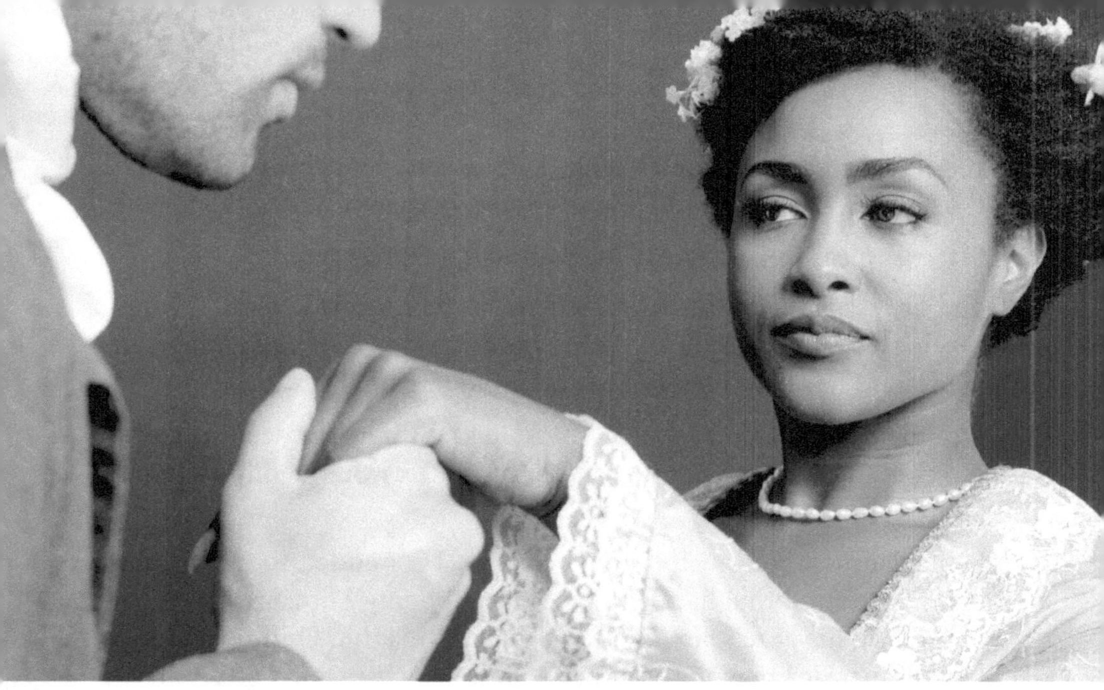

"Lady Alain, have you met my cousins?" he asked.

"Not this particular set, no, my lord," she said with a smile that drew one from him as well.

"In that case, might I present His and Her Grace, the Duke and Duchess of Roxleigh," he said.

He watched as her eyes widened in feigned surprise, and this was what he liked so much about her. She was such a practiced actress, absolutely brilliant in her studied demeanor. Nothing ever truly surprised this lady. She knew who every single person in this ballroom was. She had to—it was simple survival for her, because if she crossed the wrong path, it would be devastating for her future.

"Your Grace," she said as she curtseyed deeply, "and Your Grace. It's lovely to be allowed to make your acquaintance." Quinn heard Roxleigh grunt his quiet annoyance at her over-the-top greeting, as if she'd stepped just a touch too far into wanting something. As she rose, she caught her error and winked at Francine, passing the greeting off as playful. "Truly lovely, as I've heard so much about the both of you. I pray your life has become much more boring as of late?" she asked.

Good recovery, Quinn thought, but his cousin was still much too meticulous and worldly to be charmed so quickly.

"Yes, quite boring, thank you," Francine said with a genuine smile. She turned to Quinn, and he knew she wanted to know if she should extend an invitation to her. He gave a quick nod. "Lady Alain," Francine continued, "I would be honored if you would join us for tea, perhaps one day this week?"

"At your pleasure," Lady Alain replied with a quick dip.

The crowd shifted, and a gentleman headed toward them. "Quinn, another dance?" she said quickly. "That Lord Briskley is on the hunt for his fifth wife, and I have no interest. Do you mind terribly?"

Quinn heard Francine laugh at that and knew if he refused, she would send Rox out to the floor with her, and in turn, Rox would require a pound of flesh from him.

He had no choice but to quickly accede. He nodded to his cousins, took her hand, and brought her to the floor, stopping Lord Briskley in his tracks, sending his gaze searching for a different victim. Quinn wanted to mind but didn't. He knew she wasn't after more than he would give, and she was smart and fun to converse with.

"Thank you," she said as their second waltz was underway.

"You're welcome, though you must consider that if you keep coming to me for rescue, people will take note and believe there is more here than simple convenience. My mother, for one, is going to think she'll need to meet you." He felt her back stiffen like a steel rod had been shoved down her spine, and he turned to her.

"I'm sorry, I didn't mean that we don't suit. I only meant—"

"I know what you meant. Believe me, I do. I'm just not familiar with being around such blunt men who aren't after something a little more from me," she whispered.

"I imagine," he replied.

"I doubt you can. I only—I worry that—"

"Shhh," he said. "It's fine. Don't concern yourself. I wanted only to mention it. I don't mind dancing with you, not in the least bit. You misunderstand me if you believe any differently." Because he knew she misunderstood.

She thought she knew the truth of him, but she didn't, and he wasn't sure how he could possibly explain it to her. It wasn't exactly a simple thing to tell someone you'd known for any period of time that you could love them—*but not like that*—because you loved someone else—*like that*—but that neither you, nor she, nor they, could ever be happy together because of their particular circumstance.

Damn the world. He could reach out and touch every single thing he wanted, but he could never hold on to any of it. Like grasping at smoke.

"Quinn?"

"Yes?"

"Will you take me riding? Perhaps tomorrow?"

Quinn nearly tripped over her skirts at the shock he felt at her invitation.

"Celeste, I didn't think—"

"Please don't read anything into the invitation. I simply wish to talk, and you seem to be the only person in the world I can talk to, the only person who seems to understand certain things…"

Quinn nodded, taking a deep breath. "If you wish," he said.

"Thank you," she replied quietly. "I appreciate your friendship more than you can know."

Quinn narrowed his gaze on her, but she avoided his stare, looking around the ballroom at everything but him. The waltz waned, and Quinn brought her to a stop before bowing over her hand and kissing the back. He walked her back to Roxleigh and Francine, where a few more of his cousins had migrated. As he did so, he caught his mother's excited smile at the edge of the dance floor. A sting of electricity shot up his back to his neck. They might all be in a bit of a sticky wicket now, and it was all because he couldn't say no to this woman who did nothing but say no to him. Not that he wished to hear a yes, even if a yes might make things easier.

"My lady," he said as he drew up to the group, "since I have no idea whom you may know and whom you may not, let me quickly present Lord Trumbull and his wife, Lilly. Lord Calder—not that Calder, mind you. That's his elder brother, who should be Canford, but—"

"Elder by three minutes," Lord Calder cut in.

"Elder by law, regardless of time," Quinn said with a smile, and Lord Calder grinned.

"Well, perhaps another time for that story. And finally, this is Lord Vaughn, my own brother, who doesn't generally grace us with his presence at these sorts of things. Welcome," he said with a quick bow to his brother.

"And of course you've already been acquainted with Roxleigh and his wife." He turned to his brother and cousins. "Everyone, this is Lady Alain." She curtseyed, her hand still on his arm. "I would make a small request of you this evening," he said. "Lady Alain needs to dance, but she isn't in the market, and since none of you is marketable at present, I see an opportunity. I'm not feeling well and cannot be her champion, so won't you all please assist me?" He watched as each of his cousins gave her a quick nod like a vow of dedication.

"I thank you all," he said, took a deep breath, and turned to Lady Alain. "I'll come for you tomorrow morning at nine o'clock," he said.

She smiled and dipped another small curtsey. "I'll be ready," she said.

No, he thought, *I don't think you will be. Not if my mother has been paying attention.* He turned and walked toward his mother, as she was conveniently blocking his path to the entrance of the house. He looked past either side of her, hoping—but no, everyone saw her standing there in all her regal fittings. There was nothing to be done but take her on his arm and promenade while she let him know all about how she was going to make his dreams come true, because, quite obviously, he had set his cap for Lady Alain. Which meant his mother would set her sights on making that happen.

Damn them all.

$$Celeste$$

She and Quinn might well be in trouble. Celeste watched as his mother took his arm and they strolled along the edge of the dance floor. There was naught that she could do about that now. He had warned her, but Quinn was the only place she'd ever felt safe in society. The first she'd been introduced to him she felt some sort of thread pull tight, something that had always been there, a memory she had long forgotten.

Celeste latched on to that feeling and she'd be damned if she'd ignore him and the safety he could offer in favor of standing alone in the ballroom. She wasn't ready to be picked and plucked by the next bored peer in need of a wife who thought her to be worthy, or enough—or worse, none of the above.

Fuck that. Fuck all of them. Celeste nodded to his cousins, then turned and walked away as quickly as she could from the ballroom. She hoped to catch a moment's peace in the retiring room to collect herself and pass some time so she could leave this ball at a late enough hour, one that wouldn't call attention to her.

She was so very alone. In every single thing she did. The funny thing was that she actually preferred being alone, because that was her normal. She didn't belong here and only tried her best to fit in and fly under the radar. Her adolescence in this world had been difficult enough, but at least she'd found ways to hide in plain sight.

Celeste understood that most people liked company. She understood that most people had a goal to be a part of a couple. She didn't understand some of the other wants that everyone seemed to have that sprang from their couplings. The ultimate culmination of which, of course, was the want to mash themselves together naked, two writhing, sweaty, sticky bodies joined in some ancient, base, human need to procreate—just as an example. That made no sense to her. She shuddered.

Celeste made it to the retiring room and was thankfully met with silence. There were a string of waltzes being played, and certainly all the ladies needed to be out in the ballroom to find their futures.

She felt so lost, even when close to Quinn, even with his hands on her, touching her sweetly and gently, guiding her and protecting her. She didn't exactly feel *alone*. That wasn't quite the correct word. Perhaps *empty* was the word.

She looked in the glass next to the sink, wiping some smudged kohl from the corner of her eye with a linen square. She loved her eyes, narrow and long, unlike most of the peerage. Her face was more brown than white, her hair more coarse and dark as night. She carried the infusion of her grandmother's heritage in her blood.

Sometimes she thought she could feel her grandmother's wild roots take hold of her in a visceral way and shake her about like a rag doll. She had an uncontrollable need to move her body to the heavy beat of a drum, the pining sound of a lute, or the sweet threads of some strings.

That wasn't something she could do, obviously. She could only watch. She sneaked out of the house to the ballet whenever it came through London. The women en pointe, the rare man in his tight breeches supporting her and transporting her around the stage as though she weighed naught but a feather was so powerfully beautiful. She'd even attempted to run away with Ballet de l'Opéra de Paris, but they hadn't appreciated her raw aesthetic. They'd said she needed to have that trained out of her in order to fit in with the rest of the dancers.

She was, however, offered a job on an entirely different type of stage. Had her parents refused her when she came crawling back to them and with no other alternatives, she might have been forced to take the opportunity. At least she would have been allowed to move.

For now she would dance for herself whenever she could hear the music. She closed her eyes and listened closely to the rise and fall of the waltz. She loved listening to music through walls because then she heard only the most powerful of the notes, and she could decipher the silence between the beats however she wished to.

She rested on one of the chaises, sitting on one hip to avoid crushing the stupid bustle cage attached to her backside. She pulled her feet up next to her and tucked her toes under the edge of her dress.

Her family would be happy enough to be rid of her, to let her go and not return. They'd never cared that she wouldn't give them children, a name, a better foothold in society. They'd been clawing their way back ever since her grandfather had married *that woman* while on his travels, and Celeste had been unhelpful to that end, her skin and hair a constant reminder. They simply wished to be done with her and move on.

This year they'd said, find a husband and get out. Or just get out. She was smarter than she used to be, however, so she was looking for the perfect opportunity, and Quinn had presented one such possibility. As a person on the outskirts of society constantly watching those around her, Celeste knew more than perhaps most people did. She could see that Quinn wasn't interested in finding a wife, which meant perhaps that he already loved someone but was unable, for whatever reason, to wed her. That was what she wanted. A man who was otherwise engaged. She wanted a marriage in name alone. Protection, and no more.

She wished she could simply be free to live without a care in the world, taking from the earth to sustain herself, and giving back just enough. Impossible as it was, she had always hoped that somehow she would find her happy solitude somewhere. She'd heard stories of the beauty of nature outside London and hoped she would have a home far from society one day.

The door to the retiring room opened, and Celeste straightened, letting her feet drop to the floor beneath her skirts as she shifted, lifting the edge of the bustle cage so she could sit up straight, like a proper lady.

The women stopped when they caught sight of her, certainly unsure whether they should be in the room with her alone, or at all. Certainly frightened they would somehow be sullied by their very proximity to her. She knew the only reason she was tolerated in society was that her father's position demanded respect.

But he wasn't here to protect her right now. He wasn't able to protect her every time she left the house or attended a ball. And her mother wanted nothing more than to get her married and out of her house, certainly to raise the perception of their home in stature. Certainly to present the outward appearance of perfection, a perfectly bland, uninteresting family with ladies made for bearing children and money to marry them off.

The women finally decided to stay, and Celeste stood. She didn't need to overhear their chatter, their words like shards of ice in her heart, because the more they stabbed, the harder they were to thaw. She straightened her skirts and smiled at each woman independently so as not to call special attention to or cut any one of them. *God forbid.*

Her job thus far in her life was to bend to the wills of those around her, no matter where she was. No matter how she felt, no matter who they were, she was always lesser by right. Even on the arm of a gentleman like Quinn, who had a powerful family behind him.

She should be thankful that his family didn't seem to be the kind that would judge her because of her heritage, because of those who came before her, because of something she had no control over. At least they didn't mind her for their lesser son. There was always the possibility that if she set her cap for the heir, their reaction to her would be entirely different. She understood that. She wasn't sure how they treated the heir. And she wasn't sure whether the not knowing was a blessing or a curse.

She hoped, as she left the room and wandered toward the front entry, that she and Quinn could come to an understanding now, even if she had been pushing him away since they met. He needed to know that she would do her duty if she must, if he required it of her. She would much prefer that they just live as amiable people, and he do whatever he wished away from their home. There were no odd rumors, and she assumed that he kept a mistress or had a lover, but he'd been careful and not stirred any talk. She would need to let him know that that could continue once they married. She would not mind. She would welcome it, even.

That's what drew her to him, for while she didn't want the wifely duties, she also didn't want to be talked about—any more than she already was.

"Celeste."

"Mother," she said sweetly, even as the sound of her name tensed the muscles of her arms. She curtseyed quickly. "I'm not feeling well, and I thought—"

"You can't possibly think to take the carriage. What would your sisters do?"

Her three younger sisters who had not been so cursed by their grandmother's skin. Celeste thought there could be another reason, that perhaps they weren't actually children of her father. Perhaps her mother had believed that since her husband looked white, his children would as well, but then Celeste had arrived and ruined everything. Perhaps her mother had been so horrified by her that she'd refused to take his seed again.

"I could take a hack—"

"I suppose that's fine for you," her mother replied.

Celeste tried to not let her mother's words hurt her, because she remembered warmth from a mother when she was younger. Of course, she could not reconcile the memories of her mother when she was young with the woman who stood before her now, and so she simply tried to ignore it all. As she curtseyed again, she saw Quinn duck out the front door. "Good night, Mother."

She turned and followed him. Because if society didn't know much about him, perhaps she could find out for herself. Then she would know whether or not she could truly trust him with her own secrets.

Calder

Calder returned to his house on Sussex Square, hoping beyond hope that he could wash the memory of Quinn from his mind and his body. It never worked, however, and wasn't bound to work tonight. That didn't mean he wasn't game to try. He slammed the front door behind him and yelled to his man. "Grant!"

"I've started the water in your rooms and expect it to be heated enough any moment," he said as he walked quickly down the stairs toward Calder.

"How did you know to expect me?" he asked.

"My lord, the carriage returned some time ago. I assumed you were on foot. It's approximately three-quarters of an hour from Grosvenor here. I started the water when I saw you in the Hyde Park gardens."

Calder glanced back at the door, then to his man. "Thank you," Calder said, tossing his gloves, coat, hat, and cane at the man. "The night is yours. Bolt the door behind you." Calder wasn't a peer who liked people underfoot. He liked to have Grant available, but he also appreciated his privacy. It made him slightly uncomfortable that Grant paid enough attention to his movements that he knew when to prepare the water. He supposed that was a part of his normal duties, to think ahead, to be prepared, to assume and be ready. He imagined the best servants held all the best information about their masters—and didn't Exeter like to have the very best of everything? He should speak to his valet. Perhaps he could be bought.

"My lord," Grant said, breaking his reverie, "until tomorrow." The man bowed and disappeared, and Calder ran up the stairs to his suite on the first floor. He was stripped bare before he even reached the door to the bathing room.

Calder stepped into the steam and was engulfed by the heat of his shower. His hands gripped the silver ribs as he held on and let the scalding water cleanse his skin, if not his soul. As the heat waned, his skin flushed and his temper eased. He turned his face up into the heavy stream above him, letting the cooler water wash down his form and take most of his tension away.

Finally, he shut the water down and stepped from the cage. He pulled one of the towels from the warmer, scrubbing it across his face and through his hair, roughly soaking up all the water it held.

"I'm not sure I like this shower you've had installed. I think I much prefer to find you in the bath," Quinn said roughly.

Calder froze against the words as they came at him, deep and hard, from the doorway of his bedroom. He dropped his arm, letting the towel hang in one hand to his side, leaving evident the physical manifestation of what Quinn did to his body.

No point in hiding what had always been known to Quinn. At least that's how it felt because they'd grown up together and had never shied before.

Nearly the same age, their mothers had been together often enough to let their offspring play, and play they had, perhaps too much. Quinn had only to speak to him in that voice, and the words themselves mattered not. Calder knew what he wanted, what they wanted, and his body would ready.

Quinn was still in the clothes he wore at the dance, save his coat. Shirtsleeves open at the neck, waistcoat, trousers with a hard ridge straining the buttons, black shoes. He preferred Quinn in boots, but nobody wore boots to the ball anymore. Damn shame, that.

Calder's blood was already warm from his shower, and now it flowed quickly as his breath caught, his heart pumped harder, and his veins filled with that thick want of Quinn.

He crossed the bathing room in three steps and grabbed Quinn's shoulder, turning and pushing him hard into the wall as he came up behind him, his mouth at Quinn's ear. "And I like you better when your trousers are around your ankles and you have dirt on your knees," he said as he took a deep breath of Quinn and palmed himself. His fingers trembled slightly, but he managed to hide it as he reached around and tore the buttons from Quinn's trousers, releasing him.

"Goddammit, Calder," Quinn complained, but he pushed back into him with a shudder all the same.

Calder ignored the words, and with one hand, he took a fist full of Quinn's hair, and with the other, he shoved the trousers down his hips. "You came into my house. You came into my room. Uninvited. You came into my bath while I was naked." The fist in Quinn's hair clenched to stop it shaking, and Calder relished the quiet intake of breathe that hissed through Quinn's teeth. "You don't get to argue." Calder kicked Quinn's feet wider and stepped on the fabric between his ankles, pushing it to the floor as the other man held on to the edge of the doorway.

"I've never needed an invitation before," Quinn said, and the words were so quiet Calder nearly missed them.

Calder spit into his palm, slicking his hard length before pushing Quinn farther forward until his hands slipped and his shoulder hit the edge of the door. Quinn's hand shot out to brace himself against the other side of the open doorframe, and even still he didn't fight.

Calder stroked his cock and took the fluid from it, pushing his fingers into Quinn's arse without much foreplay, but if Quinn had wanted sweet and careful, he wouldn't have come here tonight, not like this, not when he knew the kind of mood Calder was in. Quinn knew what he was asking for when he climbed the trellis and came into his room, just like he always knew what he was in for when it came to Calder.

His fingers froze just inside that tight ring, and he forced himself to slow, forced himself to feel, to breathe and enjoy this man. Calder massaged gently, patiently waiting for Quinn's body to soften, to quit fighting him. He waited so he could gain his entry in a much more pleasing and tangible way.

He heard Quinn gasp as the muscle released and Calder pushed in, and he loved the sound that came from Quinn next—so deep, so guttural, so passionate and wanting, so damned desperate. It was the sound of a man who couldn't help himself now and never would be able to. It was the sound of resignation, the sound Calder always waited for. He lived for it.

Calder took the bottle of oil from the shelf over the sink and poured it at the top of Quinn's arse, letting it trickle between his cheeks where his cock rested. Calder slid there, slowly covering himself with the oil, the warmth and friction releasing the scent of the herbs that infused the oil inside the bottle.

"Devil, please."

"I told you," Calder said as he pressed the crown of his cock against Quinn's much more ready arse, "to stop calling me that." He thrust patiently, allowing Quinn to lose for him, then froze, releasing Quinn's hair and taking his hips and pulling him back against the cradle of his legs. "Goddamn, Quinn," he said.

That first thrust, it was always so very much. He could feel it spread out from his toes to the tip of his tongue in a numbing tingle, and all of his senses woke up. He could smell the starch in Quinn's shirt and the saddle oil from his mount. He could feel the points of his hips against his palms and the shifting of the muscles that butted up against his fingers. He could almost see the silence as Quinn held his breath, waiting for his body to accept him.

Calder rocked there, slowly, for as long as he could manage before his body demanded he take, thrust, come. "You're mine, you know," he said as he moved faster. "You'll never be able to walk away from me."

Quinn yanked one foot from his trousers to spread his legs wider, tilting his pelvis, and Calder groaned as his arse clenched his cock in just the right way with the movement, and he knew then Quinn was ready. He moved.

"You don't own me," Quinn said. "This means nothing, just like it always does. This isn't anything but what we've always done. Sate some… horrible…" Calder pushed hard, slamming Quinn's shoulder into the doorjamb again. "Fucking," Quinn yelled, the word forced from him.

"I like you better with your mouth shut," Calder said. He put his hands at Quinn's shoulders and fisted all that fabric and thrust again and again as Quinn struggled to stay upright. He heard the fabric rend, the buttons of his waistcoat strain and pop free, his shirt giving way at the front, and still Calder held on.

"Calder," Quinn choked out, and Calder released him and pulled free, walking past Quinn into his bedroom. He turned and watched as Quinn hit the floor, his shirt still on, his trousers still around the one foot, his self-respect crawling along the edge of the room toward the balcony. Calder sat in the gold chair at the end of his bed and waited for Quinn to look up to him. When he did, Calder crooked one finger, and Quinn crawled, the trousers coming off as he did so.

When Quinn reached him, he rose from the floor in one fluid motion, his shirt coming off over his head as he stretched tall and wide toward the ceiling. Calder sat forward and breathed of him, the warm scent of his skin flaring his nostrils for want of more.

He leaned in farther and licked that gorgeous cock, stem to stern, sliding the head between his lips, and Quinn dropped what was left of his clothing to the floor with a skull-dragging moan. Calder slipped his tongue between the flesh and the crown of Quinn's cock and sucked the salty fluid from it, and Quinn nearly doubled over.

He steadied himself with rough hands on Calder's shoulders, his back. Calder shrugged him off and sat back, palming his cock again with one hand, the other adjusting and soothing his bollocks.

As Quinn stepped forward, the small hairs at the back of Calder's neck stood and sent shivers through his muscles. Quinn put his hands on the back of the chair at either side of Calder's head and carefully stepped over the arms of the chair, his thighs supported by the padded arms, his knees resting against the end of the bed behind the chair. He hovered there over Calder's cock… It was his turn to wait, and his mouth went dry at the very idea of what came next.

When Quinn leaned forward, his mouth was naught but a breath away, and Calder's lips were warmed by it. "I like it when you say please," Quinn whispered heavily as he moved one hand, slid it down Calder's face, his thumb catching on his lower lip as it passed, until it skimmed the edge of his jaw. Then his hand wrapped around Calder's neck and squeezed just so. "When I do this," Quinn finished, and the tables were turned.

It was too much, and Calder's body began to vibrate from holding himself still.

Quinn was obviously prepared to wait and tease endlessly. Calder groaned. He reached up between them, one hand turning up to cup the round of Quinn's arse as he positioned his cock with the other. Calder thrust up, and as he did, the grip on his neck tightened, and "Please," did come from his mouth, just before Quinn's mouth came down over it, forcing his tongue past Calder's teeth and sucking hard. Quinn relaxed and sank down into Calder's lap, as open as one man could be for another.

Jesus, but this was the best thing in the world. This was life and death and love and the entire reason the world existed. This here, this connection, the two of them. Calder thrust again, and Quinn straightened. His neck craned, his head back as he screamed into the night, and Calder reached up and put his hands on those shoulders, the ones that she'd held when they'd danced just hours before. Calder wrapped his arms around Quinn's strong body and dug his fingers into those heavy, round shoulders and pulled him down, and he fucked him. Hard.

Quinn

uinn fought to steady himself. The only thing holding him in place were the devil's hands, hot on his ribs. He grabbed the back of the chair and leaned forward, bringing the pressure of Calder's cock just where he wanted it, but Calder pushed him back again, holding him off.

It was always a fight with them lately. Always. Particularly when they did this. Quinn wouldn't lie. It wasn't as if it had ever been sweet, by any means, but sweet wasn't something either one of them had ever really wanted. Calder bit his lip, and Quinn released the back of the chair, licking the tang of blood from the bite.

"You can't say no to me," Calder said. "You've never been able to do that."

Quinn winced because it was true, but why would he ever want to say no when yes was always so fucking good? He sank onto Calder as far as he could, just pulsing his hips, concentrating on that small movement in his arse, his own cock growing harder as it pushed against the soft skin of Calder's belly.

Calder shifted, and his arms wrapped around Quinn's back, pulling tight as his hands dug into the flesh at Quinn's sides and held him close. All too soon, Calder shifted to the edge of the chair, and Quinn wrapped his legs around Calder's back as his own back hit the floor hard, the breath leaving his body. Calder fucked him across the floor, punctuating his words with his thrusts. "I—hate—seeing—you—with her—"

"You'll have to become used to it," Quinn replied breathlessly, knowing Calder would hate the truth of it just as he did. How could he like it? How could either of them? There was no world in which he and Calder could live together, be together, like some sort of horribly twisted fairy tale.

A sob broke from his chest before he could stay it, and Quinn cried out in an attempt to cover it up. He wasn't sure then whether Calder fell for it or simply allowed him his dignity in the moment, but he gentled.

"I hate the way you can't say no to people," Calder said softly, his face so close Quinn was tempted to lick the sweat from his cheek that would slide and drip from his chin any moment now. He watched as the gentleness faded from his eyes and the anger returned. "Tell them no. Tell them you don't want to marry. Tell them to stop managing you. Tell them to stop handling you. Tell them," Calder yelled in his face.

"You tell them," Quinn spat back. Because who the fuck was Calder to expect more from him than he was willing to give? Calder stopped moving and stared at him, myriad expressions crossing his face. Quinn shouldn't have yelled. A chill ran the length of Quinn's spine as he gazed up into those eyes that seemed to be stripping the flesh from his bones and chewing the marrow.

Calder's head jerked, as if he couldn't process whatever thoughts tangled in his mind, and he grabbed Quinn by the shoulders again, slipped free, and flipped him over, covering him with his now very hot, very sweaty body.

Quinn trembled into him, and Calder's weight settled, a heavy comfort that pressed him into the floor. Calder's hands moved in a maddeningly slow way from Quinn's shoulders, around his biceps and down his sides, his hair standing on end, his breath stilted from want. He pushed his hips into the floor, attempting to release some of the building pressure, and Calder's hands wrapped around his hips, his thumbs dipping into those dimples at his spine, his strong fingers finally tilting Quinn's arse up for him once again.

"Goddammit, Devil," he begged and cursed at once, the teasing too much.

"We are already damned, the two of us," Calder said quietly, filling the shell of Quinn's ear with the heat of his breath. Calder thrust and pulled Quinn's hips back to meet his pelvis as he reached between his body and the floor to take Quinn's cock in hand, and the moment he did, Quinn came off.

Quinn struggled against it, grunting as his legs slipped against the wood of the floor from the pressure of the body above him, his hands reaching for anything to hold strong to but left wanting, grasping at air.

"Calder," he said. Calder stilled, and Quinn heard the smallest gasp—more like a stilling of his breath—as he came off as well, filling that emptiness that Quinn had brought with him.

Calder pulled back, and Quinn felt the chill chase over his skin as it met the open air of the room. He felt that loss of heat like he would have felt the loss of his own skin. It left him raw and open. Calder never was one for closeness. It was some sort of rejection of what they actually meant to each other. Some sort of rejection of a time in which their naiveté had them believing they could spend their lives together. Somehow.

If Calder knew and understood that, maybe Quinn would tell his family to fuck off, but since Calder was of no mind to be honest about them, about their relationship, about how he felt… What would be the point in destroying his own life? You don't leap from a bridge without a net.

Quinn closed his eyes and breathed for a moment as he listened to the water running in the bath. He wondered if he would be welcome to stay this time, or if he would have to leave. Why did he continue to do this to himself? Calder was right about him. He couldn't say no, and he never would. Calder was his world and had been for a very long time. He couldn't remember a life without that knowledge, without knowing the feel of his skin, the shift of his muscle, the growl of his voice.

He opened his eyes. His knees were going to hurt. So were his elbows and his shoulder where Calder had shoved him into the doorjamb. His—well, all the usual places. Suffice to say, he would be sore tomorrow. He touched one finger to the bite on his lip and pulled it back a little bloody. Calder was in a mood tonight after seeing him with Celeste.

What had he expected? It had to happen. He had no excuse for it not to happen. He wasn't some secret spy who disappeared at the pleasure of the Crown. He was but a businessman, the spare—not the heir. He wasn't needed unless something terrible happened to his elder brother, Wilder, and he prayed nothing ever did. Everyone loved Wilder, himself included, and Wilder—he was born to lead even if he was in a bit of a tangle at the moment.

Quinn came to his feet without touching his knees to the floor, wincing as he stretched his muscles, tendons, and joints back into place. He glanced at the bathroom, heard the water running still, and knew it was the shower and not the bath. Calder knew Quinn disliked the shower. He supposed that was his cue to leave, but he didn't want to. Not just yet.

He walked past the bath and stepped between the silver ribs that wrapped around his…what was he? More than a lover, much more than just a friend, not merely a cousin either. He was just more.

Quinn watched for a second as the water sluiced down Calder's back, the rivulets running his spine and splitting at the round of his arse, running down the half-moon shape of his hips. The man was beautiful when wet. He wanted to drink him. Maybe Quinn could get used to this caged contraption. He followed the trail of the water with one finger.

"We've already had one discussion about invitations tonight, Quinn. Must we have another?"

He took Calder's arm and turned him around, pushing him against the bars. "Yes, we have, and like I already said, I've never needed an invitation before, so I don't understand why I should need one now."

Calder opened his mouth to argue, but Quinn pressed into him, filling his mouth with his tongue, biting his lips to still them, holding his head steady with both hands.

He kissed him like that until neither one of them could breathe, allowing the water to rush their forms, to sink in. It was an intense sort of feeling to be surrounded so completely by touch, as if the water were a thousand trailing fingertips.

Quinn broke away, but he didn't go far. His hands slipped down to encircle Calder's neck, his thumbs tracing his jaw, Calder's day beard scratching at them. "Why don't you understand?" he asked, watching his mouth, inspecting the marks from his teeth, the swells from his sucking, the evidence of his existence on this man. It hurt. He wanted more, so very much more.

Quinn watched as Calder's mouth tilted on one side in that snide, defensive smile of his, and Quinn gave his head one shake. "Don't—don't you dare try to edge your way out of this with me. I've done nothing— nothing you haven't forced me to do by your own inaction."

"Is that so?" Calder asked. Calder's hands slid around Quinn's sides, his thumbs playing with the line where the cheeks of his arse met his back, occasionally swirling in the dimples on each side of his spine. Quinn couldn't breathe. Calder was the embodiment of love and hate all at once.

He felt it in every touch, saw it in every glance, and tonight Calder was in a mood, and Quinn had known it before he came here, but he came anyway. So he would accept Calder's belligerent abuse and return only patience, as he always did.

He leaned his forehead against Calder's chin and let the feel of his hands sink into his skin. "You are the biggest fucking arse I've ever met. Everyone thinks you're the best of us…but they're all wrong, aren't they?" Quinn took a deep breath and pushed away from him, then he turned.

Shaking the water from his hair, he crossed the bathing room, grabbed a towel from the heater, and went into the bedroom to dry off. He was exhausted and knew no good would come of him staying. He needed to go home. He could try again tomorrow, because Calder wasn't going to listen to reason tonight, and Quinn couldn't be here anymore. It hurt so much, having him so close yet so far away. He needed to leave before Calder managed to truly start a fight.

He heard the soft footsteps behind him as Calder approached, and Quinn leaned over to dry his toes and clean his mettle from the floor. Calder's fingers swept up from his neck to the seam of his arse, then around to cup his bollocks. "Stop," Quinn said as he stood and turned.

"Says only your mouth," Calder said, nodding toward his half-risen cock.

"I'm perfectly aware you can get a rise out of me without much effort, as are you. It doesn't mean anything."

"Sure it does. It means you like it when I fuck you. It's very simple."

"It's not that simple."

"No?" Calder asked. "And why not?"

"Because it's you, Calder. It's you."

Calder tsked as he shook his head. "Poor Celeste. Does she know?"

Quinn felt his temper slip its tether. "Why?" Quinn yelled. "Why must you be such a goddamned shit? She's not a bad girl. She's sweet and lovely and wants nothing from me that I don't want to give."

"No? And how much do you want to give?" Calder snapped.

"Are you truly asking, or are you just baiting me again?" Quinn asked, and Calder turned away, but not before Quinn saw the change in his eyes, just a quick flash of jealousy. Funny how he could do that. Calder. He could hide almost anything. Almost. But Quinn saw it, because Quinn had become good at seeing past Calder's well-practiced tells. "Calder…Devil, please talk to me. If you're hurt, I want to talk to you, not be abused by you," he said.

"Excuse me?" Calder said. "Hurt?"

"Mad, frustrated, angry, annoyed, whatever it is you feel, I want to talk to you about it. I'm not trying to belittle or demean you. I'm the last person who would do that, because I know you fight that. I know you act like more of a man because, for some reason, you feel like less of one, but—" Calder's jaw clenched, and Quinn knew he'd gone too far.

"So—we're done here, and you can see your way out," Calder said stiffly as he pulled a robe from the end of his bed and put it on.

"Fuck! That's not what I—wait, please—"

Calder kept moving.

Quinn wrapped his towel around his waist to follow. "Devil!" he yelled.

Calder paused at the door to the hallway, but he didn't turn, and Quinn stopped. "I told you—"

"I know. Don't call you that," Quinn said, cutting him off.

Calder's gaze shifted up but didn't quite meet Quinn's before he turned away and pulled the door shut behind him.

Quinn ran for the door, but when he opened it, Calder was gone, and Quinn knew he'd never find him in this ridiculous house. He slammed the door and yelled, then went to collect what was left of his clothes.

eleste bit her lip and turned from the open door, but biting her lip wasn't enough, so she covered her mouth with both hands. She couldn't believe what she'd just witnessed.

She slid down the wall, rested her forehead on her knees, and covered her head with her arms. She wasn't sure what to do next. When she'd followed Quinn here after the ball, this was the last thing she'd expected to see. Well, fine, possibly not the last thing, but it certainly wasn't in her top ten, by any means. She gazed up to the sky and pinched the bridge of her nose. How was she ever going to look him in the eyes and not think of this?

She couldn't. There was no way. That was…the most amazing thing she'd ever seen. Her body felt like it was on fire, like…she wasn't sure how to describe it even to herself. Her skin was vibrating. It was alive, as though her blood sang and pooled in her belly, dripping slowly to places she'd never felt before.

Perhaps this feeling was the one that people had forever been trying to describe to her, but she'd never understood—having never once experienced it. Not even when she'd tried to touch herself.

She wanted to touch herself now, right here on this balcony outside Quinn's cousin's house. She didn't, of course, but she wanted to.

Oh dear God, Quinn and his cousin. She heard a noise and squished herself as far into the corner of the balcony as she could, tried to make herself smaller, bowed her head to hide behind her riot of black locks. She glanced sidelong over her arms and saw Quinn, still just a towel on, walk to the balustrade and tilt his head up at the sky. His chest heaved—was he crying? Her heart skipped.

Calder had been quite mean to him. He'd been…she'd always thought Calder to be the most respectful and gentlemanly of men. Not that she'd had much interaction with him, but what she'd had, this was someone else altogether, so angry, so…passionate. The thought of it sent goose bumps across her skin, and she clenched a fist against her mouth once more to prevent any sound.

Quinn looked down, covering his face with his hands and running them through his hair. He turned and went back into the room, and Celeste leaned over, looking through the door as he dropped the towel—I should stop looking, shouldn't I?—and reached for his clothing.

She didn't stop looking. She couldn't stop looking. She had never seen such beautiful bodies. She'd wanted to reach out and touch them, but at the same time, they terrified her. She would rather touch a statue, something safe, something that wouldn't want, or need, to touch her back. Those bodies, she wanted to watch them move, she wanted to see them dance. She knew it would be amazing. She wanted to see them do what they'd just done, again and again.

She kept her eyes on Quinn as he yanked on his ruined clothing. She resisted the urge to help him, wanting so very much to console him somehow, to help him button his shirt and find his coat. He had one button left and six holes on his trousers, and she could see that if he just crossed the top button hole across the front to the opposite remaining button on his trousers, that one remaining button might just keep his trousers on until he could make it home.

But she didn't.

She couldn't.

And she felt horrible because of it.

She felt it was such an invasion of his privacy to watch this, and of course, that made her feel even worse that watching this—watching this man pick his dignity up off the floor and attempt to put himself back together—was much more intimate than watching Calder fuck this man across the floor.

She turned away and leaned into the wall and tried to breathe. She shouldn't have followed him. She shouldn't be here. If she could take it all back…she stared up at the sky.

"I'm sorry. I'm so sorry. But I wouldn't take it back," she whispered at the sky. "God help me, I wouldn't take it back."

She heard Quinn coming toward the balcony and turned away again, hoping for one more moment of blind luck in which she wouldn't be discovered.

Calder

alder shut the door to the room across the hall and stood as silently as he could. He knew Quinn wouldn't give chase, because Quinn always gave up. Quinn always had some excuse. And Calder wasn't going to trust Quinn as long as he was so easy to send away. He sank into the chair next to the entry and rested his head in his hands. His gut tensed and churned as he considered the night. There was so much he should have done differently, so much he could have done differently. But he hadn't.

He really needed to get himself together. He had important things to do that had nothing to do with Quinn, and quite obviously, Quinn had important things to do as well—a girl, for one.

A *woman*, actually. Celeste was rather stunning for a female, and he'd always known Quinn would find one eventually. Because Quinn wasn't quite like Calder—he was more dedicated to what his family expected of him, and they expected him to marry, and so he would…even if it made him miserable. Because it's what was expected of him. In a vicious circle with no way out, like an ouroboros, Quinn was eating his own tail, and Calder could have no part of it.

If Calder disappeared, Quinn wouldn't follow. He would simply allow it. Calder would step aside so Quinn could settle down with Celeste and forget he ever existed, just like the last time Calder had gone away. Except, the last time Calder had gone away, there had been no Celeste, and he'd known that Quinn would be here to welcome him home. Because whenever Calder came back, so, too, did Quinn—straight to his bed. But what if the next time Calder returned, Quinn already had a warm bed, even if it wasn't quite what he wished?

Calder closed his eyes.

Quinn always waited.

Calder shook his head.

Quinn always waited.

It was almost a mantra, because Quinn—he always waited. He may not give chase, but he always returned. So if Calder made to India, Quinn wouldn't follow, and Calder would have the space he needed to breathe and somehow come to terms with Quinn being married, then he could return and somehow—*somehow*—Quinn would make his way back to him. Quinn would be here for him, because Quinn always was.

So Calder would pull a Warrick and disappear, leaving Quinn to his woman, until he was too weak to stay away. Because Calder was too weak to stay away from Quinn, and Quinn always waited. Calder looked down at his hands to see them shaking. He shook them out and stood. He paused, listening for the slamming of the front door, but it never came. Quinn probably had left as he'd arrived, over the balcony like some Shakespearian hero. And like a Shakespearian hero, he would return.

Who am I trying to convince?

Calder paced the room, hoping for some signal that would never come.

He walked to the windows that looked out over the street. He would have to deal with Quinn if he stayed in London, but Calder was here for now. If he could avoid him, it would be easier. And Celeste…why did Quinn attempt to push that woman on him?

Unlike the other girls who may expect something from you, she won't. And he'd said it with that intense gaze of his that he used when he said things like, *Let's go for a ride, shall we?* Or, *Let's go to the library.* Or, *Care for some brandy? Wink. wink.*

There was only one reason Quinn and Calder went for a ride, and that was the destination. They never went to the library, and he certainly didn't drink brandy. All that ever meant was, *Let's go somewhere to fuck.* Anyone paying two bits of attention would have noticed them always leaving together. Perhaps since they were cousins, nobody gave it a second thought. Quinn and Calder certainly never thought twice about how it appeared to others.

Convenient, that. Possibly a bit too much a convenience and more a curse. To be together as he wished would bring down half the Trumbull

lines, destroying his parents and Quinn's parents and all of their reputations and futures. There were too many girls who needed marrying off to do that.

Impossible. Quinn needed to marry, and Calder needed to leave so that Quinn *would* marry.

And so he would quit London. As quickly as possible.

Calder turned to return to his room. He'd no idea what the future held for him and Quinn, so instead of thinking about it anymore, he would simply go to bed now and avoid Quinn altogether for the time being. He let his robe slide from his shoulders and tossed it at the corner as he walked to his bed. He stopped when a shadow shifted in the far corner by the windows.

Now…shadows in the corners of old homes in London were generally nothing to consider, especially when the gas lighting could hardly chase away all of the darkness, just like the candles that came before. Shadows were simply a part of life when England went dark.

But this shadow moved like a man.

Calder suddenly wished he'd kept his robe on.

He feigned a sudden interest in his fingernails as he watched from the corner of his eye, surreptitiously inspecting the doors to his balcony to see they were fully closed. There were two problems with that. One, it meant there was no breeze, and two, Quinn had left them open when he arrived, and he wouldn't have shut them when he left.

Calder considered calling out to Quinn, but if it wasn't him…

There was nothing to be done. Calder stood tall and bluffed. "Come out from the drapes, or I'll run you through with my knife and never think on it again."

He heard a stillness that came from fear, saw a hand wrap around the edge of the fabric, and push it aside. *What the devil?* If Calder had made a list of the people he would consider being behind the drapes in his bedroom, this person would not be on it. Not on the page, not in the mentions, not even under consideration. A cold sliver ran down his spine like chilled mercury, while his blood pushed through his heart. He narrowed his gaze on her.

"What is it you want from me?"

Celeste

eleste stared at the man across the room, all hard lines and anger, and every bit of his attention on her. She shrank within her own skin as he watched. Wished it were true somehow, that she could simply melt into the floor, never to be heard from again. It would be easier than this.

"I—" She shook her head. She didn't know what to say. When Quinn had left the balcony, part of the trellis had pulled away from the house and gone with him, and it currently lay on the ground below the window, taunting her like only an ivy-encrusted old ladder to freedom could.

She'd watched as Quinn walked away from the house and hadn't looked back, as if he hadn't been concerned at all that the trellis to Calder's bedroom was damaged, as if he hadn't been concerned for her, as if he didn't have to apologize for destroying her only escape route. She wished that he'd somehow known she needed to be rescued, because she would rather have dealt with his ire than this man's. He'd left her there to fend for herself. As if he'd known.

She'd almost called out to him, but had had the sudden thought that she could get through the house and out before Calder returned to the bedroom. *His bedroom.* So she had turned and come inside. She had shut the door behind her and started to walk across the room, but it simply wasn't to be. When the door creaked open, she'd thrown herself behind the drapes and prayed he hadn't seen her. Alas…

"I asked you a question, and I expect an answer. If it's your intent to trap me to marriage, I would make you aware that the rest of your life would be so inconceivably miserable, you'd wish for death."

Her breath left her in one fell swoop, like a punch to the gut. *How can he think—*

She looked around the room as she tried to get her wits about her. Of course he would think that. He didn't know her. She tried to argue, because that was the last thing she wanted from this man. But she felt like a fish out of water, her jaw working with no words coming out. "No…" she said slowly, finally. "Please…no."

"You have one minute to explain yourself before I find a way to get you from my house without incident."

"Incident?" she squeaked.

"There could be an incident."

"What sort of incident?"

"The very sort of incident young ladies like yourself attempt to avoid at all times."

She shook her head again.

He simply raised one eyebrow as he shifted and placed his hands on his hips, which drew her attention to them, thus bringing the sudden and awkward realization to her that he was standing there absolutely stark naked. "You're naked," she said.

"This is my home," he said as though she were simple. "These are my private chambers. It's night. I have no invited guests. Is there a reason I should be clothed?"

"It's indecent."

"Again, in my bedroom, in the dead of night, by myself, I'm not allowed my own freedoms?"

"But you're not alone."

He wagged one finger at her as if scolding a child. "But I should be. This is my home, and I don't remember inviting you to it."

"No, you didn't," she whispered. "But I'm here now, and we can't possibly—I can't possibly…you can't expect me—" She swallowed the lump that prevented her from finishing a sentence and closed her eyes tight.

"Do you believe, for some reason, that I wouldn't be able to manage a conversation without my clothing?"

She shook her head. At least she thought she did.

"Do you think, for one moment, that I wouldn't be able to *handle* a small thing like you without my clothes on?"

Please don't handle me. "Please." His eyebrows rose in question. "Don't. Please don't," she repeated.

"Why are you here?" he asked.

Celeste looked to the balcony door behind her, wondering how far away Quinn really was. Would he hear her scream? Should she scream? Did she need to scream?

She cut her gaze back to a very impatient Calder and took a deep breath. "I don't know, exactly," she hedged. She didn't want him to know she'd followed Quinn. It seemed a very bad idea to let him know she'd seen them. But what could she tell him? What good reason could she have for being here? "I saw the light, in the room…" She shook her head the minute the words were out, because she knew it was nonsense.

"Are you some sort of voyeur? Do you often break into gentlemen's homes in the dead of night to see what it is they do with their—" He stopped suddenly as some horrible realization dawned on him. Most likely that she had seen them together, him and Quinn. *That* realization. That truth. His face twisted in anger.

He rushed at her, taking her arms and pulling her flush against his body, her toes barely sweeping the floor. As it happened, he was perfectly capable of handling her while completely naked, and she was thoroughly unnerved by that fact. "How long have you been here? What did you see?" he yelled.

"Nothing," she choked as she tried to catch her breath. Her heart pounded so hard it felt like it kept her lungs from expanding. "Nothing, I just…I just climbed up, and the room was empty."

"Absolute fucking nonsense!" he yelled. "What are you here for? Did someone send you?"

"No, please," she said. "Please, let me down."

His hands tightened on her arms, and his gaze narrowed to the sharp edge of a razor as his face got within a breath of hers and she cringed as he shook her once. "Not until you answer all of my questions."

She nodded. "I will, I will, I promise I will, please," she begged.

His grip on her relaxed, and her bare feet met the floor, but he didn't release her. He pulled her to the chair at the end of his bed as she stumbled beside him, the chair he and Quinn had only just… *Oh God*, she thought as she closed her eyes. *Not there. Let me sit anywhere but there.* She struggled anew, her body convulsing as though it had a mind of its own.

Calder simply pushed harder against her resistance and used his foot to sweep her legs out from under her. Her backside met the cushion and knocked the wind from her, the metal ribbons of her bustle cutting into the backs of her thighs.

"It's going to be a long night for the both of us," he said quietly, "unless you start explaining." He released his grip on her arms and stood, unashamedly, directly in front of her. She thought she would choke. In all her life she'd never expected to come this close to…a man. A naked man and his…appendage. But here she was, and she stared. It was long and thick and had the shape of a knitted sleeve over a tall, upside-down mushroom.

She'd always hoped if ever she married that she and her husband would be civil and accomplish what needed accomplishing with their clothes on, somehow. He would get her with child and leave her be.

"Were you using Quinn to get to me? Is it a title you're after?" he asked, jerking her attention back to the present. Calder hadn't moved. He simply looked down at her in that menacing way.

"No. I don't want your title. I don't want any title. I don't want you."

"Then why are you here?"

"I don't…I can't—" She lifted her gaze to him, met his eyes, and pleaded with all that she was. "Please believe me, I mean you no harm."

"How could a little thing like you harm me?" he asked with a quick laugh. But it wasn't *said* jokingly. It was rough. Because he knew she could harm him, and if she wanted to get out of this room, she had to convince him of the opposite. *Impossible.*

"I can't. I have nothing. Nobody would even believe me if I were to say—you must know of me, you must know that nobody would dare believe anything I had to say against any peer, particularly one so esteemed as you."

"For example?" he bit off as he leaned down toward her just a bit. Good God, but he was good at terrifying.

"For example?" she parroted, and his eyes narrowed on her again, and she knew he was becoming more frustrated.

"What is it you saw that nobody would dare believe?"

"Anything—anything at all. Nobody would believe me. They would believe nothing I said."

"You had better pray that to be true."

Celeste pulled her feet up to the chair suddenly, wishing her shoes and stockings weren't underneath the trellis, because her toes were rather cold. She'd had to remove her shoes and stockings to climb, though.

She hid her face behind her knees, covering her head with her arms as her corset bit into her abdomen and she did say a prayer. She tried her level best to stifle the tears she felt pricking her eyes. Why had she followed Quinn? What had she thought to accomplish? What would Calder do to her? "I'm sorry," she whispered.

"Are you?"

Celeste jumped when the voice came again from just in front of her, so very close. She looked up. "Yes, truly, I mean you no harm."

"You understand by saying that that it sounds like I should have reason to believe that you could harm me in some way?"

"Yes, I understand. But I care for Quinn. I would never—"

"And what exactly does Quinn have to do with this?" he asked.

Damn it all. She had just given herself away entirely.

He turned and walked for the balcony, looked out over the edge. When he turned back toward the room, his gaze stopped at the spot where she'd been standing, where she'd watched them. "Everything, I see."

She started to shake her head, but he pointed at her. "Don't."

Calder turned back to the balcony and whistled, then he crossed the room, swept a towel from the floor as he walked to a writing desk, wrote a missive, and sealed it. He stood and wrapped the towel around his waist and took the letter and several coins and went back to the balcony. He peered out into the dark, whistled again, and a moment later tossed the missive and the coins down below. "Twice that on delivery," he said.

He turned back to her. "It seems we have a little time to spend getting to know one another."

Celeste blinked, and the tears fell, scorching her cheeks as they cut down her skin, pooling on her hands. "I'm sorry," she said again.

"That's been established, regardless of whether I believe it or not. Try something else." He pulled a chair up to hers and placed it directly in front of her. He sat down and stretched out his long legs, folded his hands across his middle. The towel he had on shifted and fell open on one side. He didn't fix it.

Celeste could see the shadow of his penis, the dark hair that led to it. If he wanted to discompose her further, it was working, because her heart started to race. He was simply so damned confident, and that alone terrified her.

He waited.

"I have—have to—have to marry," she stuttered.

Calder stayed silent.

"I was hoping to marry Quinn, he—he seemed—he seemed amenable, and we'd—we'd had some conversation on it." She put her hand over her mouth and tried to calm her heart so the words would come more reasonably.

Calder stayed silent, and her heart calmed a bit.

"He doesn't love me," she said quietly, watching to see if he reacted. He didn't speak, but his gaze narrowed on her once again. "And I don't love him. We made a good friendship. Something we could sustain…" Calder still didn't move, didn't react. "I followed him after he left the ball. I followed him…here." She swallowed hard.

"There it is," he said as he sat up straight and leaned forward with his elbows on his knees, bringing his face close to hers, once again sending her heart to shudder against her spine. "Why did it take so long for you to come to the simple truth of it?"

"I was afraid."

"Of?"

"You."

"You should be," he bit out.

Celeste let her feet slide to the floor, unfolding her body so she could breathe a little better. It seemed she just couldn't get enough air. It seemed the world was spinning. It seemed she had made the biggest mistake of her life.

And Calder simply waited.

"I'm sorry," she choked.

"I'm afraid sorry is not going to do you any good at this point," he replied.

Celeste heard the whimper as her heart seemed to ricochet through her chest, her breath stuck in her throat. She went to stand, to relieve the pressure from her corset—and then nothing.

Quinn

e wasn't even five minutes home before the butler knocked on the door to Quinn's rooms. "Sir, you have a missive. The messenger awaits a response."

"At this hour? Fuck's sake, this is obscene," Quinn said. He took the paper and savored the jolt of electricity that shot down his spine when he saw who it was from. He broke the seal and read, the words swimming on the page. He blinked hard and read it again.

"Sir, you have a response?" Yeats asked, to remind Quinn he was waiting for him.

"No, I'll go," he said. "Just have the messenger wait for me out front and have my horse brought back around."

"Yes, sir."

Quinn closed the door and stared at his hand on the door knob for a moment before looking back at the note from Calder. Perhaps he'd changed his mind? Perhaps he just wanted to be together however they could? Calder never asked him to return, never invited him over by hand, never requested his presence in this blunt manner.

There was no physical proof of their existence in each other's lives save for the marks on their bodies that often faded much too soon. And most telling, Calder never referred to himself by the nickname Quinn had given him when they were children. But those words…

Return now,
—Devil

…in one simple sentence…Quinn was not only chilled to the bone, but impossibly excited about their future for the first time in a very long time.

He went to the wardrobe and pulled out a pair of trousers, since the ones he had on were held up by a single oddly placed button-and-hole combination. He pulled his boots on, grabbed his coat, and headed belowstairs.

"Quinn!" The voice was so joyful it stopped him in his tracks, and he turned.

"Mother," he said as he walked to her and bussed her cheek.

"Where are you off to at this ungodly hour?" she asked.

"Calder's. I shouldn't be long."

"This late?"

Quinn stopped. It was late, of course. He hadn't considered the time after reading Calder's demand. If he'd left the ball at half past nine, it must be nearing midnight. To put a point on it, the long-case clock in the entry bonged a half past something or other, and Quinn pasted an easy smile on his face.

"We are bachelors, Mother. There's nothing for us to do early in the morning, so we're allowed the luxury of playing cards late into the night," he said with a smile.

"Is this about earlier, at the ball?"

"What about the ball?"

"You must know the exchange between the two of you was noted by several people."

Quinn thought for a second. "Just a momentary disagreement, Mother. We've known each other the whole of our lives. We're allowed disagreements, are we not?"

She shrugged. "I suppose you are." She patted his shoulder. "You two have always been up to no good in the dead of night," she said, but something in her eyes concerned him.

"Nothing has changed, then," he said.

"This all must change once you marry, you know," she said.

He didn't take the bait, though. He had to leave.

"Don't wait up. You're a lady, and you should get your rest. Certainly someone will be coming to tea early tomorrow."

She smacked his shoulder. "Don't you get rude, child. I can still make your life miserable."

"Don't I know it," he said. He smiled and bussed her cheek again. "I do love you, Mother," he said. He turned for the entry as she called back.

"And I you. You're such a good son."

Quinn almost tripped when she said it, but caught himself. Something was off with her, but there was no time. He went down the steps, handed the waiting messenger the coins as instructed, and walked to the groom and his waiting horse. "I'll manage her tonight if I return. No need to wait up," he said.

He mounted Silk and pulled her to the street. It wasn't far to Calder's house on Sussex. He'd walked it many a time. Tonight, he wanted speed, because he wanted to know what it was that was of such urgency.

He leaned into her neck and let her take her head. The streets were nearly empty tonight, and save for a few sharp turns, he never pulled the rein, because he wanted to be at Calder's more than anything. More than anywhere. More than ever.

He brought Silk up in the mews behind Calder House and put her up in one of the stables. He thought about leaving her ready, but decided against it, letting her have whatever rest she could without the saddle. He managed her quickly and walked through the back garden. The light in Calder's room was still burning. The pile of ivy and shattered wood below the balcony where it had pulled away from the wall under his weight was like an accusation.

He went to the rear door and pulled the latch, letting himself inside and running the stairs to the bedroom. When he opened the door, his first instinct upon seeing Calder in his rooms, naked, a woman at his feet, was to simply shut the door and run. Because that's what you did when you intruded upon a private moment like that.

Because if everything he knew to be true about Calder was false, nothing in his life mattered.

His hand tightened on the door knob, and he forced himself to steady. He watched as Calder bent and put his arms under the woman and pulled her up against his chest as he stood. Naked.

"Get over here and help me, Quinn."

"What—"

"Help me and then we'll talk. Quinn, come," he said.

And Quinn did. He took one step and then another and then…he recognized that silk dress. He recognized that dark hair and that smooth skin—a chill ran his skin. *Celeste.*

"What the fuck are you doing with her?" Quinn asked.

"What the fuck do you think I'm doing?" Calder threw back at him.

"I—I've no idea," Quinn replied.

"Well, let's figure it out, shall we? I asked you here, Quinn, because once you left and I came back to my rooms, I found your future wife hiding in my drapes. Care to ask why?"

"Why?"

"That's a goddamned good question," Calder said stiffly as he laid her out on the bed and looked to Quinn. "One she has yet to answer because she seems to have fainted."

"What did you do to her?"

"What did I—really? I just had the shock of my life, but you ask what I did to her?"

"She's passed out, and you're hale and whole"—Quinn looked him up and down—"and naked. Yes, I'm asking."

"And she is in my bedroom. What is it with the both of you? This isn't a parlor. Coming here uninvited isn't normal. This is my bedroom."

"I've never needed an invitation," Quinn said quietly, remembering their earlier argument.

"But she does," Calder said.

Quinn moved to her side, checked her pulse and her breathing. "We should probably loosen her clothes so she can get more air. She's probably just in need of air, nothing like…nothing like… Damn all this female clothing."

"Nothing like you?" he asked.

Quinn shook his head but didn't answer.

"How will we get her redressed and home if you take her clothes off? That mess is a production."

"I don't know, but I would prefer to take a breathing woman home as opposed to one who isn't," Quinn replied.

"Point," Calder said.

Quinn lifted her shoulder to look at the back of her gown. Removing her clothes wasn't to be necessary, because she spoke before he managed anything. "I'm sorry," she whispered.

"It does no good," Calder said, as if they had been in the middle of a conversation before she passed out and only just picked it up. "We've been over this. Your apologies mean nothing."

"Devil, stop. Why must you—"

"Why must I? Again, Quinn, I am in my home. I didn't intrude upon anyone. She came into my home, *my bedroom*, and I would appreciate it if that fact was remembered as you take that sort of tone with me."

Quinn nodded. "I understand that, but she's—if she's apologizing for something, she truly means it."

"I want to know why she's here, Quinn. She followed you here. Quinn, think for just a moment about what you did after you arrived and what *we* did before you left. Think on that, and then tell me *again* how cordial you wish for me to be right now!" Calder turned and stalked over to the balconies, and Quinn did as he was told. He considered. His palms grew cold and damp, and his head grew heavy.

"Fuck," he said to himself as he turned to look at her.

"Yes, you could say that," Calder said to the night sky.

"Can we start with you putting some clothing on?" Quinn asked quietly.

"My clothes go on and hers come off. How telling of you," Calder said.

"Goddammit, Devil, not right now!" Quinn yelled, and Calder turned to look at him, the gaze cutting, angry, and hurt. It was the hurt that cut him to the bone. "I'm sorry, I—it's all just so—" He shook his head. "I can't really think straight with you naked and angry," he said under his breath. He looked back to Celeste, who was pulling herself up in the bed against the headboard, desperately trying to keep her gaze turned away from Calder.

"I promise I have nothing to say, not to anyone, not ever," she said quietly, and Quinn walked over to sit next to her.

"I don't understand. Why did you follow me?" he asked.

"I wanted to talk to you. I thought if I followed you, we could have a moment away from all of the—everything," she said.

"That's not quite true," Calder said. Quinn ignored him.

"You expected to be allowed into my home at night to speak with me? How did you get here?"

"I hired a hack. I told my parents I didn't feel well," she said.

"And now? How long has it—it's been hours, Celeste. They're probably looking for you," Quinn said.

"No. They'll assume I'm in bed sleeping. They won't check. They don't care enough to check."

"Celeste—"

"No, don't. I understand, really. I'm not what they wanted. At any rate, I could probably—"

"Pardon me," Calder said suddenly, breaking into their conversation. "But do you mind getting back to the whole part about you following Quinn and ending up in my bedroom? You seem to have skipped something in the middle there, like, why did you follow him up the trellis? I assume that's what you did, climbed the wall as he did? And why? Why did you follow him to the balcony? You know full well this isn't his house."

"I thought…maybe…" She twisted her hands in her skirt as she pulled her legs over the side of the bed to the floor, putting her back to him. "I thought perhaps he had a mistress, and I wanted to know who. I wanted to see her. I wanted to see the woman who would make him happy when I couldn't," she said.

"What do you mean 'couldn't'?" Calder asked.

She looked up to Quinn with those pleading eyes, and Quinn stepped between them, blocking her from Calder. He wasn't going to allow her secrets to be forced from her. Nothing good could come of that. "You don't have to do this," he said.

Calder yelled, "Yes, she does! I demand an explanation for why my entire life has just flashed before my eyes. I deserve to know what happened tonight, *in—my—rooms.* I am owed an explanation as to why I may have to disappear."

Quinn turned to him. "Look, Devil, I told you there was something about her. I told you that you should talk to her—"

"Are you referring to your cryptic message at the ball tonight? What exactly did you wish to take away from that?"

"Only that there may be ways for us to live—"

"That's enough. You're defending a woman who broke into my home and—just in case you haven't quite put it together yet—watched us fuck. Quinn. Watched us from the balcony. The two of us, in my bedroom. Fucking."

"You keep saying that. I'm aware it was in your bedroom."

"Because it was, and you seem to be ignoring every pertinent fact at the moment! I can't—" he stopped. "Get her out of my house. Get out, both of you. None of this matters. I was planning to leave for India anyway. This just…moves my timeline up."

"Calder, wait, please." Quinn panicked. This wasn't what he wanted. This wasn't… Calder couldn't leave him, not right now. "Calder, listen to me—"

Calder grabbed him by his coat and yanked him up, nose to nose.

"Get out of my house. You don't seem to understand the damage you and your woman have done here. Get. Out."

"Calder—"

"Out," he said, but he didn't yell. He simply said it, turned, and walked from the room as Quinn fell to his knees.

"No," he said. "No." He felt like his gut had been opened up, and everything that made his body work had followed Calder from the room. He sat there, on his hands and knees, just trying to catch his breath, forcing his body to calm. He needed to keep his wits about him. He couldn't deal with an episode, not right now.

"Go after him."

Quinn shook his head, the voice so foreign to him in this moment. "I can't."

"Quinn, go. Go after him," she begged.

"He won't allow it."

"How can he stop you?" she asked.

Quinn sat back on his knees and looked up at her. She *had* destroyed everything, and for what? "What did you…why?"

"Why what?" Celeste asked.

Quinn felt an eerie sort of peace come over him as he stared at the door. Quinn stood. "I'll see you home."

"You need to find him, Quinn—"

"No, Celeste. Calder doesn't want to be found, and if he doesn't want to be found, he won't be. I'll see you home."

Calder

alder went around to the mistress' room and ducked through the closet to his own dressing room. He dressed quickly, trying to block the sound of their murmured voices through the door. He left through the back and went straight to Warrick House to see if he had received any new information about Exeter and his men. Calder was certain he would be interrupting something—considering Gray and Lulu's exit from the ball—but he didn't actually give a single damn about it.

When he got there, when he went through the mews to the back of the house and heard the crack of whips, when he heard the unearthly groan that came from the ballroom at the back of the house, he changed his mind entirely.

He watched from the gardens outside the ballroom as Lulu wielded two bullwhips high over his cousin's head, knocking the crystals from the chandelier one piece at a time. They rained down around them both like shards of a broken rainbow. He sat hard on the bench in the garden and watched for a while as she teased him—and it was a tease, because he could clearly see the want, the pure desire in Warrick's gaze. It was something so powerful and raw it stole Calder's breath, because he knew that feeling.

Quinn.

He closed his eyes and turned away. He wasn't going to interrupt this. Whatever this was. He'd known for quite some time that Warrick wasn't typical, but the depth of what Warrick considered to be his depravity had still been no more than speculation on Calder's part. But this, seeing this, seeing Warrick and his pure response to what Lulu was doing, seeing that want and passion and something like love…Calder could not possibly be happier for him.

Warrick was settling into a life that had terrified him, a life he'd never had any interest in, a life he'd been forced to take control of, and while Calder had had concerns, they now shattered like the crystals of that unfortunate chandelier.

Quinn.

He should go back. He should find Quinn and make things right. Calder didn't want to lose him…but that woman—and Quinn had taken her side. He'd made his choice clear, and Calder needed something to keep his mind of off all of it. He stood and walked to the side of the house. He popped the latch on Warrick's study window and climbed in.

Calder knelt beside the desk and pulled the hidden drawer open that Warrick kept for all the correspondence they'd collected in their investigations of Exeter and the rest.

Calder sat in Warrick's chair and leaned back with his feet up on the desk. He went through a few of the papers and letters he'd already seen, rereading them for any hints to follow up on. There was nothing. These men were doing as they usually did, and it was all painfully aboveboard. He put the paperwork on the desk and picked up the more recent missives that were neatly stacked on top of Warrick's desk, probably from this afternoon. One packet caught his eye. He broke the seal carefully and inspected the sealed missives inside.

It was odd that the packet contained sealed missives. Addressed missives. As if they'd been intercepted and collected to be sent to Warrick. He shuffled through them, examining the addresses…

Exeter. Expected. The man was horrid and had a hand in so many pots Calder wasn't sure how he ever had a hand free to shake at all. The bastard and his underground group of self-righteous, misogynistic, old-guard peers needed to be stopped. Their penchant for dealing in underage girls and arranged, paid-for marriages was not something that a modern England should put up with. However, Her Royal Highness wasn't of a mind to call negative attention to so many of the men who'd helped to secure the Empire of India for her.

It would be easier to deal with them in India than in France, but either way, if they were ruined abroad, the story could be changed before it reached home, and England would remain unsullied—the queen's perfect Diamond Jubilee façade would remain intact. Just as she wished. Calder just had to figure out how to make all of this happen. He flipped to the next missive.

Hepplewort. Not quite expected, as he'd been dead near on two years or more now, but the paper was older and stiff, so someone had found it, or kept it until now. Who and why was now the question…

Soundringham. Not at all expected. Soundringham was an earl and a high-level confidant of HRH, and Calder had never heard ill of the man. To his knowledge, Soundringham had never been associated with these other men, so this needed more investigation.

Bentleigh. Expected. His contract for one of Francine's sisters had been broken by Trumbull. So if he still tended to the circles, it was no surprise. He did finally obtain a wife. Where she'd come from Calder wasn't certain, as she wasn't a child of one of the more established families, and he hadn't heard any rumors that she'd been purchased in the fashion these men were partial to.

Warrick. Calder froze. Warrick being one of these men was not within the realm of possibility. Certainly it wasn't Gray—if it had to do with this business, it was his father. Neither of his brothers had ever held the title. The letter could be old, like the one for Hepplewort—but it didn't look it. Or it could be from whomever sent the packet. He ran a thumb over the address as he considered whether to open it or leave it for when Gray was available. He set it on the desk with the others and picked up the large packet again. He turned it over and inspected it. There was no information beyond Warrick's address on the front. The handwriting did seem strangely familiar, but he couldn't place it. His boots hit the floor, and he leaned forward, tracing the well-honed scrawl with one finger. He put it aside and shuffled through the letters again. He took the one addressed to Hepplewort and, since the man was long dead, broke the seal.

H—

As you have allowed your contracted bride and her sisters to be taken from the convent, subsequently breaking their own contracts with Bentleigh and Ringolsby, we have made the decision that you are too much a liability and can no longer enjoy our brotherhood.

The interest you have garnered from the Trumbull family is more than we can accommodate, as they have the close attentions of Q.

You must manage on your own. Do not contact any of us again for a wife or any other merchandise.

Effected August, 1880

X—

He checked the writing with the packet. It wasn't a match. Where would this have come from? What other merchandise… Did he refer to the bawdy house they'd set up in India? Calder closed his eyes and set the missive on the desk, as it would need to be categorized with all the other papers they'd found and saved over the past few years. He didn't want to think on that. He looked back over the missive without touching it. X was most likely Exeter. Calder had always thought the man to be the head of the enterprise, even if Gray thought there was someone else pulling the strings. This missive would be some verification of that.

Merchandise. Calder shuddered. If the merchandise were more women of some sort… It wouldn't be brides. Their brides were bought and paid for in daylight, where everyone could see, legally and respectfully in the most disgusting of traditional ways and possibility. The merchandise could be more prostitutes, but their whores were kept in other countries. They'd never deigned to bring any of them to London.

He pulled the first missive addressed to Exeter and carefully broke the seal.

X—

The shipment is ready. We appreciate all you have done to prepare the house. We only need to arrange the papers and transportation. R is prepared to accompany, considering you have become too close to the wrong people as of late.

You must not visit the house until we deem it safe.

Your child needs to do her duty to your title as was arranged.

If this doesn't happen, you will no longer be accepted.

Certainly you understand the danger therein. We will contact you when relevant.

—S

No date. Certainly this was more recent. S was Sandringham more than likely, and apparently they still expected Cecilia...Lulu to destroy Warrick. The house he referred to... Exeter had recently purchased an old inn in the bottoms. He also had several properties to let in India, the most recent of those an old haveli in Jodhpur. Perhaps one of them was the house they referred to? They couldn't keep Exeter from his own property. He couldn't remember having found any other properties, but he now had more names to add to the search as well.

He inspected the missive addressed to Warrick. The seal was a large M. He carefully slipped the seal in case he needed to close it again.

Grayson—

I've missed sparring with you. Won't you come out to play?
Come back to the only place you ever called home.

GMJ

Madoc? Fuck. Calder stood. His hands shook as he read the words again, and again. Not possible. Not at all possible. Calder rubbed his temple as he read the words over and over, and he knew one thing for sure: Gray could not be involved in this. He could not. Not with his new bride, his new life, finally coming to peace with who he was. If this were true, Grayson's peace would be coming to a swift end. The two facts could not coexist. Calder was fairly terrified by this information.

With trembling hands, Calder put the missive in his coat pocket. He wouldn't allow this sort of bait until he knew the truth for himself. He had checked the packet to be sure there were no other missives when it hit him. He turned it over and compared the writing to the address on the missive for Gray—it was a match. He couldn't leave any of this, because if he'd had the smallest recognition, Gray would certainly see it.

He found paper and ink and wrote Gray of his intention.

Gray—

I opened the packet. I must act on the information post-haste, so I've taken it with me. Lord E has lost the rein—there's someone new. If you receive more, forward it to the haveli.

Watch the usual men—add Sandringham.

I'm for India as soon as possible. If Rakshan is amenable, I'll take him with me.

I'll send word as I'm able,

—Devil

He left the note in the drawer of Gray's desk, checked his pocket for the missives and the packet, and left the study to find Rakshan's rooms.

Warrick's valet answered after a single knock. "What's this?" he asked.

"I'm afraid I need to return to India. I hoped you would be interested in coming with me."

"Of course, but I thought there were other things we needed to manage before we could leave."

Calder considered the missives from the desk, knew Rakshan would understand. "I fear something irreparable is imminent."

"But Warrick—"

"Is part of the problem." Calder shook his head. That wasn't what he'd meant.

"What is it?" Rakshan asked as he put his hand out, somehow knowing Calder had something. Calder put his hand in his pocket, slid his thumb along the sharp fold of one side, pulled the missive from his coat, and handed it off and watched as anger, fear, and finally determination crossed Rakshan's face.

"Give me one hour. Meet me at the Iron Duke."

Calder nodded and turned to go.

"Calder," Rakshan called out to him before he got too far.

"Yes?"

"Do you believe it?" Rakshan asked.

"I don't know what to believe. I only know that Gray cannot see this letter, and if it's true, it must be handled before he finds out."

"I pray you're wrong about all of this."

"I pray every night, but I fear God has stopped listening to me," Calder replied. Rakshan seemed to consider his words. "One hour," Calder said. He turned and left the way he came.

Quinn

Quinn waited until Celeste was inside, watched as she lit one lamp in her room and moved the drapes like she said she would. She was safe. Nobody had seen her.

But Calder was gone.

Quinn turned Silk back to the main road and steered her toward home.

uinn had no idea when Calder would turn up again. The last time he'd seen him this angry, it had been nearly a year before he'd returned to London, bringing with him some wild stories from India. Stories Calder had never shared with the rest of the family. He regaled Quinn with the vibrancy of the people, the sounds, the smells, the passion of it all. It had seemed so impossible to him, until he'd met Rakshan and seen the truth of it when the two of them spoke. It was no wonder that Queen Victoria wished to rule over the country. It wasn't just for trade routes, certainly. It was the wish to be master of that incredible culture and beauty, but something that beautiful could have no master. Something like that was untamable and should be left to flourish with the people born to it.

Quinn heard a crack and started, only to realize one of Silk's hooves had snapped a twig on the ground in the park. He'd no idea how long he'd allowed her to wander, how long he'd been in his head, how long since Calder had been gone.

Could he get him back? If he followed him, he would never get him back. Regardless, following would require knowing where he'd gone, and Calder would run farther, harder, like he had before. That was a simple fact, and he knew it even though he'd never tried to prove it.

When Calder left, he didn't want to be found. Quinn had been very well trained, apparently. Always waiting patiently at home for him. But this all felt very different. It felt very wrong. Somehow, it all felt very final. And that unsettled Quinn on a level he didn't truly comprehend. He was exhausted, like his veins were filled with syrup, and yet his body vibrated, telling him he needed to move, to run.

He heard another branch break, and he flexed his hands, moving the blood through them, taking up the rein, and moving Silk back toward the road. His family home was the last place he wanted to go, but he had nowhere else to be. He knew he should have taken rooms away from the family house so he wouldn't have to answer questions about his behavior. It was too late for that now, and he couldn't very well return to Calder's house. Not after what had happened tonight. He wished he could forget it all, start the night over, never mention Celeste. There was no chance of that either, and now he would have to wait until Calder somehow let him know that it was acceptable to approach again, as per usual.

Quinn was never the one to request Calder, though he had at times made it known that he wanted him. Needed him. Calder would make himself known at a society event where Quinn was in attendance. Calder would invite him to do something, and Quinn would accept. They would be very nearly inseparable until Calder left again. There was a distinct pattern to it all, but what if Calder didn't return? What if this time he didn't come back? What if this was over?

It wasn't over. It couldn't be. Quinn wasn't ready for this to be over. He didn't think Calder was either. The wait was bound to gut him, regardless. Perhaps he shouldn't wait. Perhaps he shouldn't do what they'd always done. Perhaps he should try.

Silk stopped, and Quinn looked up to find the broad façade of Calder House, dark and quiet. He hadn't planned to come back here, but here he was. The house felt abandoned, dark, closed, somehow wanting and lonely. He turned Silk and went around to the mews. He put Silk up for the night and went to the back gardens.

Something moved in an upper window, and Quinn ran for the house, letting himself in like he always did—well, as he often did. As he would have to now, until the trellis was repaired. If it was repaired. What if Calder chose to not repair it? What if Calder was here, and Quinn wasn't welcome? Impossible. He was always welcome. Except when he wasn't. Wasn't he?

He paused to shake off the mess of thoughts and vaulted the stairs, running straight to Calder's room.

"Devil?"

There was no response. The drapes shifted in the breeze from the open balcony doors, and Quinn knew he was still gone, and he wasn't coming back any time soon. He felt the knowledge shift and settle in his bones. It relaxed him as much as it pained him. So Quinn did something he never would have if Calder had been here. He walked over to Calder's bed, stripped naked, and pulled down the heavy sheets. He crawled beneath them.

He tried to sleep. If he could have, he would have. It would have been nice to surrender, dislocate from his thoughts, and simply float away, but all he could see was Calder walking away from him.

The door shutting.

Silence.

He watched the drapes sway quietly in the breeze and wished he could fade away, but he was wide awake. He steadied his breathing. Calder. What had happened?

Celeste.

Quinn should have warned him, told him more of what he wanted from her, for her. He'd thought maybe she could make it so that they could hide in plain sight.

I hate the way you can't say no to people. Tell them no. Tell them you don't want to marry. Tell them to stop managing you. Tell them to stop handling you. Tell them.

Quinn winced, remembering the force of the words Calder had said. He closed his eyes, Calder's face just above his while his body pressed him to the floor, his cock pinioning him to the spot. Quinn closed his eyes, relishing the soreness that came back so readily.

Quinn couldn't tell his family anything. How was he supposed to tell them this? He would lose everything. He would lose everything, and they would lose each other, and Quinn couldn't live without Calder. So he would wait, and he would behave, and he would follow these erroneous rules that had come to be the structure of their life together, and Calder would come home, and he would be here, waiting for him.

The bed dipped behind him, and Quinn feared moving, feared opening his eyes, feared facing any sort of reality in which Calder wasn't next to him.

A hand ran down the length of his side, from just under his arm down past his hip, gathering blood as it went, warming his skin, and sending sparks through his extremities. It slid around his thigh, skimming up past his rising cock to slide along the crease between his hip and abdomen, wrapping around the narrowest part of him and resting against the ridge of muscle there. Quinn flexed his muscle only to make it feel like more of a solid connection, but the touch faded, so Quinn froze and didn't move again. He just waited and let his skin soak up the sensations.

"I dare you to move," Calder whispered to the nape of his neck, ruffling the short hairs there.

The hand slipped around his waist again, smoothing the skin of his abdomen, the hair that ran from his navel to his penis. The hand wrapped around his cock, bringing him full and heavy. The hand pressed him against his own belly, making friction where there had been none.

Quinn couldn't help it. He thrust into the hand tight on his cock. All of his muscles tensed from that push. "Calder," he whispered, and he rolled to his belly, burying his face in the pillow and offering himself up with the push of his hips.

Quinn knew one thing for certain—whatever he wanted, Calder could have. Anything at all, because at some point in the dead of night, Calder had returned, and Quinn wanted to make sure Calder knew how very much he meant to him. Calder had crawled into bed and wrapped his big body around him, his big hand around his cock, and it felt like peace and forgiveness, and right now Quinn would do anything. Calder need only ask it of him.

Quinn groaned, pushing into the grip, keeping his eyes tight, and just breathing deeply of the man he loved. Loved. He loved Calder, like his own family. More than his own family. More than himself. Calder was everything to him.

"I dare you to pretend that today never happened," Calder whispered, and Quinn tensed his muscles until they couldn't move. "Quinn… I dare you… If this never happened, none of it ever happened. I would still be here wrapped around you. I dare you to move, to prove it to yourself now…"

Quinn jerked, breaking the hold on his cock as Calder vanished. Quinn's eyes flew open, and he pushed himself up, his hips pushing hard into the soft tick of the mattress. He flipped over, his arms flying out to steady himself, and searched the bed. He was alone. His hands tangled in the sheets as every one of his muscles melted and tensed anew. Calder wasn't here. Quinn was surrounded by the smell of the man, by his linens, his clothes, his things, but he wasn't here.

Quinn couldn't let him go, not like he always did. He couldn't just wait until he came back this time, because if none of this had ever happened, Quinn simply didn't exist.

It was naught but a dream…but it manifested in a realization.

I hate the way you can't say no to people. Tell them no.

Quinn closed his eyes as he sank back to the bed, letting the smell of Calder on his pillows soothe his tension.

Tell them you don't want to marry. Tell them to stop managing you.

He turned over toward the pillow, wrapped his arms around it, breathed of Calder. Prayed that at the very least this small piece of reality didn't disappear.

Tell them to stop handling you. Tell them.

He would. As soon as he found Calder, he would. He would tell his mother and his father. He would accept their judgment, promise to hide for fear of their shame, do whatever they wanted of him so that society wouldn't judge them. Until then, Quinn would wait. He would wait for as long as it took. He wouldn't do as Calder expected. He wouldn't run home. He would be here when Calder returned. He would prove himself, as if yesterday had never happened.

Calder would come home to him, like he always did, and Quinn would be waiting.

Quinn heard the long-case clock in the main hall and got out of the bed because he had somewhere to be, and he was going to have to borrow some of Calder's clothes to get there.

Celeste

eleste watched the world lighten outside her bedroom window. She hadn't slept a bit. How could she after last night? She was concerned for Quinn after what had happened with Calder. She'd never seen someone so angry with her, probably because she'd become very good at avoiding the ire of others.

Being born with attributes that automatically drew annoyance, she'd learned well to avoid upsetting people further. That hadn't happened last night. She had truly angered Calder—and Quinn, too, most likely, even if he hadn't shown it. At the very least, she'd absolutely hurt him and damaged his relationship with Calder by her actions. She wouldn't be surprised if he chose to never speak with her again.

Please speak to me again, she thought. She would miss his friendship terribly if he didn't.

She turned away from the window. How could she fix things? How could she help? Now that she knew the truth of their relationship, the truth of who Quinn was, perhaps she could. It wasn't unheard of to marry a man who favored other men. It happened often enough, even if nobody spoke on the subject. It simply was.

Perhaps she could be that person for them—for Quinn. Except Calder was titled and would require an heir, meaning if she were to help them, chances were that she would have to marry Calder to give him the legal heir, and Calder was set to be Duke of St. Cyr, and she could not be a duchess. She could not.

Could she carry a child? Could she lie still enough for a man to put his seed where it needed to grow? She closed her eyes against the sting that followed the thought. She had thought about it before, and though she'd been resigned to it, she didn't want to. She didn't even want to be touched, not like that.

Beyond that, Calder frightened her entirely. He had been altogether different from when she'd seen him within the realm of society. She couldn't imagine Quinn being with someone who treated him so dismissively. Or perhaps he had been that angry only because of her. It would be understandable, considering. Except that he'd been angry with Quinn long before she showed up. And why? Calder had stormed out of the ball after Quinn spoke to him, after he'd danced with her. So perhaps it truly was all her fault.

She needed to speak with Quinn.

Celeste reached for the book she'd been reading. The words floated above the page, not making a bit of sense. When the ladies' maid she shared with her sisters entered, she sat up straight and tried to be the perfect mistress she was expected to be.

"My lady, you've missed the morning meal. I've had a tray arranged. You have an invitation from the Marchioness of Cheshire for tea this afternoon. What response do you have?"

Celeste turned toward her and threw her legs over the edge of the bed. Quinn's mother? She wasn't sure, now, if she should attend tea. Quinn had said they were to go riding today at nine, so she could ask him then. What if he didn't even show to go riding? In that case, she certainly shouldn't go to tea with his mother.

She shook her head.

"I'll send your regrets—"

"No—" she blurted out. "Sorry, I meant…I mean, please let her know I will be there. I need to ready for riding at nine. Would you please alert the stable master?"

Abigail nodded. "The tray should be up shortly, and I'll help you ready for riding as soon as you've finished."

"Thank you, Abigail, as ever," Celeste said with a smile. She hoped she hadn't been too much trouble.

After she breakfasted and dressed, she went down to the sitting room to see if her mother or father were there. Even if they were quite disappointed in her, they were her parents, and she tried to love them. The room was empty. She could see the door to her father's study down the hall, closed tight. She startled when she heard the mantel clock go off in the sitting room behind her. The waiting began, but it didn't last too long, and Celeste hurried to the door before the knocker could fall a second time, beating the butler there and opening the door.

"Quinn," she said with a smile, and her worries melted.

"My lady," he said with a bow. "If you're ready, I would ask to borrow a horse if I may, as I left Silk behind. She had a long night."

"Of course you may," she answered and turned in time to see the butler nod and head toward the back of the house. "Do you have an idea where we shall go?" she asked.

"When?"

"Riding. I wasn't so sure we should go to Hyde Park and make that sort of statement because of what happened yesterday. I thought perhaps Grosvenor."

"Don't mind about yesterday," he said with a smile. "Everything will be fine."

"What part of yesterday?"

"The ball. We'll set my mother straight to be sure she doesn't do anything that might make you uncomfortable. She just gets excited."

"I see. Have you spoken with Calder? Quinn, I don't want to come between the two of you." She kept her voice low, even though nobody else was about.

He turned away as he considered, his gaze much too distant. "No need to worry. You could never come between us. We do that just fine without any outside help at all. Calder will come back. He just needs to find his way again."

"He was so angry. I've never seen anyone so very angry," she said quietly.

"He was angry. That much is true, but he'll be back. About last night..."

"Yes?"

"Generally, when I'm with him...he is a better man. Even as last night seemed evidence to the contrary. That wasn't a very true representation of him, truly, please believe me."

Celeste nodded as the stable master came around the front of the house on Beelzebub with Mephistopheles in tow. She pointed. "Shall we?" she asked.

"We shall," he said, and he turned and offered his arm. She rested her hand on his elbow carefully, just hovering there, barely grazing his coat. He put his hand over hers, pressing it down to his arm. "We are familiar enough, you and I, Celeste, as much as we need to be, as much as we can be, so don't be afraid of me."

She nodded and followed him down the steps to the horses. He turned to the master. "Lovely gray. His name?"

"Mephistopheles," he said with a grunt.

"What a…friendly name for a horse," Quinn said. He turned to Celeste, who was already atop her gray. "Should I be concerned for my life?" he asked, and his face alone made her laugh. This was the Quinn she adored. Light and free and humorous.

She smiled and turned her horse toward the street. The twins bore the names of her father's choosing. Though she did prefer to call them Topher and Elza, to avoid the inevitable questions.

"Why would you name your horse after the devil?" he asked as he caught up to her on the street.

"I wouldn't. My father, however, doesn't like horses. He thinks of them as a necessary evil and thus has named them to suit."

He looked at her horse. "I'm afraid to ask," he said.

"Beelzebub," she replied with a smile. "They will answer to Topher and Elza, however. When they wish to, at any rate."

"Oh, that's much better. Dare I ask if they are a set of four?"

"They are not, no. We do have a team of four for the carriage. They're Friesians. I know you're familiar. Azazel, Baphomet, Lilith, and Lucifer."

"Truly? Roxleigh would not be happy to hear Friesians being named as such," he said.

"He wasn't, in fact, but once my father purchased the team, he had the right to name them as he wished."

"He renamed four of Rox's Friesians after demons?"

"Yes, he did."

"God's balls," Quinn said, and she laughed.

"Well, we do refer to the mares as Lucy and Lili, so that's not quite so bad," she said, attempting to quell him.

"Not so bad, no, but a mare named Lucifer?" He set his gaze to the road as he considered, and she watched him. They settled into a good canter, crossing the park close to her house. When they slowed again, she spoke.

"Quinn, after last night, I thought—"

"What, Celeste?" He seemed frustrated that she'd brought it up again, and Celeste wasn't sure if she should try again, but it was too important to just move on.

"I don't know, we didn't all leave on the best of terms. Did you find Calder?"

"No, I didn't, but he'll return, and I'll be waiting. I'm going to move some things to his house, stay there."

"Are you?" she asked.

"Yes, I need to…" His voice faded, and he didn't finish the sentence. He considered something for a time, and then he looked up to her, his expression resigned. "I must be there when he returns. You must understand. If I lost him, it would end me. So I must believe he'll be back. He has to come back," Quinn said quietly.

She nodded her understanding. "I'm so sorry for what I've done to cause the two of you such grief. I had no idea,"

"Why did you follow me?" he asked.

"I wanted to know…I guess—I wanted to know that you had a mistress—not to know anything about her or you or to intervene. I think I wanted to know that if you married me, you would be able to find that particular enjoyment somewhere else."

He stopped his horse, and she turned Elza, walking around Topher and bringing her up alongside, so they could speak face to face. She waited patiently as he considered.

"I wasn't aware you were quite that serious about marriage," he started. "I didn't—do you prefer women?" he asked finally.

"No, I—Quinn, I'm sorry, I don't know how to answer that." She stared at her gloved fingers woven through the rein. She wasn't sure she could explain how she felt, because she wasn't entirely sure she knew how she felt. After all, she really had no experience either way. She just had this idea that she didn't wish to have that particular experience with anyone.

Quinn reached out and ran his hand from her shoulder to her elbow. "No, don't. You can explain, or not. I won't force it from you. You don't owe me anything. But consider that our conversations are well past chatting about the weather at this point."

"That they are," she said. "Considering last night, I feel as if I do owe you more—"

"No, you owe me no more than the apology which you've already given freely. Besides, I happen to know how difficult it is to answer those type of prying questions when you don't wish to."

"If we'd married…I assumed you liked women," she said.

He shrugged. "I like women fine—" He stopped and looked away.

"I don't understand. I mean. Calder—"

"It isn't about a man or a woman, Celeste. It's about Calder. That's… that's all it is. I love Calder. There is no way around that," he said.

She considered that. That perhaps in another life he would have fallen in love with a woman first, and his entire life would have been easier. Or perhaps not. Perhaps it would have been more difficult for having not had Calder in it.

Whatever it was, she could feel the strength of Quinn's resolve in his feelings for the other man and knew what had happened was even worse than she'd thought. "I am sorry that what I've done has caused such difficulty between the two of you."

"Whatever difficulty there is between us was already there. You are simply a match to a flame," he said.

"Have you ever been with a woman?" she asked.

"Are you asking if I've fucked a woman, Celeste?" he said rather gruffly, and she shied.

She swallowed past the lump in her throat. "Is this your revenge? Are you just trying to discomfit me?" she asked.

"Perhaps somewhat, but more I'm just trying to be quite specific in answering your questions because I believe we owe each other that at least."

"So, have you, then? F—" She closed her eyes. Thinking it was one thing. Saying it out loud? Something else altogether. "Fucked a woman," she whispered.

"Yes," he said.

"When?"

"Have we already come to this conversation?"

Celeste shrugged.

"In the past when Calder traveled, I would take a mistress to sate my need with a willing woman. The first time I did so was by the hand of Calder himself. He'd arranged for a beautiful creature to come to me, a woman Calder had paid very well for the purpose. He always knew I liked women as much as men and it was his way of giving me permission while he was away, and since then it simply became the way of it. I knew Calder wasn't abandoning his own want either. He's told me of the handsome men he's had on his travels," Quinn said.

"That's—" She didn't know what that was. She assumed when you loved someone they were all you thought of.

"Inappropriate?" he asked.

"Maybe not quite that word."

"You must understand—Calder and I have been part of each other's lives in this sense for a very long time. We've never followed any rules because there were none. This wasn't something that was done. There is no Debrett's handbook for sodomy."

Celeste coughed and looked around to be sure nobody had heard him.

Quinn laughed and continued. "As I've grown older, I've changed and so has he, and though I've seen other women whilst he's been away for longer periods, my tastes have changed. They've narrowed to one man."

"Calder."

"Calder."

"So you would have been happy to marry me and continue on with Calder?" she asked.

"I don't know. I knew you were different, and since I wasn't allowed to ask you to marry me in the beginning—"

"Oh, yes, that." She smiled at the memory. "The first night I was out, you took pity on me and asked me to dance, and I told you I would dance with you—but nothing more, and if you offered for my hand, I would refuse."

"Yes, and I said, 'What if I asked you to dance and didn't ask for your hand until the fifth dance?' And you said—"

"'We'll see about it then, but your chances aren't looking good,'" she said.

Quinn laughed. "My heart shattered in my chest," he said with a dramatic hand over his heart.

"Oh, it did not. If anything, I thought you looked quite relieved, and now I know why," she said as she pulled Elza around so they could continue to the park. "I think that was what endeared you to me so."

"That I didn't look like I was after your money?"

"More that you didn't look like you were after my body," she said quietly.

Quinn broke the silence. "The third time we danced, you agreed to be my dance partner only for as long as I didn't ask you to marry me," he said quietly.

"I did, yes."

"Why?"

"I was being a bit selfish at that point because I didn't want to lose you as a friend. I liked you and…I didn't want to do this to you."

"Do what to me, exactly?"

"Quinn," she said so quietly she wasn't sure he would hear.

"Ah, so we've come up against the thing where you don't want me to understand you. Is this the reason why you followed me last night?"

"Yes. No. That's not what it is. It isn't about understanding me. I'm not a thing to be understood."

"I think perhaps you do owe me something," he said, and he was probably right in that.

She nodded. "Ask me again sometime, perhaps when I understand myself a bit better."

"Unfortunately, I won't be much for dancing for a bit," he said as he watched Topher's ears twitch.

"I wouldn't expect you to."

"You saw us," he said. "Everything—all of us?" he questioned.

Celeste recalled the two of them in the doorway and how she'd nearly gone back over the balcony and down the trellis when Calder had shoved Quinn's shoulder into the doorjamb as he pushed him over and came up against his arse. But she hadn't. She'd slid down the wall next to the door, and she'd watched as Calder sank into Quinn, and the looks on their faces were so similar, so welcoming, it felt like finding home.

Celeste closed her eyes as she remembered Quinn straddling that chair over Calder's lap, and her breath left her lungs in a rush as she visualized Quinn on the floor under Calder in perfect clarity. She shifted uncomfortably in her seat. She looked away. She nodded.

"How much of us?" he asked quietly.

"I saw it all." Her voice was rough, and she had to clear her throat. "You had the right of it," she said as she looked back to him. She owed him that much, but he turned away from her, hiding something in his expression.

"That was very private," he said finally.

"Yes, I'm sorry," she said.

"Even more so than usual," he said.

"Even more than—"

"That, last night, it was quite…personal. Of course, those sorts of things are all personal, they should be private, but last night, somehow, it was even more so. What happened—I can't explain," he said finally.

"You don't have to, Quinn. I am so very sorry. I never…I had no idea what I was doing. I shouldn't have done. I—"

"He's not usually so very angry with me. Rough, yes, powerful and possessive—" He visibly shuddered and shifted in his seat. "Yes, absolutely. But that anger? That was different. That was new," he said quietly.

Celeste reached out and ran her thumb across his lip where he had a small cut. He shook her off, and she turned away to let him have his privacy. They rode on for a while in perfect silence. Celeste wasn't sure what to do. She wanted to fix things, but had no idea how.

She couldn't even figure out her own jumbled emotions, much less help Quinn with his, and trying to find Calder was certainly out of the question. She should probably stay about as far away from him as she could possibly manage.

"Where is he?" she said aloud, before she realized.

"I don't know."

Calder

alder rolled over and looked at the sooty window, the offending light fighting its way through the grime and beating its way into his skull through the thin veil of dawn, demanding attention. Demanding he wake and greet the day with force and determination. Calder rolled back over and put his head under the pillow, telling the dawn to fuck right off because he wasn't interested.

He lay there for a while, with the previous night replaying in his head, trying to figure out what had happened and what brought him to this itchy, uncomfortable mattress in the rooms above the Iron Duke. At least he remembered where he was. He hadn't drunk enough to forget that. Maybe that wasn't a good thing. He needed to rise and get his things together so he and Rakshan could follow the few leads they'd found and prepare for their trip to India.

Calder wanted to look into the properties mentioned in the missives he'd read the night before, and he also wanted to apprise the queen of what was happening. He knew she would be interested, and he knew she would be quite unhappy if he didn't keep her apprised of the situation—regardless of his opinions on the matter—and she was, of course, the queen.

He turned back toward the window and threw his feet over the edge of the bed to the floor, letting them drag his legs down and his body upright. He shouldn't have let Rakshan get him so very drunk last night, but the mulled wine had been delicious and something he hadn't had for quite some time, forgoing the pleasure of the drinking for the quick result of hard liquor.

Calder had a feeling that Rakshan's purpose was merely to get to the bottom of Calder's anger. He also had the feeling that Rakshan had done it to help convince him to talk about what was troubling him. He'd been successful in some ways—of course he had—but just how successful remained to be seen, since Calder couldn't remember being put to bed. Calder knew he could trust Rakshan, simply because Warrick trusted him, and Warrick trusted no one.

Perhaps he should find Quinn before leaving for India. He didn't feel right leaving with so much between them. The ache in his gut was more than last night's wine, or so he thought. He pulled himself from the bed and put last night's clothes back on. He would need to return home and change, as well as pack for the trip.

It should be safe for him to return home, because Quinn would be back in the welcoming arms of his parents. Tucked upstairs in the same rooms he'd had as a child. The same rooms they'd first been together in. Perhaps that was why he stayed there? But no—Quinn wasn't maudlin. He wouldn't stay with his family simply because of some ridiculous memories. Would he? He stayed for convenience, Calder told himself, that was all. Perhaps he would have Quinn meet him there.

He scrubbed his hands across his face, then whacked his cane against the floorboards to let Dodson know he was awake. A few minutes later, Lucy arrived with a bowl and a silver ewer of water. She put them on the side table and swayed toward Calder. As one of the oldest inns in London, the Iron Duke had yet to be retrofitted with plumbing on the guest floor.

"Thank you, Lucy, that will be all," he said.

"Are ye quite certain, milord? I've got a few minutes before Ol' Dodsie will have need of me," she said as she ran a finger down his chin, scraping his night beard with her fingernail. He caught up her hand, looked at her palm, and pressed a kiss to the center of it. He was going to have need of a new pub if he couldn't convince Lucy to leave him be. *Accidentally* dumping her in the chicken pen had been the only thing he could do to escape her the last time she'd tried to have her way with him.

"Quite certain, dear Lucy, but I appreciate the effort," he replied. He released her hand and turned her for the door, giving her cushioned backside a little push. He needed to clean up as much as possible so he could get on with his day.

℃

Calder sidled up to the tap for a bit of the hair of the dog before walking out to the inordinately bright London day. It wasn't often they were treated to a stronger sun these days, and it happened to be a bit welcome. He could use a bit of sunshine to warm the ache in his bones.

He walked outside, letting the door swing behind him as he held his hand up to shade his eyes and look out over the park in the square. Two riders caught his eye and salted his blood. His heartbeat rushed his ears deafeningly, and he saw nothing but red.

Quinn and Lady Alain. Calder should have gone to a different pub, a different inn, somewhere they were not so familiar with—an area they didn't frequent. If Calder had thought this through better, he would never have seen them. He would still be happily ignorant.

How quickly Quinn had recovered. How soon he was back to her. Apparently, it would be nothing at all to push Quinn away from him and into the lady's bed.

Rather suddenly, Calder didn't care whether or not he had intended for them to become closer in his absence. Rather suddenly, he wanted to spook her horse and watch her carried off into the sun. His hand tightened on his cane, and he tapped the side of his calf methodically, trying to ease his tension.

Quinn

uinn turned to Celeste. "He'll be back because he always comes back. I don't need to know where he's gone. I don't. I only need to know that he'll be back," he said. He wasn't sure who he was trying to convince. Topher shifted and bumped Elza. They ricocheted back and forth there for a moment, his leg rubbing up against Celeste's through her heavy riding skirts. Her hand released the rein and reached out, smoothing down his thigh and tapping his knee.

"If you believe it, I believe it," she said.

Quinn looked away across the park and wondered. He'd been shaken last night, but somehow in the light of day the world didn't seem so very dire as it had in the night. He wondered at that for a moment, that last night it had felt as though something had shifted, something had been lost, and something had changed and was irretrievably broken. His thumb smoothed over the leather of the pommel as he considered this, tried to reconcile it. He still felt somehow different.

"I'm not so sure," he said finally, and her hand stilled on his thigh. "I don't know what it is, but something…I'm not so sure about anything anymore. I tried to be. I believe I've been trying to convince myself of something, but it simply isn't working." The horses shifted restlessly, squeezing Quinn's and Celeste's legs together tightly between their big bellies, then bringing them apart and breaking all contact. Quinn looked over at her in time to see her eyes widen, her hand coming up, pointing across the park.

"Quinn, I know where Calder is," she said.

Quinn followed the length of her arm, gazing out past the tip of her finger as if a beacon, across the cobbled street to the tap they all loved. His breath left him. His throat tightened.

"Calder—" His voice was bare and mostly unrecognizable. He turned his horse without a second thought for Celeste, moving toward him. Calder had been watching them, for how long he didn't know. "Calder!" he shouted without regard for who heard him. "Please!"

Calder turned and rounded the corner by the Iron Duke, and Quinn put his heels to the gray and leaned into his neck, and Mephistopheles responded in named fashion, recklessly abandoned and determined upon the point to which Quinn steered him, and Quinn had a sudden newfound respect for his mount.

He pressed his knees to turn him, and the horse rounded the corner as if he were on rails, taking the turn without so much as a slip, but Calder was nowhere to be seen. Quinn sat back, bringing Topher to a reluctant canter, jumping and skipping uneasily as if that run had not been enough for him. He fought the excited horse as he spun in the street, and Quinn tried to focus everywhere at once, looking for any sign of Calder, his heart racing, his pulse heavy and loud.

He saw nothing. The mews at the back of the Iron Duke seemed abandoned and still. The street was calm, as though nothing had happened. Quinn shook his head as he tried to clear his mind against the blood rush because he needed to be able to concentrate.

No man had shoved his way through the crowds. It was as though nothing out of the ordinary had transpired here. People looked up to Quinn as though he were the only thing amiss and Calder had simply vanished. Again. Quinn wanted to scream as he searched the street behind the pub for any sign of Calder, fighting the horse and his panic.

Celeste. Damn.

He pulled Topher out of the turn and back toward the square. He should not have left her side. He should never have abandoned her in the park like that. She wasn't safe in London on her own. Even in broad daylight she could be accosted because of her skin—regardless her station. Possibly even because of it.

He found her quietly walking Elza in the tall grass as if nothing had happened. He attempted to slow his breathing and calm his nerves as he steadied his mount. Now was not the time for this. He approached her as if nothing untoward or out of the ordinary had transpired. Damage mitigation was the name of this game. He couldn't be one to somehow tarnish her reputation with a public cut. Hopefully nobody had noticed.

"Celeste," he whispered as he came close enough. "I apologize. That was incredibly callous of me." He said it with a smile in the event anyone was watching them. Her family cut her enough in public, he could not be thought to have done the same.

She returned the same brilliant smile, if a bit more convincing than his felt. "Not at all, Quinn. If you hadn't gone, I would have," she said. "Though, more than likely, that would have made the situation worse."

She was magnificent. Quinn took a deep breath and vowed to give her all of his attention until he returned her home—just as soon as he could manage to control his own anxieties.

"I'm assuming you didn't catch him," she said.

"No, I didn't, but I shouldn't have left you alone like that either. That was terrible form," he said.

"Please, Quinn, if you hadn't, I would have thought much less of you. In fact, we should make our way back to my house, and you can go find him," she said, one small hand on his arm. "Since he is quite obviously still here in London, you should try to find him."

Quinn was still torn. Calder hadn't simply left this time. Calder had run from him. And what had Quinn expected?

He looked back up to Celeste and considered what Calder may have seen—the two of them laughing, the two of them chatting amiably, the two of them riding closely and comfortably. Quite simply, the two of them, together. After last night. His jaw tensed to the point of an ache, and Quinn rubbed his thumb along his temple as he tried to think this through, but his heart picked up yet again.

After last night, if positions were somehow reversed and Quinn had seen Calder so cozy with Celeste, he would have run as well. His chest tightened, and he felt as though his lungs would be crushed beneath an invisible weight. He couldn't lose Calder. He simply couldn't. Everything had gone wrong in the last twenty-four hours. Absolutely, positively, everything that could have gone wrong had.

Blood rushed from his head, and his vision narrowed. He felt lightheaded and reached out to steady himself. "Celeste—"

Darkness.

Celeste

As Quinn slumped over in the saddle, Celeste had at least three things run through her mind. One, he was dead. She immediately dismissed this. Two, he fainted. This was entirely possible, considering he had warned her about his episodes. She much preferred that idea to the former. And three, she'd truly ruined everything.

Once again, Celeste had come between these two men, without malice—certainly—but without thought or intention as well. As it happened, none of that truly mattered. What mattered was only that it did happen, again, and Calder had reacted badly, again—and rightly so.

She grabbed on to Topher's tackle and Quinn's coat to hold him steady and tight against Elza as she attempted to keep him from hitting the ground between the horses. She spoke sweetly and gently to keep the horses calm as she scanned the park for any sort of help she could find. Anything at all.

She saw nothing, then she saw a man running toward her from the east end of the park. *Please be no one of import. Please be no one of great stature. Please be a nobody that anybody would listen to.*

Her pleas were ignored…of a fashion, because he happened to be one of the most powerful dukes of the realm. The saving grace was that the duke also happened to be Quinn's cousin Roxleigh, whom she had only just met the night before.

He came up to the horse and Quinn, knocked his boot loose from the stirrup, and mounted Topher behind Quinn, sitting on the horse's rump and wrapping his arms about Quinn to steady him at his chest.

"Follow me," he said. He took the rein from her and led the horse out of the park and around to the mews behind Roxleigh House.

She hoped Quinn would be well. He'd told her that he had these episodes at times, but she'd never been witness to one. He'd said it prudent she know, considering they were together often. He'd told her not to worry, because he would be fine even as he had no control of them. She worried anyway.

This wasn't exactly how she'd thought the day would go. She considered everything that had happened as she followed, because she had to figure out, above all else, how to extricate herself from the situation. She needed to keep her distance from Quinn, at the very least, until he and Calder could work things out. The last thing she wanted was to come between the two of them yet again. She shivered as her mind drifted back to the night before when she'd watched them from the balcony.

You're mine, you know, you'll never be able to walk away from me.

Calder's fiercely possessive words juddered though her system, but not for the want of hearing them, solely for the want of witnessing them again—directed at Quinn. That fully realized heaviness of passion and want. The thickness of his voice as he ground out words that could not have been more true. She'd felt the truth, the want, and the plea in those words.

We are already damned, the two of us.

And perhaps they were. And perhaps she was, as well, for wanting so very much for them to be together again. What was it between Calder and Quinn that pulled her in so desperately that she felt as though she would do anything for them to be together?

Certainly this wasn't normal. Certainly others didn't feel this sort of connection to people they had no intimate relationship with. She closed her eyes and felt large warm hands wrap around her waist, shocking her back to the present. She looked down to find Roxleigh pulling her from the saddle.

"I should return home," she said absently.

He narrowed his eyes on her. "You have no interest in staying with Quinn?" he asked.

"I do, yes. I'm sorry, I just…" She closed her eyes. What a disastrous turn.

His hands tightened on her again, and she allowed him to remove her from the horse and place her on her feet. "I apologize. I'm a bit—" She looked around, saw Topher being managed by one of Roxleigh's grooms.

"Where is Quinn?"

"I had the men take him inside. Come," he said gruffly.

She felt as though he was peeling her apart by bits and pieces, looking for something, but just what he looked for she had no idea. She nodded once and followed him across the gardens to the house. They skirted the back of the house, which was nothing but a massive ballroom, and entered through a small door in an attached orangery.

"They've taken him to the green parlor, this way," he said, as though she knew what any of that meant. Perhaps he just wished to fill the emptiness between them, but it felt a bit forced, as though he wasn't amenable to entertaining ladies. She nodded out of habit, but as quickly as he moved, he wasn't looking back to be sure she'd heard him at all.

He wove through a series of passages, and they arrived as if from a dark cave into the bright, warm room that must have been the green parlor. Quinn was sprawled on a large settee, and Francine knelt at his shoulder, speaking quietly and mopping his brow with a cloth. She turned when Roxleigh came up beside her, left the cloth on his forehead, and stood, her hands going to Roxleigh's person as if drawn by some magnetic force.

Celeste blinked, feeling like she was once again intruding upon a scene she had no business intruding upon. "I beg your pardon for my…" She stopped. She had no idea what to say. Lady Roxleigh smiled at her, and she was instantly put at ease.

"Quinn?" Celeste said and looked down to him. His head turned toward the back of the settee, and his arm came up to cover his face.

"He is well," Lady Roxleigh said. "He has panic attacks occasionally. He just needs a minute, and he'll be fine," she said.

"Panic?" she said.

"Er…yes. You've probably never heard that. It's just what the family calls them." She looked up to Roxleigh, who was doing absolutely nothing but watching her. "His heart races, and he can't seem to control it, can't calm himself, and he passes out."

Celeste walked over and sat at the edge of the settee next to his leg. She lifted his hand and held it. Tears pricked her eyes that what happened in the park this morning had caused him such distress. "I'm so sorry, Quinn."

He stirred at her hip, and she smoothed one hand down his cheek. She turned to Roxleigh. "Thank you," she said.

He shrugged, just a small lift of one shoulder. "He's family. Do you know what set him off?"

Celeste knew her eyes went wide, and she thought she should probably close her mouth because she didn't know what to say, and therefore, sitting here with her mouth hanging open was a bit untoward. She snapped it shut and turned back to Quinn.

"Was it Calder?" Lady Roxleigh asked, and Celeste went cold. "I only ask because they had a bit of an argument last night. The two of them have always been quite close."

Celeste turned enough to see Roxleigh squeeze one of her hands. Did they know? She turned away again. "We did see him outside the pub, but he left before Quinn could catch up to him." She heard a rustling of fabric, and Roxleigh moved into her line of sight.

"I appreciate you staying with him. I'm thankful I happened to be leaving the house when this happened, but I do have business that I need to attend now that he's safe. I will bid you good day." He bowed slightly, his hand on his waist, then turned and left. Francine followed him, bussed his cheek, and pulled the bell next to the entry.

"I'll get some tea, shall I?" she said. "He should wake up pretty soon, and it would be nice for him to see a familiar face. Not that I'm not familiar, but I wasn't there when he passed out,"

"Right. I'm supposed to go to tea with his mother today," Celeste said quietly.

"I'll send a note. She'll understand," Lady Roxleigh said.

"Thank you, Your Grace," Celeste replied.

"Please do call me Francine. You're a friend of Quinn's, and that's enough for me. Titles still make me a bit twitchy," she said with a smile as she came to sit in the chair next to the settee.

Celeste wasn't entirely sure what she meant by that, but there was something warmly familiar about the way she spoke.

"Celeste, please," she replied.

Quinn groaned, and Celeste turned back to him. "What…" he said, and she squeezed his hand.

"You're safe, Quinn, I'm here," Celeste said, but he didn't respond, and watching closely, she could see that he wasn't actually awake at all. Her heart sank in her chest, dragging her shoulders down as though she wore a heavy coat. She fought it, trying to straighten her shoulders and sit properly.

A man bearing a large tray entered and placed it on the butler in front of the settee. "Will that be all?" he asked.

"Sanders, please send word to Lady Cheshire that Lord Wyntor is here, as well as Lady Alain. Tell her they send their regrets, and I will share them another day soon," Francine said.

"Yes, ma'am," he said, then turned and left.

Francine turned back to the tea. "Cream and sugar?" she asked.

"Sugar only, thank you."

"So the two of you were riding in the park? Are Quinn's intentions honorable?" Francine asked with a smile.

"What do you mean?" Celeste asked.

"Well, it certainly isn't riding in Rotten Row. He obviously didn't intend to make any sort of statement today, but you did dance together last night, enough to be noted, and he did ask his cousins to guard you from the onslaught of eligible peers."

"I suppose he did." Celeste paused to consider it. "I suppose we were on our way to figuring these things out," she said. "We're friends. We would suit. Isn't that the way of things under the best of circumstance?"

"Love would be the best circumstance. Barring that, yes, friendship would be a lovely beginning."

"That's all I wish for, nothing more."

"Nothing? You don't want…"

"I don't want more than…" She sighed and melted a bit. She wished she could be honest with someone, anyone. She felt a hand on hers, and she looked up to find Francine with the most compassionate expression she'd ever seen, and something inside her shifted and opened and—

"I don't like to be touched," she blurted out, and Francine pulled her hand back, but Celeste caught it. "That's not what I meant. I don't mind this. I…" She shook her head, and Francine seemed to consider her.

"You mean in the way a man might touch a woman he's married to," she said.

Celeste looked up again as she tried to decide whether to try to explain away what she'd said or just fall into it and hope Francine could be trusted. Celeste could tell that Francine was being delicate, and from what she'd heard about her—which wasn't much, because nobody dared speak badly of a Trumbull—Francine was not generally quite so delicate. "Yes," she said finally. "Intercourse. I'm not interested," she said.

There it was. She was out with it, and it felt glorious, and she soaked it in, because any moment Francine would ring her parents, and she would be off to the asylum, this time with a diagnosis of hysteria. At least then she would never be able to come between Calder and Quinn again. Any moment Francine would do it. But instead—

"You've not suffered any sort of trauma, have you? Is it because someone has treated you badly?"

"No, nobody has ever touched me in that way, and I don't think I want to ever be touched in that way, by anyone."

"Women?" she asked, and Celeste froze. Cut her gaze to the entryway to see if anyone was listening, to see if there was a man with a straitjacket looming behind the curtain. "I'm sorry. I'm blunt. Please believe me when I say that I'm not judging you and would never do you any harm because of your sexual orientation." Celeste nodded and Francine held up the cup of tea. She took the cup and ducked her head, sipping slowly.

This woman spoke a different language than she did, but it was altogether familiar, and goose bumps rose across Celeste's arms as a chill spread from her ears to her toes. "Sexual orientation?" she asked carefully.

"Yes—gay, straight, lesbian…er…homosexual, sapphist, etcetera," she said.

"None of those," Celeste replied. "None at all." But part of Celeste wanted her to keep speaking like this, to keep asking her questions, because the words she used were sneaking into her memories and pulling some long-unused threads.

Francine considered her. "None of the above. Asexual?"

Celeste didn't know what that meant. She shrugged.

"All right." Francine said. "Can I ask you one more question? It may seem odd."

These questions haven't been odd? "Certainly," she said warily.

"Are you truly from London? Were you actually born here?"

Celeste froze, the cup halfway to her lips. She set it back on the saucer, then on the tray when the shaking of her hands made the china rattle.

"Whatever do you mean by that?" she asked.

Francine studied her in a most uncomfortable way. "I mean…wow, this is a difficult thing to ask," Francine said. "Finding Lulu was so much easier."

"I find simply having out with it is the best course," Celeste said as she tangled her fingers together and held them as still as she could.

"Were you born in this century?"

Celeste froze. Her inclination was to say no, but she didn't know this woman, so she stayed her reaction to the question. She had shared too much already. The memories Celeste had of her childhood were so vastly different from everything she knew now that she chose to ignore them.

To survive, she'd built memories from scratch with the people who should have been there.

Celeste didn't truly understand why. She remembered wishing she could live anywhere but where she was, and she remembered thinking that had come true. She also remembered she'd been about ten when it had happened, and her mother had blamed her strange behavior on her heritage, her grandmother, a sudden illness…everything.

She'd been sent to the Royal Earlswood Hospital in Surrey to recover.

What was Celeste doing here?

"Celeste?"

She looked back to Francine, realizing she'd been lost in her thoughts. She reached for her teacup, if only to have something to do with her hands.

"You don't have to answer that. If what I suspect is true, you must be terrified, and I simply wish you to know that you're not alone, should you wish to talk."

"You're not concerned for Quinn?" she asked into the teacup. She could see Francine's smile without looking.

"I'm not concerned for Quinn as far as you're concerned. Though I am concerned for Quinn where Calder is concerned," she said, and that did bring Celeste's attention. "Listen to me, don't say anything you aren't comfortable saying. If everything works out, I would hope that we could be friends. I need more women in my life who aren't over-tightening their corsets. So to speak. I need some honesty and reality. Finding people who are real and aren't the typical societal belle has been lovely. I'm looking forward to getting to know Lulu, and Perry's friend Hugh recently married a woman who is…well, perhaps we don't need to get into details just yet. Know that I look forward to your friendship, should you be in need of a friend. I've realized it's quite lonely as a woman in the Victorian era."

For the first time, Celeste saw a genuine sadness in her eyes. This odd woman, she could come to trust her, and what's more, Celeste thought that perhaps she could come to like her as well…very much.

"What are you women tittering on about?"

Celeste startled and put the cup on the table with a loud clink and stood, allowing Quinn to pull himself up and put his feet back on the floor.

"Nothing at all, Quinn," Francine said.

He rubbed his eyes and leaned back into the settee, his head falling back over the top of it as he took the cloth from his forehead and dropped it to the floor.

"Are you feeling better?" Celeste asked.

"I…" He seemed to consider. "How did I get here?"

Calder

alder had watched from the Iron Duke as Quinn panicked and lost his seat, and it had taken every ounce of his anger to stay him and keep him from running to Quinn's aid. He'd nourished that anger by concentrating on Celeste and her hands on his Quinn. Calder had very nearly broken, but when he'd seen Rox running from his house to Quinn, he'd known he would be safe.

Calder had simply run around the building and gone in through the back because he hadn't expected Quinn to give chase, and when he had, when Calder had heard the hoofbeats bearing down on him, he'd known he would have been run down in a matter of moments.

Calder tossed clothes into his portmanteau as he remembered the panic he'd induced in Quinn. He had done that. He was at fault. He had been the cause of that, and it pained him. He did regret that. He regretted it most soundly. Hurting Quinn in that way wasn't something he savored, and Calder was newly determined that this all had to stop—and the best way for it to stop was for him to leave and never to return. He refused to be the source of such difficulties.

Calder would send for the rest of his things as necessary, once he had an idea how to have them sent without them being followed. Of course, Quinn wouldn't follow, so what did it matter? Until today, Quinn had never followed him directly. Perhaps it would just take some time and Quinn would give up the wait and let him be. If Calder didn't return this time, in theory, Quinn would move on. Considering he already had someone to move on with, it didn't seem all that extraordinary a thought. Quinn and Celeste could be happy together, because Quinn wasn't like Calder in that

Quinn appreciated women as much as he did men. So Quinn and Celeste would be happy together—he repeated it to himself, beginning the mantra that would hold him together while he disappeared. Quinn and Celeste would be happy together. He would leave, and everything would settle, and Quinn…he could be happy with Celeste.

Calder closed the bag and put it next to his bedroom door. Quinn was safely at Roxleigh's. Calder wasn't sure how long that would last, so while it had been the best possible time to return home and gather what he needed, he also needed to get out of here quickly. Once done packing, he would send word to the queen, letting her know he could not present himself in person because the immediacy of his departure was unavoidable.

He sat heavily in the green chair at the end of his bed, running his hands across the heavy velvet upholstery on the arms of the chair to disturb it, only to smooth it once again.

"My lord, Rakshan awaits you in the parlor. Do you have any further instruction for me?" his man said from the entry as he reached for his bag.

"Close up the house and forward any missives to Warrick. I will let my mother know that if they wish to visit London for an extended period, they may avail themselves of the house, but I will ask she give you notice to prepare. Beyond that, tell no one. It is nobody's business, as usual. If Quinn comes…tell him to speak with Warrick." Quinn would never speak with Warrick. The very idea of approaching Warrick would stop Quinn in his tracks, because he'd always been afraid of him and was even more so since he'd returned from India. His man bowed quickly and left, and Calder went downstairs to the parlor.

"Did you find anything at all on the properties?" he asked Rakshan.

"He seems to have a notion to run a hotel. He's not attempting to advertise in any way, however. The establishment has an entry with two secure rooms—a bar and a parlor, most likely. The rest of the floors have rooms equipped with beds and a water closet and not much else."

"Toilets? In every room?" Calder asked.

"Yes, every room has a toilet and a shower," Rakshan said with a nod.

"That's more than most hotels can boast at the moment." Calder scratched his chin as he considered it. He needed a shave.

"I agree, but the uppermost floors are the most concerning. This

particular establishment has two floors that would be considered private, the first with rooms much like the more public floors, except two beds to a room and only one shared water closet on the floor. It's larger, but not like the lower floors."

"And the uppermost floor?" Calder asked.

"I'm not sure if it has been remodeled, or if it is as it was before he purchased it. It seems to be set up as a nursery," Rakshan said, and Calder watched as his face tensed, his eyes going dark. "There's a schoolroom and several smaller beds. Books, toys, children's things," he finished quietly.

"You're still working on the assumption they intend to set up a private whorehouse?" Calder asked.

"I can only hope not. For what would the purpose of a schoolroom be to a whorehouse?" Rakshan said, and a knot in Calder's gut twisted. He reached out to the mantel over the fireplace to steady himself, wrapping his hands around the edge of it until the blood left and his knuckles turned white.

"I don't want to know the purpose of this house. I only want it to fall into disrepair from never having been used," Calder said. "Why would they put such a place in the bottoms?"

"Oh, you misunderstand," Rakshan said. "This isn't the property in the bottoms. That property seems to be a holding area of some sort. Close to the docks, storage areas, cots, showers, an area set up for several seamstresses. I imagine this is where the women and children will be brought when they arrive. Where they will be made presentable."

"Where is the house you spoke of?" Calder asked.

"My lord, it's here on Sussex Square, just across the park."

Calder dropped his hands, clenching and unclenching his fists to get the blood moving again. He felt like using them to cause a certain lord some damage.

"What else did you find? Is there more?" His voice was foreign to him.

"No, the house is empty. The holding house is empty. There's nothing… and Exeter left for India three days past."

"Does Grayson know?" Calder asked.

"In generalities only. I informed His Grace that we would be returning to India, of course, but he is yet unaware of the letter."

"He cannot know about that letter, not until we know for certain if it's true…and even then there may be a remedy for which Gray—"

"Do you intend to do him harm Madoc if he is alive?" Rakshan asked.

"I have no intentions beyond finding him and figuring out what he has to do with the group of men we're watching. Beyond that…there are a multitude of possibilities."

Rakshan inspected him carefully, then nodded. "I will not help you if this is a suicide mission. I will not help if there is revenge or murder in your intent."

"I do not at present intend anything. I only know that Gray has a wife, and a new life, and a new possibility, and I refuse to let a dead man take those things from him. What I know is that I'm prepared for all eventualities, Rakshan, but what those eventualities are…I know only as much as you do."

"Understood," Rakshan said.

"I should be off. I'm leaving today, and it will take at minimum of three weeks to arrive in Jodhpur, and that's if everything goes perfectly. Which… it seldom does. Are you coming or following?" Calder asked.

"I gave my case to the footman," Rakshan said. He stood and followed Calder out as the last bags were strapped to his carriage, and with the snap of a whip, they were gone, the carriage and her passengers sucked into the afternoon fog that had settled over London. A month of travel. A month of nothing but sitting on trains and steamships and having nothing to do but think of Quinn. Perhaps this wasn't the best plan after all.

Quinn

Quinn wanted to shrivel up in a ball and disappear. How mortifying to have created such a scene in Grosvenor Square. In full daylight, while courting a lady. He was an utter fool. He sat there with his head thrown back, listening to Celeste and Francine talk about absolutely nothing. Better than the nothing so many women nattered on about—embroidery and shopping and the like. At least Celeste and Francine spoke on books and food, two of Quinn's favorite things in the world, but how much could one say about a book? It was good, you should read it should be plenty for any person to know. What was this need for dissecting every small bit? Honestly, Alice fell down the rabbit hole, so it was her own damned fault she went through the looking glass as well and had need to defeat the Jabberwocky. Quinn wanted to scream.

He groaned and was immediately repentant when he felt a warm hand at his knee, as he hadn't wished to draw attention to himself. He stood and walked to the front window that looked out over the park. He couldn't even see the side street that led to the pub from here, because the smog had laid in so thick.

"Why did you bring me here?" he said, stopping their conversation immediately.

"I didn't, actually. Roxleigh saw us in the park, and he came when you collapsed and brought you here," she said.

"Like a woman?" Quinn responded as he turned from the window.

"Well, I'm certain I don't know what you mean by that," Celeste said. "He brought you here in the only way he could manage."

"Don't be an ass," Francine cut in with a glare, and he was instantly shamed. Francine was very good at putting all the men of his family in their place with a single look, only because she was right.

"No, I apologize Francine, Celeste, truly," he said, but he knew she wasn't finished.

"There's no need for apology, Quinn, just stop being so sexist. It isn't demeaning, what happened to you. It happens. That Gideon was outside and saw you and was able to help Celeste and bring you safely here should be considered a good thing, not something demoralizing. Simply because you're a man and he carried you doesn't make you less, and it certainly doesn't make you a woman," she said.

"So he did carry me? As if I needed another reason to avoid him." Quinn turned back to the window. His cousin's wife took some getting used

to, but he, as well as the rest of their family, had not only become used to her points of view, but had also begun to understand and assimilate them. Rox and Perry had even been attempting to change their peers, and as difficult a task as that was, at least they tried. This notion that women deserved equal rights like men…it had been terribly foreign to all of them, but she was persistent. And not merely persistent, but understanding, and lovely, and compassionate, and in everything she did, she proved herself to be one of the best and smartest people he knew.

He felt a hand at his shoulder and looked

down. "I realize I can't change a world that will take many decades to catch up with my thinking," Francine said. "I understand the difficulty in that, and I know that it has pained all of you to be forced into it so suddenly."

"And I do apologize for my rudeness. My temper has its own mind at times."

She turned him toward her from the window with her hands on his shoulders, took his face in her hands, her touch cool and soothing. "I can see what a wonderful man you are, Quinn, inside and out. Please know that no matter what you may be hiding, I'm here for you. I love you, and I will never abandon you," she said.

Why would Francine say something like that? Did Celeste tell her about him and Calder? Did Francine know about him?

Quinn glanced over to Celeste, who was sipping her tea and didn't seem to have heard any of what Francine had said. She wouldn't have said anything—he convinced himself—not after all the apologies and promises.

"I like Celeste for you," Francine said. "She's lovely, Quinn, and she's special. She needs a safe place to call home, and I think you could provide that for her and still be happy."

He looked back to Francine, then shook off her hands. "I should be getting her home. They'll be looking for her," he said.

"No, they won't," Celeste replied, and he knew then that she'd heard everything Francine had said to him.

He walked over to her and sat, turning her to face him.

"We need to talk."

"I agree. But first you need to find him," she whispered. "So take me home." She stood and took his hand, and he followed. He looked over to Francine with an unsteady smile, and the one she returned warmed him to his toes. She was quite unsettling. Roxleigh truly was the luckiest man he knew in this world, and possibly the next.

Q

After leaving Celeste at home—and she was right, nobody had missed her a bit—he went back to Calder House. It was dark and silent. Yeats was there, and he let Quinn know that Calder had closed up the house and left no forwarding information for anyone other than Warrick.

So Quinn went to Warrick House, but nobody answered the door, and Quinn was actually relieved in that, because Warrick truly scared the daylights out of him, even more so than Roxleigh. Of all of his cousins, Warrick was the most mysterious, the most detached, and the most frightening. That particular branch of the family tree had been shrouded in darkness until only recently, and it had all started with the death of the previous Warrick, whom nobody seemed to mourn. Quinn hadn't spent much time with those particular cousins as children, because his mother and father hadn't been keen on the current duke, and when Warrick had been sent away, there had been no point in him visiting at all, because his older brothers had been as awful as their father.

He knew Warrick's mother had tried to find him, to no avail, but the queen…she'd forwarded his letters patent to him after his father and older brothers were killed, and he was forced to ascend to the title. Warrick had only recently returned by that demand. These facts didn't particularly tell him much about Warrick, other than that the queen was the only person who'd known where he was—because his family certainly hadn't—and that fact alone only told him that Warrick had been, in some way, in service to Her Royal Highness, which made him not merely powerful, but a force.

With no help from that quarter, Quinn set out to all the places he knew Calder would not go. White's, back to the Iron Duke, to his favorite bookshop near Harrods, Rotten Row, his mother and father's house… He hadn't truly expected to find him in any of these places, and he didn't, but he didn't want to admit to himself that he was simply wasting time.

Quinn had considered that Calder may have gone to one, thinking it safe because he wasn't expected to be there, so perhaps it wasn't entirely wasted, and yet…Quinn wasn't putting much effort into his search. Somehow, Quinn knew that he wasn't going to find him anywhere—and he didn't. Quinn was just turning himself in circles, because if he stopped—it meant the search was over, and he would have to accept that Calder was gone. That wasn't something Quinn was prepared to face just yet.

He returned to his parents' house. The one he should have left years ago. The only place he had and the one place he didn't want to be anymore. He felt like he didn't have a home. He didn't belong anywhere. Without Calder or the expectation of Calder, Quinn was truly lost. He looked up to

the façade of the house and tried to think of anywhere else he could be. He was still wearing the clothes he'd taken from Calder and really did need to bathe and change. He should have Calder's things cleaned so they would be ready for his return.

There were things Quinn should do, and he didn't want to do a single one of them. He wanted to curl up in front of Calder's fireplace, in Calder's clothes, and wait there until Calder came back. Somewhere safe, somewhere with a friendly face. Somewhere he wouldn't feel so very alone. Goddamn, but he was a mess.

Celeste

After Quinn escorted her home, Celeste decided to stay in her room the rest of the day, reading, in an attempt to avoid everyone in the household. She did have the distant hope that someone would wish to talk with her, but she didn't seek anyone out.

She moved through this house like a ghost, one that nobody paid any mind to. Her questions about Francine and her past, coupled with her concern for Quinn and Calder, unsettled her to such an extent that even reading was difficult. She had to reread pages over and again as she tried her level best to pay attention to the story.

She finally gave up and took up her quill and diary, curling up in the window seat by the balcony.

What I remember from that day I don't actually remember because I'm not a reliable witness to my own history. I have been, and continue to be, treated for a mental illness that never existed. Or perhaps it did. It depends upon how I feel in any given moment.

Some days I fight reality, and some days I don't.

Some days I believe in my memories, other days I believe in theirs.

What I remember from before that day was the warmth of a mother. Something I haven't felt since, don't expect to ever feel again. I feel the loss of that like a weight upon my shoulders.

What I remember from that day is pain, because I was hurt. I don't remember how, I only know I was chasing…something.

What I remember from that day is pain, because I lost everything I knew to be true.

What I remember from that day was waking up in the arms of the stranger who would become my father. Or perhaps he already was and I did deserve to be locked away.

Regardless, what I remember from that day…were the two boys that came to my aid.

One dark, one light.

An angel and a devil.

What I remember from that day is a name…

And no matter how I fight that memory, the name never fades. It has taken up residence in my soul and is whispered with every beat of my heart.

Quinn.

She wrote, and wrote, and wrote, until her fingers bled blue, darkness stole her sight, and her neck had a kink in it.

She wondered if there had been supper, since nobody had come for her, or called for her, or even sent a servant to fetch her. She wasn't truly hungry at any rate, so there wasn't much point in searching anything out. She stood and twisted the knob to open up the gas line a bit for the lights in her room and went to the wardrobe to remove her dress. She remembered pushing buttons to turn lights on. She pushed the memory away, something that had become second nature to her because those memories were dangerous.

She loosed the dress, untied her petticoats, and shimmied her way out of all of it. She released the steel busk of her corset, letting it drop to the floor, and she took her first true breath of the day.

She caught a glimpse of herself in the cheval mirror next to her wardrobe, the flickering of the gaslight casting long shadows across her body. She supposed she was pretty for a woman with brown skin. She supposed someone could appreciate the way she looked and put up with her for the right amount of money, like her mother said. She supposed someone would see past the flaws that society insisted she had, to see who she truly was inside.

She slid her fingers along her grandmother's strand of pearls that she now always wore at her neck, the silky smooth surface against the pads of her fingertips a calming reassurance that someone loved her even if that someone had never existed for her.

This grandmother, she was certain, would have loved her regardless of the tone of her skin. This grandmother, she was quite certain, would have taught her how to better love herself in her own skin as well. But society, as it was, attempted to teach her something altogether different. Outwardly she accepted it, but inwardly…

She smoothed her fingers over her eyes, smudging the kohl, making her eyes appear even more oval and drawn out. She sucked her lower lip, plumping it and bringing the blood to it before she wet her lips to give them a bit of a shine. She loosed her hair from the pins, pulling them free and dropping them to the floor, the pricking at her scalp a welcome reminder that she was alive and well, and much more so than many others who resembled her.

She wondered where her grandmother was from, who her people were, where she might have fit in. No one in her family dared speak on it, and so she had no idea. Chastened by the thought, she dropped her hands and stood tall and straight in the mirror, a proper lady—if mostly naked and improper. Hands held gently just below the pinch of her waist, buttocks thrust out to flatten her abdomen and support her bustle further. The men loved a big bustle, oh yes, they did.

Her gaze followed the long line of her neck, down her shoulder to her hands hanging gently from her wrists. She pressed them against her belly and faced the mirror, truly inspecting her body, this thing she lived in but mostly ignored because it was her enemy in the eyes of her family.

She thought her body beautiful. The color of her skin was rich. It wasn't pasty, and you couldn't see her veins through it. But then again, her body also didn't work the way other bodies did. Until last night, she'd never felt anything like lust. Until last night, she'd believed herself to be exempt from the messiness of physical love. Until last night, she'd been wrong.

She smoothed her hands across the waist of her drawers, down her naked abdomen to her— What did she call it? She stared at herself in the mirror as the whisper of a word she'd never been allowed to say appeared in her mind. Pussy. She touched herself, but she felt nothing, just as she always had. She slid her fingers between her legs, one hand over the other, searching for something to pleasure and finding nothing but skin. It seemed that last night had been naught but a fluke.

She pulled away and turned from the mirror, casting her gaze about the room. It wasn't so different from Calder's chambers, if smaller. They both had the basics—a bed, a fireplace, a secretary, a chair. She paused, then pulled the chair away from the secretary and turned it toward the mirror.

She sat down and spread her legs, matching the way Calder had sprawled in his chair at the end of his bed as he teased Quinn mercilessly, waiting for him to come to him. She closed her eyes and remembered. Quinn had stood, and Calder had licked his cock, and oh! Celeste felt the first twinge of that lust she'd experienced yesternight.

Celeste spread her legs farther, as Quinn had, putting her knees over the arms of the chair, stretching them as wide as they'd ever been. She ran one hand down her face to her neck and squeezed, just like Quinn had done Calder. *I like it when you say please,* he'd said. *When I do this.*

She squeezed her own throat just as he had Calder's, and her other hand went straight to her pussy, sliding much more easily against her sensitive

skin, which was now wet, and—oh God, this is it. She pulled back from the sudden fear of it, the friction so strong, so sharp, it sent strings of sensation through her body.

She looked up to the mirror, her body flushed, her chest rising and falling heavily, her pussy so wet she could see it glistening at a distance. What did she want? She closed her eyes. She wanted to watch.

She closed her eyes to her own body and went back to Calder's room. To he and Quinn fucking in that chair. Fucking. It wasn't sex. It wasn't intercourse. It was fucking. There was no other word that fit but that crass, improper, perfect word.

He didn't use his penis, he used his cock. And he didn't make love to him, he fucked him. Just thinking the words flipped some buried switch in her.

She wished she'd been privy to a different angle, because she hadn't been able to see everything from where she'd been, only the profile of their sweaty bodies writhing together on that chair. At the moment, though, that was enough.

Her hands came back to her body. This time, she kept her eyes closed and concentrated on them. They were both so strong, so powerful, so incredibly passionate. They didn't have a clean and easy kind of love between them. It was messy and hard and beautiful and—oh God, did that feel good!

She found that elusive spot that women spoke of, calling it a nub, a button, a bud, a whole host of appropriate terms for such an inappropriate little thing. One of her legs rose and fell of its own accord when she touched it, as if this one tiny thing were the strings to her puppet. Her body tensed and relaxed as she moved, her wetness loud in her ears.

She slipped her hand from her neck, and her forearm grazed one of her nipples through her chemise, and she nearly came off the chair to standing at the sheer shock of it, the web of fingers shooting out in all directions from that point, one she'd not known about. She brought her fingers there and pinched, rhythmically matching her other hand as it brought that bud to an impossible hardness, and once, twice—she was certain she yelled as her heartbeat stalled then picked up twice as fast, and she could feel it rush her veins, pushing her blood and concentrating in every muscle in her belly before releasing with a flood of sensation that racked her body with convulsions.

Le petit mort, she thought. And wasn't that the truth of it.

Her legs slipped to the floor as she lost control of her muscles, her body sliding after as it turned to jelly and the contractions waned to pulses. She lay there, the pulses finally calming to shivers, a puddle of eased want, her hands holding her breast and her pussy as if to soothe them. It's all right, it's all right, we're still here, it's all right.

Oh God, but now she understood, and all she wanted was more.

Quinn

uinn's hands tightened on the wood of the balcony doorway as he watched what was one of the most erotic little episodes he'd ever seen in his life. It wasn't as if he'd never seen a woman bring herself off, but a prostitute doing that for him to watch seemed so very mechanical in comparison to this.

He tried to control his breathing as he watched his little Celeste slip from the chair, shaking and shuddering in a loose ball of flesh on the floor. He leaned his forehead against the cool of the glass as he brought himself down.

When he looked back up, she was still lying on the floor, her body calming yet still jerking occasionally, her knees drawn up, and her chin tucked to her chest. She didn't look like she intended to move, and he knew she would catch a chill rather soon.

He wanted to go into her room and wrap her up safe and warm, hold her until the crisis passed, until she drifted off into a sweet and silent dream. He imagined that wouldn't exactly be welcome. He imagined Celeste would react to his spying much the way Calder had reacted to hers—and wasn't this just a wicked turn of events?

Quinn really didn't want to upset her greatly. Then again—after everything that had happened in the last twenty-four hours—he really did. He hadn't wanted any sort of revenge against her. He'd never been a vindictive person. He understood what she'd done and truly had forgiven her, but…his hand moved to the handle of the door and pushed.

The mechanism clicked, and he pulled the door wide easily, and even still Celeste didn't stir. When his gaze caught her face reflected in the mirror, he could see she was sleeping that extremely peaceful sleep only an intense climax could bring. He kicked his shoes off and tiptoed to the bed. He pulled the counterpane from it and approached her on silent feet.

Quinn slowly covered her body, careful not to drag the fabric against her still sensitive skin. He wrapped her up in the heavy quilt and lifted her carefully, walking to the bed and laying her down. She snuggled into the heavy bedding, one hand curling beneath her chin as she settled in. Quinn went around to the other side of the bed, tossed his jacket over the window seat, and he lay down on the bed facing her.

She really was one of the most beautiful people he'd ever met, and that she was such a lovely person on top of it…it was a tragedy that London Society had it out for this girl. He supposed that her family's indifference to her stirred that ire quite a bit more than was necessary. His family knew more than most that closing ranks and refusing to bow to society was the only way to protect their own. That and status.

Celeste was a true diamond—one that he could no longer think of as a girl. Celeste was most absolutely a woman, and what a woman she was. He was learning so much about her.

Quinn knew he loved Calder. He loved him with every ounce of his being. But there were many, many ounces to him, so perhaps he could give her just one of them, just a single ounce to carry her until she found her own place, whether that be with them or someone else. Obviously, she was a passionate person. Obviously, she would need someone to explore that side of herself with. It just couldn't be him. Because of Calder.

Quinn closed his eyes. He wished for something simple for all of them. Wasn't that what everyone wished for? A small home in the country where nobody would bother you? Where you could live freely however you wished to. Where you could be yourself without fear of anyone else? Some people had managed it. The Duke of Castleberry and his duchess, for two.

Everyone knew they had some sort of arrangement with the Baron Endsleigh, and nobody bothered them. One, because they did what they did away from London, away from society, and when they did come to the city, they were compliant and respectful and didn't push themselves at anyone, and two, because Castleberry was entirely too powerful to deal with. A blessing, that.

It wouldn't work with he and Calder, though. Calder would have to give up his claim to St. Cyr to be with Quinn, and giving that up would render them fodder for the wolves no matter where they lived. No social power, no standing, no protection, no chance. If they did this, if they brought down that much of the family, Quinn believed the family wouldn't do as they'd done in the past. Quinn didn't believe their family would protect them from society. The two of them, who they were, what they'd done…it was too far beyond the bounds of society.

Celeste was right. He needed to find Calder and at least speak with him, explain things to him, tell him that he and Celeste weren't anything to each other beyond friends, even if it didn't change anything between them.

At some point, Quinn drifted off to sleep and dreamed of the perfect world, the one he had only just wished for. He and Calder were not alone in their little cottage. There was a second bedroom, and in it was Celeste.

Q

He opened his eyes to find hers wide and frightened, the sun just barely dawning as it tried to reach through the heavy smog of the night-burning coal fires. He reached out, placing one finger against her lips. "Don't worry, sweet Celeste. Nothing happened. Nothing is happening. You haven't

forgotten yourself. Don't be worried. I did naught but put you to bed," he said as quietly as he could.

He felt her nod once stiffly in agreement as her hand disappeared, and her eyes grew bigger as she, he assumed, realized she was mostly quite naked inside the cocoon of her quilt.

Celeste tried to sit up. She was lying on part of the quilt, and it wouldn't budge. Quinn stood and walked around to her side of the bed, lifted her up, and placed her against the headboard. He sat at the edge against her knee. "How soon will someone come for you?" he asked.

"Not until I ring for them," she said, and he nodded. It was sad that they left this daughter to herself. He supposed for all of his intent and purpose at the moment, it worked out to his own satisfaction. "How?" she asked quietly.

"I came last night to talk to you. I couldn't find Dev—Calder anywhere. I don't know where he's run off to, and I simply couldn't go home. So I came here, climbed your trellis—you should have known that a possibility—and I found you," he said.

"And how…how did you find me?" she asked, her voice timid and not a little bit frightened.

He put one hand on her covered knee to offer a bit of comfort. "I found you in much the same state you found Calder and I…" he said, letting his words fall away as quietly as he could. Her head started to move slowly back and forth, as if she were trying to process the truth of it but simply couldn't.

"No, I…but I'm—I was—"

Quinn palmed her cheek and ran a thumb over her cheekbone, warming her skin as he stopped her movement and turned her to face him. "Please don't be frightened. Please don't be ashamed—"

She jerked away from him, nearly knocking him from the bed as she yelled. "I'm not ashamed! I'm angry! How could you?" she asked.

"How could I? How could you?" he replied, only a bit perturbed by this. He knew he deserved her reaction just as much as she'd deserved Calder's.

"It's not the same! I wasn't with anyone. I was…" She closed her eyes tight. "How could you just watch?"

"How could I just watch? Did you wish me to join you?"

"No!"

"Then I would pose you the same question, again. How could you?" he said quietly as she turned away.

She and the counterpane slid, and she fell to her side, covering her face and the rest of her in the bedding. "Go away," she said. It wasn't very determined, and the blankets surrounding her started shaking, and her voice hitched with a sob.

He reached out to her shoulder, or what he thought was her shoulder, beneath the thickness of the fabric. "Celeste, I am sorry. But I'm not going to leave just yet." His hand massaged her shoulder, and he shifted and moved her so he could reach her back, pushing and kneading and rubbing through all the fabric. "You're so tense," he said.

"What do you expect?" the pile of blankets said, before shifting to allow him better access.

"Listen to me, please. You trusted me, and I trust you. At this moment, I could use a friendly face, and I hate to say it, but you really are the only friend I happen to have who understands all the goings-on."

She stilled, and one hand searched out, fisting the fabric and bringing it down below her chin so she could look at him. "Quinn, I don't know how to be around you right now. I am beyond mortified."

"I understand that feeling, you know."

"I know. I know. Oh God, how did this happen?"

"The trellis," he said with a smile.

"When I leave this house, I'll be sure that all vertical garden finery will be removed from the exterior of my new home."

"Sounds like a fairly good plan," he said. "I would hazard to guess that Calder will follow suit." Quinn pulled his hands back and turned and put his feet on the floor. "I really should go, but I know not to where. Since I still live with my parents, I…" He exhaled and fiddled with his thumbs.

She reached out and squeezed his shoulder. "I have always found your parents quite cordial," she said.

"Please don't misunderstand. They're wonderful as parents go. I just need privacy. Somewhere away from them would be nice. I should have moved out sooner, but I think part of me always believed I would eventually be living with Calder, so there would be no point in letting a flat, but that… well, it simply never happened. How could it?" Quinn smiled to himself. It felt good to be able to say these things aloud to another person. It was an experience that he'd never had, for obvious reasons. Until now, he hadn't known he was missing it.

"What made you believe that?" she asked, and he wondered at that, truly considered.

"I suppose because we'd spent our lives together, that we'd always talked about living together here in London. I just—he was different when he came back from India. He'd run off and been hiding, or whatever he did there, but when he last returned, he was frightened, truly frightened, that someone would discover us and do something. That's when we started this—whatever this is—where we would see each other in public, and I would follow him home, or elsewhere. Sometimes, we did just go to the pub, to White's, for a ride, whatever. There was every reason for us to be together, but no way for us to be together. He wanted to tell our family, to take whatever they gave and disappear, but I just…I couldn't. I love my family too much to hurt them in that way. They need me."

He stood and started collecting his clothing, then sat in the chair before the mirror to put his shoes on. When he looked up, Celeste gazed back at him from her reflection in the glass. "Celeste, I do apologize. I'm not quite the husband you need, not quite the husband you should want for, certainly."

"You are everything I could ever want in a husband, should I ever want for one. Strong, dedicated, thoughtful…what more could a woman wish for?"

"A man who wants her for the woman she is," he replied quietly.

"You know me better than most people."

"I think I know you better than you right now," he said.

"You still don't understand me at all."

"What do you mean? What is there to understand?"

"I don't want…I wish to be left to myself. I don't want to be touched. My presence could validate your life with him. Why is that not an option?"

"Because you didn't mind me touching you. Just then, you allowed me to massage your shoulders, your back," he reminded her.

"That's quite different. I actually have a great need for that sort of care. I receive it so rarely I yearn for physical compassion of any sort. Beyond that—" She pulled her knees up beneath her chin, dragging the quilts with her. He wanted to turn around and show her a bit of that compassion now, but he thought that perhaps she'd begun to open up to him solely because they were not in direct contact, so he stayed.

"I think that it's possible you merely fear what happens because it is so unknown to you, and now that you've been introduced to your passion, I have no doubt your…interests will increase."

"I don't know that I agree with you. I would think I would have had some sort of flutterings at one point or another."

"Did someone mistreat you?"

"No. To be perfectly honest, I'd never felt any sort of attraction for anyone until—" She stopped, and he watched as she covered her face and fell over to her side in the bed again.

"Until?" he pressed gently.

She mumbled. He couldn't tell what she'd said, so he waited. He saw her shift, saw her little face peer out at him from the blankets once again. "Until—" she started. She closed her eyes tightly, tucking her chin to hide from him as her finger did a little twirl in the air.

"Until you saw us?" he asked quietly, keeping his eyes downcast, keeping all censure from his expression, all judgment stayed. He saw a small movement in the mirror and looked up to find her nodding. He wasn't sure how he felt about that. He wasn't sure if the fact that her realization came from watching Calder fucking him excited or horrified him. He looked away again. "Had you ever seen…" He let the sentence hang in the air between them.

"Never," she whispered.

"And when you saw us, did you want to be with us? With Calder?" She shook her head. "With me?" Again, she shook her head, and he was disappointed, which confused him, because he wanted Calder. He twisted the laces of his shoes. "What did you want?" he asked her, but he was trying to answer the question for himself as well.

"I wanted…I don't understand what I wanted. I still don't understand what I want."

"And last night?" he asked.

"Last night, I thought of you, the both of you, and felt things I never knew existed. So I managed—myself."

"You managed yourself. That's a lovely way to put it," he said with a smile.

"I'm not sure what to call it."

"I could teach you," he said to her reflection in the mirror.

"Please don't."

"You haven't discussed this with anyone?"

"I've never had need to understand it," she whispered.

"You mean to tell me, you'd never—"

She shook her head quickly to cut him off, as though she simply could not hear him say it.

"I expected you to be a virgin. I did not expect that you would be so chaste as to never know, never even understand, what your body is capable of."

"I had no interest in discovery. Until last night, those bits of me felt like nothing more than flesh. Like my ear or my knee. I didn't know they could do these things," she said, and her voice sounded so impressed, so reverent.

"Until us." Quinn felt a warmth spread through his chest at that.

She nodded. "Until you. I had always wondered why everyone was so enamored of the act. I had touched myself, but had never felt anything until I thought about…" She caught his gaze in the mirror and swallowed heavily and closed her eyes. God, but she was amazing, and he wanted to know so much more of her.

"Celeste…" He waited. She didn't look up to him. "Celeste, please look at me," he said, and after a moment of patience, her eyes fluttered open, and he caught her gaze again and held it. "I feel incredibly privileged to have been a part of your awakening, no matter how small a part I may have played. I am honored that I could do that for you."

eleste sat up in the bed, careful to keep the quilts in place. She thought he would have been angry, or disturbed, or at the very least upset somehow, but to feel privileged? She didn't understand. She also couldn't seem to break the hold he had on her. She couldn't look away.

"I understand what it is to not know yourself," he said. "To not know your body and what it wants from you, what it needs from you. To not understand the things your body is trying to tell you." He looked away, and she was both relieved and disappointed. "When we were younger, Calder and I, we didn't know what we were doing. We didn't understand what our bodies were already attempting to tell us. You must understand, as cousins of an age we spent a great deal of time together, either at his family estate in Loughborough or here in London at my family home. Nobody paid us any mind. For the most part, they were trying to get rid of us, as we were young boys, boisterous and obnoxious. So as long as neither of us was hurt, they didn't much care what we were up to, and so…we spent a lot of time becoming friends and exploring our worlds and eventually…each other."

"They never knew?"

"Nobody ever happened upon us, no."

"You've loved him the whole of your life, haven't you?" she said.

"I have, without question, loved him for most of my life. The fact is that I don't know who I am without him, and I won't know how to go on if I lose him. He, on the other hand, seems to do just fine without me."

"I very much doubt that." It seemed to her—by evidence of Calder's temper—that he was rather more fond of Quinn than Quinn believed. Nobody was that angry out of simple self-preservation. At least, she didn't think so. He'd been angry because he'd seen his world, a world with Quinn, disappear before his very eyes because of her.

"If it's not true, why does he leave?" he asked, and she knew he was truly questioning.

"He's frightened, perhaps just as much as you are. It must be such a difficult thing to love someone and want to be with them but have no options wherein that would be a possibility. Even if it were possible, somehow you would never be acceptable by societal standards, by London, by his peers. He's afraid even your family would disown you. He said as much that night."

"He did. I've always believed that to be an excuse for him to not care."

"I don't believe he's making excuses, Quinn. I think you should listen to what he's saying, because he said it rather baldly. He didn't mince words or dance around it."

"You've only just discovered lust, and yet you think yourself an expert?"

Celeste started to argue the point, but caught that teasing gleam in his eye and gave him a smile. "Don't be an arse," she said, and he tilted his head and gave her the full force of his flirty grin. She groaned and fell back to the bed.

"Quinn?" she asked then.

"Yes?"

"Tell me about Francine," she said quietly. "Why…" She stopped, unsure what she wanted to ask, and Quinn's gaze seemed to come to a sharp focus on her. "She's different."

"She is. Was there a question there?" he asked.

"I'm not sure," she replied. She wanted to know why she was different, but she wasn't sure how to ask the question.

"Francine's story is her own to tell, but if you need to know whether you can talk to her about things, you can. She can be trusted absolutely. Is that what you're asking?"

"Yes," she said, taking the chance he afforded. "Yes, I just…it would be nice to have a woman to speak with, is all."

His gaze softened, and he smiled. "I'll take my leave." He stood and walked over to her on the bed. "I will return shortly. How long will you need, to ready for a ride?" he asked.

"Perhaps an hour?" she said, though she knew she needed a bit more.

"You'll have two. Listen, I want you to consider what we've discussed whilst I'm gone. I want you to truly consider whether you could share your body with another person."

She nodded, his finger running the length of her jaw, tipping her face up to his, which was entirely too close. She trembled against that touch, but he seemed to ignore the reaction.

"Prepare to ride. I've an idea." Quinn bussed her cheek and walked to the balcony, carefully peering out into the London morning. "As good a time as ever, I suppose," he said, then he crawled over the balustrade and disappeared.

Celeste watched after him for a time, part of her wishing he would return. He would have made a wonderful husband, that man. She would have been quite happy to have him. Now she wasn't sure what to do. She didn't want to remain with her family, but her other prospects were dismal. Celeste stood and hurried to the doors, closing and locking them. Thinking better of it, she unlocked them and turned back to her room.

She threw the quilt on her bed and went to the wardrobe for her clothes before she called for breakfast. Quinn had plans today, and she was to take part in them, and that one small thing could not have made her happier.

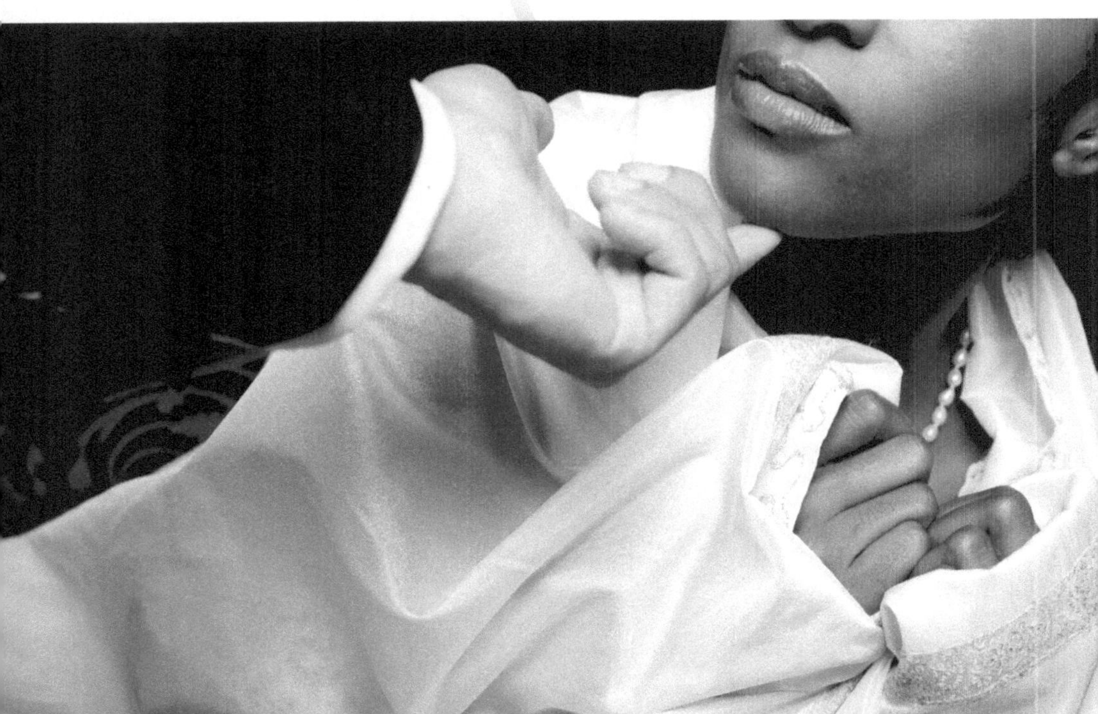

Quinn

uinn hadn't truly expected Warrick to be home. Or perhaps it was that he'd hoped he wouldn't be. Hopefully it wouldn't take long to glean any information about Calder from him. The heavy door opened, and Quinn took a calming breath.

"This way, my lord." Quinn followed the butler through the main entry to Warrick's study, where he found him working quietly at his desk, the windows at his back casting an eerie glow around him, his face dark and ominous.

"Lord Wyntor, Your Grace," the butler said. He bowed as he closed the door behind him. Quinn wasn't sure what to do, so he waited.

"Come," Warrick said, and as Quinn walked toward him, the length of the study seemed to extend impossibly before his feet as he moved. "What?" Warrick said, without even looking up from the paper he was writing on.

"Your Grace—" was all he said, and Warrick looked up to him, cutting him off rather soundly with a glare. "I…"

"Grayson," he said stiffly.

"Grayson—"

"Sit." And so he did.

"Grayson, I came to inquire about Calder. He left rather suddenly yesterday, and his man sent me here."

Grayson sat back in his chair and studied him. This was a bad idea. "What do you know of it?" he asked.

"Naught other than that. His man told me he was to forward

communication to you, and—well, that was all, really. He gave me no further instruction."

"Why do you seek him?" Grayson asked.

"I just—" Damn if he wasn't sure what to say. "I—we…we had been talking about my pending marriage to Lady Alain, and I had hoped we could continue the conversation, as I'm unsure—"

"There is no pending marriage."

"Well, not in so many words as yet. I wanted to—"

"You're looking for him to stop you," Grayson said, without a hint of question.

"No, I merely wished for some counsel as to whether he thought she and I—"

"Stop."

Quinn watched him for a moment, not sure whether to try something else or simply get up and leave. Warrick's eyes narrowed as though he homed in on him, a hawk targeting its prey by narrowing its line of sight. "Do not lie to me," he said, and Quinn's hands went cold, as if his heart had stopped beating, and all of his blood had chilled in his veins.

"I don't know what you mean," Quinn said.

"You do. I know Calder…quite well, Quinn. Do not attempt to play me the fool."

"I wouldn't—I don't wish to," Quinn said.

"Come back to me when you can be honest. And not until then." He dismissed Quinn with the wave of his hand and went back to his paperwork as if he'd never been there.

Quinn stood. His skin felt like it shrank on his bones, and he tried to move away, unsure what to say. Warrick said he knew Calder *quite well.* Well, damn, what did Warrick now think of him? His blood pounded in his ears.

"I beg your pardon," Quinn said finally. He bowed and left the study as quickly as he could.

"Quinn?" He turned to find Lulu coming down the stairs, covered head to toe in grime, wearing trousers of all things.

"Your Grace," he said with a quick bow, his voice tremulous.

"Lulu, please. We are family, yes?" she said as she took one of his hands in both of hers. She was less formal, like Francine, and though she was new to his family, she seemed to be warming to them rather quickly. "You're shaking like a leaf. Are you quite well?"

He tried to nod, but he wasn't sure his head actually moved. Her cool hand came up to his neck, pushing his cravat down and touching his pulse. His mouth opened as he attempted to work his jaw, to no avail. Finally, he managed a breath, followed by some sound. "I should go."

"I'm sorry, Quinn. I can't let you leave," she said, and she pulled his hand to her chest between hers, chafing it. "Does this happen to you often?" she asked, and he could do nothing but stare at her. She turned for the study and attempted to pull him along. He refused to move. He could not go back in there. "Quinn, come on, you need to sit down."

"No, I…Grayson—Warrick—he doesn't want to see me. I should go."

"What did he do?" she asked as her eyes narrowed on him.

"I can't." He looked down and pinched the bridge of his nose. It was everything coming together in the wrong possible moment. It was that last night with Calder. It was Celeste watching them. It was Calder's anger. It was Celeste's fear. It was his shame in the park and at Roxleigh's. It was Calder running from him, and last, but not least, it was speaking with his cousin who didn't wish to speak with him.

"Quinn? Quinn!" Her voice faded as his temple thudded, and he lurched toward the stairs and sat down. He was determined to control this.

"Gray," he heard her say. "Did he see you? He seems to be having a panic attack," she said, and his head seemed to clear a bit as he looked up to her.

"What…what did you say?" Quinn asked.

"A panic attack? I—oh. Gray?" was all she said, and the light disappeared behind the hulking form that was his cousin.

"What do you do for a panic attack?" Grayson asked her.

"He needs calm, some water, and probably for you to quit being so menacing. Can we get him to the study?"

"Come," Warrick said, and Quinn felt Lulu take his hand and pull him up, her arm going around his waist as she led him back to that study. She walked with him to the settee before the fire, sat down with him as Grayson rang for the butler and asked for a service and some water.

"Breathe for me, Quinn," she said as she took his hands and massaged them. He closed his eyes and concentrated on that small contact between them. He opened them to see Grayson looking down at him as though he were the enemy.

"Oh God!" he said as his heart raced again.

Lulu turned to look at Grayson. "You're not helping. Gray, either sit down or go to your desk, but quit looming."

Quinn watched as Grayson sat in the chair across from her, her every movement caught by his rapt attention.

"Quinn, can you see the embers in the fireplace?" He nodded. "The painting above the mantel?" He nodded again. "How about the lamps on both sides of the fireplace?"

He looked and found them both. "Yes, I can, but—"

"How about the coffee table here in front of us?"

"Yes," he said, succumbing to her questions.

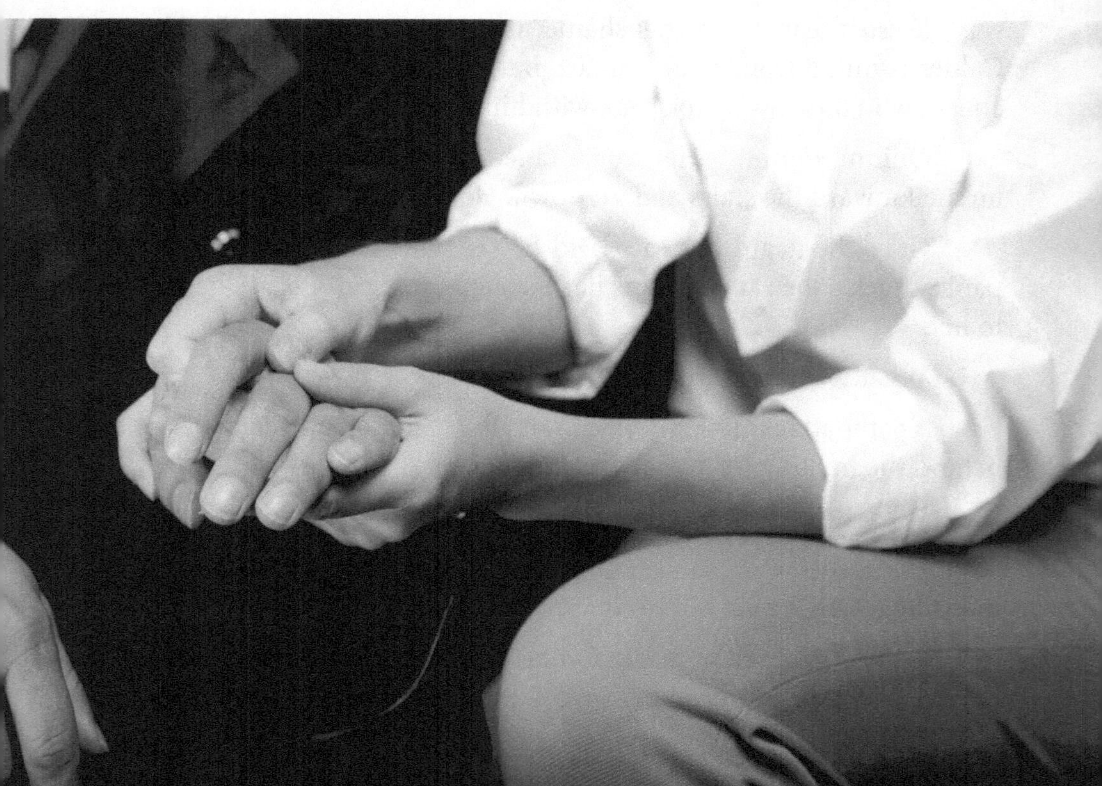

"Quinn, do you feel the floor beneath your feet?" she asked, and he nodded. "Do you feel the soft cushions of the settee?" He thought about it, nodded again. "How about my hands? Do you feel my hands on yours?"

"Yes," he replied.

"The sofa at your back, do you feel it?"

"Yes."

"And my voice, you can hear me?"

"Of course I can."

"Do you hear that bird singing outside?"

He nodded, his eyelids growing heavy as she spoke to him.

"Quinn, it was lovely to see you at the ball last night. Who was your partner again?" she asked.

"Lady Alain," he replied.

"She is beautiful. Is she nice?"

"Yes, we're friends."

"Perhaps more than that?" Lulu asked gently, and Quinn thought about it. He supposed they were a bit more than friends at this point, but he was just as confused about what he and Celeste were as he was about what he and Calder were. *Calder.*

"Perhaps more. I don't rightly know what, though," Quinn said finally, and Lulu nodded.

"That's always a difficult place to be," she said.

"What—" Grayson cut in, questioning, but she silenced him with a look, and Quinn was astounded. Truly, completely, and overwhelmingly astounded. He looked over at Lulu, who was smiling at him, still chafing his hands.

"Are you planning on attending the family supper next week?" she asked.

"I wasn't exactly planning. My mother has made it known that I'm expected."

"Ah, yes, the mothers in this family seem to boss everyone around."

"It's not all bad," Quinn said.

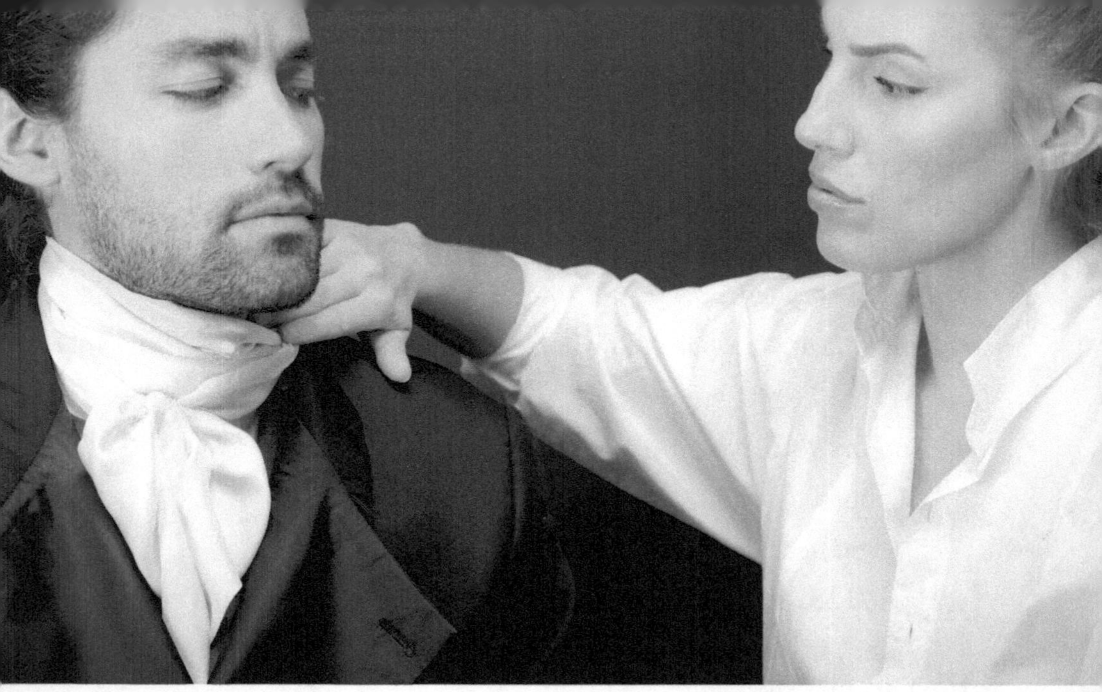

"No, it isn't. I quite like that the women of the family seem so powerful," she said with a grin, one Quinn couldn't help but return.

"I feel better," he said. He pulled his hands away from hers. She once again pushed past his cravat and felt for his pulse. He didn't even dare to look up at Warrick. He could feel the tension emanating from him like the pulse of a wave at low tide. She pulled back and gave Quinn some space.

"What happened?" she asked Warrick as she wrapped those cool fingers around Quinn's wrist and held him.

"We discussed Calder," Warrick said.

"What about him?"

"He's quit London," Warrick said.

"Why?" she asked him, and he narrowed his eyes on her. She merely returned the look.

"He's looking into a matter Quinn is not privy to," Warrick said finally.

Quinn slid his wrist from her grip and put his elbows on his knees, leaning over into his hands. "I really should go. If he cannot tell me anything, then he cannot. I just needed to—" He shook his head. "I was just concerned…" He scrubbed his hands through his hair and looked up to Lulu. "Really, I should just go." Quinn thought he could make it out of the house now, as long as he didn't look at Warrick again.

"You're quite concerned for Calder," Lulu said. "Quinn?" Her hand went to his chin, and he looked up to her. "Oh, Quinn."

Oh no. He had to get out of here.

She turned to Warrick. "Is there a reason he should be concerned for Calder?" she asked. He just shook his head once. "For some reason, I don't believe either of you," she said, and one corner of Warrick's mouth tipped up in a slow grin.

The butler brought the tray in, and Lulu handed Quinn the glass of water, which helped to further clear his head.

"Look, I don't know what's going on right now, but I don't like it, Gray," she said, and he nodded.

"Quinn should be more honest in his intention. That is all I asked of him."

"You don't understand," Quinn said.

"I understand more than you know," Warrick responded as he leaned forward in his chair, and Quinn felt his entire body tense again in preparation for…what he didn't know. To flee? Possibly.

Lulu looked back and forth between them as though she watched a badminton match. "Quinn," she said, "what do you need from Calder?"

Quinn closed his eyes and wondered at the truth of it. What did it matter if he said something here? Most of the family still avoided Warrick, for obvious reasons. Perhaps he could parlay it into some sort of joke if he let it get out. He just could not betray Calder like that. He looked up to find Lulu watching him very closely, too closely. "You love him," she whispered, and Quinn didn't argue.

"Lulu," Warrick warned.

"What could you mean by that?" Quinn said without any conviction.

Warrick was the one to respond. "You know exactly what she means," he said, and that's when he knew what truth Warrick was looking for. Perhaps this was all merely Warrick attempting to protect Calder. Quinn could not fault him for that. So he looked to Warrick, met his eyes for the first time since returning to the study, and allowed him to know the truth of it. The whole of his body shook.

"I do know," Quinn said with little more than a breath.

"You're aware that sodomy is illegal in England? It may no longer be a hanging offense, but if convicted, you spend your life in prison," Warrick said with little question.

"Grayson!" Lulu was horrified. Quinn waved her off. He understood Warrick only wanted to be sure he understood the severity of what he admitted to, what Warrick already knew, apparently. He obviously would not relent without some sort of verbal confirmation from him.

"I'm aware," Quinn replied quietly.

"Grayson, do you need further evidence than that?" Lulu asked.

Warrick shook his head. "He's returned to India on service to the Crown, Quinn."

Quinn felt like he could once again breathe. "He's…" Wait, did that mean he wasn't as angry as Quinn had thought? "He never said anything about leaving. He never said—"

"We weren't expecting him to leave so soon either," Warrick said, and Quinn understood. It felt like the confirmation he'd been afraid of this entire time.

"When is he expected to return?"

"When he has the information he seeks, and no sooner."

"Months," Quinn said.

"At least," Warrick answered.

"Years?" Quinn questioned. Warrick remained silent. Quinn was cold. At least two months without him. At the very least.

"Quinn," Lulu said, squeezing his hands. He looked over to her. "There's not much I can say to keep you from worrying. If Warrick learns anything he can share, I'm sure he will, yes?" She turned to Warrick, and he gave a single nod to the fact.

"I'm sorry to have been such trouble," Quinn said. "I really am, and I should be off." He stood to leave.

"Quinn," Warrick said, and he stopped and turned back to him. "I will send for you if I can, but the last time—"

Quinn nodded, cutting him off. "Yes, thank you," he said, and he left, because what he'd refused to hear come from Warrick's mouth was how long Calder had been gone the last time, because Quinn didn't want to be reminded of how long Calder had been gone the last time, and Quinn simply couldn't face hearing the fact that it was entirely possible Calder would be away for more than a year.

Celeste

Quinn reached up and put his hands around Celeste's waist, helping her from the horse to the green of the lawn. "This is lovely, but I wasn't quite expecting it," Celeste said as she looked up to him, attempting to discern exactly why he'd thought a picnic at the Royal Gardens would be a good diversion.

"We're always going somewhere or doing something. I thought it was nice this morning when we simply sat and talked. You don't agree?" he said.

"I do agree. I just wasn't expecting it."

"I thought we could use some privacy. Even when you say your family won't come to your room, I'm still a bit on edge at your family residence," Quinn said as he pulled a rug from the satchel on his horse and spread it out. He took her hand and assisted her to the ground before turning back to his mount. When he returned with the basket he'd attached to the saddle, she smiled up at him. "Besides," he said, "it's quite rare to have such a lovely day in London as of late. The black fog and all."

"It has been rather heavy. I hope it abates somewhat."

"We should go to the country. Certainly we could stay with family somewhere. The St. Cyr estate in Loughborough, Eildon in Roxleighshire, or Perry's Westcreek estate. Have you ever been outside the city? Would you be interested? There would be plenty of things to do, and of course an abundance of chaperones should your family have concerns."

"I haven't ever been outside London, so perhaps," she said.

"If you've never seen the air outside London, you definitely need to," he said.

She was watching him carefully, trying to discern his mood, as he seemed a bit off. "What is it, Quinn?"

"Hmm? Oh, nothing at all. I just think I would like to get out into the country for a bit, show you some fresh air."

"Quinn?" She waited. He just chewed on the piece of bread he had and stared off over the lake. She ran her hand through his hair and tugged the end. "Quinn," she said again. His gaze dropped to the bread in his hand as he picked pieces off and tossed them into the grass.

"He's expected to be gone for quite some time. Apparently it was planned. His departure moved up a bit from what was originally expected. Last night," he said.

"Can you write him?"

"No, I'm afraid there will be nothing from him for a time. It is as it is."

Celeste had no idea what to do next. This was definitely not the news she'd expected or hoped for.

"At any rate, for now it's just you and I," he said with a smile, and she attempted to return it, but apparently she wasn't nearly as practiced in diversion as he was.

"Perhaps a trip to the country would be welcome. I have no doubt my parents would happily be rid of me for a time. Particularly if they believed it was in effort to snare you as a husband," she said.

"Ah yes, a husband. We shall see about that."

"We shall?" she asked.

"Listen, Celeste, I have some ideas about your…predicament."

"My predicament?"

"Yes, the predicament in which you are convinced you wish to be left alone."

"That isn't quite what I said."

"Close enough. Did you think about what I said before I left?"

"I did."

"And?"

"I don't rightly know," she said, because she didn't. And she felt a bit improper speaking on this in the middle of a park. "Should we really be discussing this now?" she asked.

He glanced around them and back at her. "There isn't a soul who cares what we're speaking on, Celeste. It's as good a time as any."

She nodded, but still wished she could change his mind, and the subject. He turned and sprawled across the rug, leaning on one elbow, his head just at her side.

"May I touch you?" he asked.

"To what purpose?"

"Naught but to enjoy the day."

"Fine, then," she replied, and he laughed at her. It was naught but a quick burst, and she liked hearing it from him. He fascinated her in the way he could shut off parts of his mind from considering certain things. He'd done that several times with her already, changed the subject and lightened his mood and hers. She felt his hand at her knee, his thumb swirling there, calming her nerves, and she relaxed.

"How soon could you leave?" he asked.

"I only need to pack and inform my parents. I could be ready within a day or so."

"Good, then. I'll speak with my mother today. She'll make the arrangements, and we'll be off."

"That simple, is it?"

"That simple."

"You're running away," she said.

"There's nothing to run from."

"Memories," she said, bringing him back to the subject he was actively avoiding.

"Perhaps." He turned to his back and rested his head on her knee. He took her hand and pressed it to his chest, his thumb running the edge of her palm, over and over… "Celeste, for the moment it's just the two of us, and apparently both of us want for something other than what we have. So what shall we do with ourselves to while away the time?"

Celeste laughed at that. "Well, when you put it that way, I suppose we should ignore the problem and simply have some fun."

"Agreed. Warrick knows of Calder and me," he said suddenly, and Celeste froze, looking down on his closed eyes. His smile was tight, as

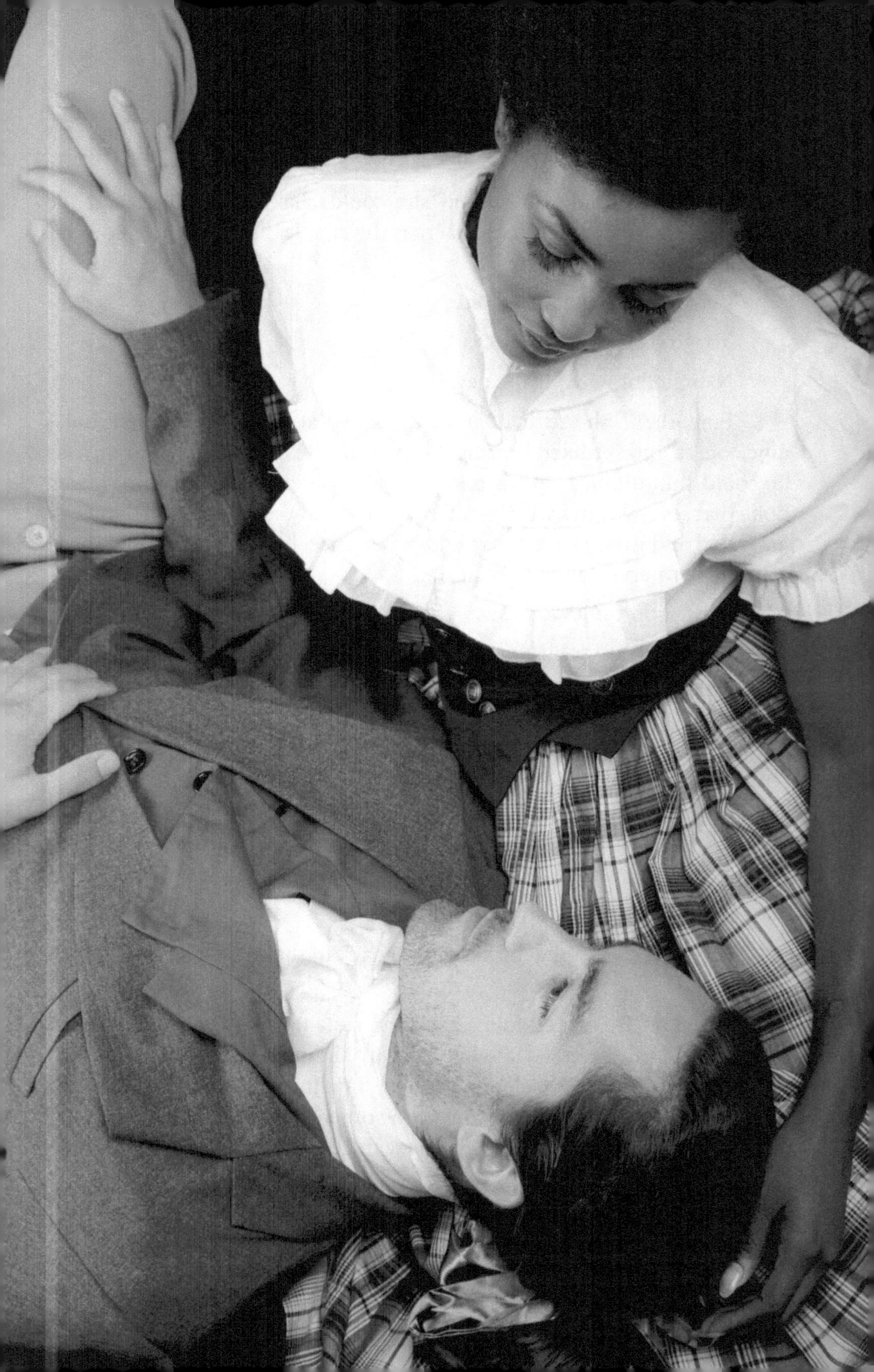

though he forced it to stay upon his mouth. She flipped her hand under his and held his tight in her grasp.

"Is this why you wish to leave?" she asked.

"Perhaps part of it. I think he already knew about us. He did already know of Calder's inclinations. When I went to see him today, he seemed to know that Calder and I…well. He knows now, that much is certain."

"Does it worry you?" she asked.

"I'm not entirely sure how I feel about it. I bartered away my most closely held secret in order to obtain information about Calder which is perfectly useless to me. Yet I did obtain the information. I don't believe Warrick would do me harm unless I crossed him. So, I must endeavor to never cross him. Rather simple, that."

"He frightens me," she said absentmindedly as she looked out over the lawn. The sky was muddy, but the sun still managed to shine through the haze a bit.

"He frightens everyone. That's the truth of it."

"Yes. Well."

"Are you finished with the food? We could visit my mother now." Yet another quick subject change. Today felt like a whirlwind, and she was merely along for the ride.

"Yes," she replied, now that she understood his restlessness. She didn't think he was going to find any semblance of peace until Calder returned, which meant she and Quinn were going to be on the move quite a bit.

They arrived at Wyntor House not long after, and Celeste was overwhelmed by the sheer size of it. At four bays and five stories, it was quite the façade. "It's massive," she said as she took his lapel in her gloved hand, and he set her on her feet.

"It is. My family doesn't spend much time in the country, so it rather needed to be. In fact, it has overtaken the house next to it there—so while it only looks to be four bays, it's actually six."

"Six bays? Your family is not so large, Quinn."

"No, but my mother likes to have us close to her, and when my brother threatened to leave because he wanted his own home, she purchased the house on the right and added a single door between the two from parlor to parlor. She's still required to knock."

Celeste laughed. "Well, that's not all bad, I suppose."

"No, not particularly."

A voice came through the entry. "Quinn!"

"Give me a second," he said. He released her and walked to his mother. "Mother, I've brought you a gift."

Celeste waited patiently at the carriage as Quinn spoke with her.

"You've not brought me a gift, child, you've brought me a guest. Don't be impertinent," she said, and she was so sweet and lovely that Celeste couldn't help but smile. "Francine and Lulu are here. They're walking the gardens. We were about to take tea."

"Perhaps we should return another day?" he asked.

"Not at all. The sooner Celeste comes to know the family, the better. Don't you agree?"

"She's a friend, Mother," he said.

"Those are the best kind. Come now," she said.

Quinn motioned to Celeste to join them and took her to his arm and led her into the small entry where he kissed his mother's cheeks and introduced them.

"You've been taking up quite a bit of my son's time as of late. Are you here to make your intentions known?"

"Mother," Quinn warned.

"Yes, dear, tea first, intentions after." She turned and left them at the entry, disappearing into the house as her voice carried throughout, asking for tea and cakes and an audience in the garden room.

"She's lovely," Celeste said.

"Come, come!" his mother's voice echoed back at them.

"Quite lovely," Quinn agreed, but something in his voice unsettled her. "Shall we?"

"Absolutely." He led her though the small entry hall, but when it opened up into a massive foyer more than three stories high through the center of the house, Celeste nearly lost her breath. "Good Lord, Quinn, but this is a sight. It's beautiful."

"It is. Perhaps I'll show you the galleries later."

"I would like that," she said as she craned her neck to take in the colorful glass of the domed ceiling and the intricately carved wooden balustrade bordering the staircase. Each floor was a different masterpiece of color and theme. She felt Quinn tug her arm, and she followed him, trusting he wouldn't let her run into a wall, because she simply could not look away from that grand entry.

They took tea in a room at the back of the house that was hidden behind a massive vaulting staircase that wound around to all three of the open floors. His mother was truly one of the loveliest ladies Celeste had ever had the pleasure of meeting.

"Francine, Lulu," Lady Cheshire said, "I believe you've been introduced to Celeste?"

"Yes, ma'am," Francine said with a smile and a hug, and Celeste sank into it for what was possibly a bit more than appropriate before she released her and looked to Lulu.

"Briefly," Lulu said, and she smiled and nodded to her.

The room was as bright and airy as any room in London could be with the current fog. What sun there was filtered through, giving a hazy look to the room. They sat around the tea butler on two large comfortable settees, just two duchesses, a marchioness, Quinn, and a nobody having a chat.

Celeste was a bit taken aback at that, as she was at their refusal to let her use their titles. *Adeleine, Francine, Lulu. Adeleine, Francine, Lulu,* she repeated in her head to remember. On top of all that, his mother served the tea. Celeste was unnerved. Lulu kept darting her eyes to Quinn as though she wanted to say something to him, but he wouldn't meet her eyes, and Adeleine just looked as thrilled as she could be, while Francine smiled warmly at her.

"Celeste, how are you faring this Season?" Adeleine asked when she handed her cup over, and Celeste shook off the reverie.

"I've had no incidents of consequence," she replied.

"No? That certainly is something. You and Quinn seem to be getting on well."

"Mother," Quinn warned quietly, and Celeste watched as Adeleine didn't even flinch.

"We do get on well. He's a true gentleman, my lady. You should be proud," Celeste said.

"Oh, I am inordinately proud of my sons," she said with a beaming smile.

"Even Jerrod?" Francine cut in.

"Of course Jerrod!" she said with a laugh. "Oh, my poor Jerrod. He'll find his way soon enough. He has time, he's young still." She patted Francine's knee. "And how are you doing with your…" She waved her hand in a circle, and Celeste looked to Francine for explanation.

"I'm pregnant," Francine said to Celeste as she twirled her hand in the air much as Adeleine had. She gave Celeste a great smile, and Celeste flinched.

"Oh, I'm sorry. I forget being pregnant isn't something we get excited about in public," Francine said. "I am excited, so I do forget. And I'm doing fairly well. My morning sickness has passed for the most part, and I believe I'm just starting my second trimester. Hopefully, we'll leave London soon so I can get fresh air for the rest of my pregnancy before I give birth."

"Francine," Adeleine said sweetly.

"So sorry, my laying in…or whatever they call it." She grinned. "Actually, the whole thing was supposed to be kept under wraps, but word somehow got out. Gideon is none too happy about that either," she said.

Celeste sipped her tea. Perhaps she hadn't been around women enough? Perhaps they spoke this boldly outside society within close families? Or perhaps it really was just Francine. Perhaps…Celeste's heartbeat kicked in her rib cage.

"I've no idea how you do it. Just the thought of being pregnant gives me hives," Lulu said.

"Hives?" Celeste squeaked, inspecting Lulu's hands, face and neck—the only bits of her visible.

"Not literally. I just mean I don't ever want to do that. I don't want children."

Lady Cheshire cleared her throat and smiled at them. "Ladies, I believe you're frightening our guest," she said.

Lulu turned to Francine. "I'm not used to this yet."

Francine wrapped an arm around her and squeezed. "It takes time. You'll be fine."

Celeste felt cold even as her heartbeat picked up, pushing the blood through her veins. She could feel her pulse everywhere. She wanted to know what Lulu was talking about. She wanted to know what she wasn't used to. She wanted to know why Lady Cecilia was going by the name Lulu.

My name was Grace.

The blood drained from her face, and Celeste felt lightheaded at the sudden realization.

"Celeste, do you paint or play piano or anything?" Francine asked suddenly.

"What?"

"Piano? Painting?" she repeated.

"I've been trained in both, but I'm not particularly good at either, really," Celeste mumbled, but she couldn't seem to catch her breath.

"What is it you like to do?" Lulu asked.

"I—um…"

"It's all right, Celeste. It's just between us," Francine said, and she felt Quinn squeeze her hand, reminding her that he was sitting next to her, but her mind spun, and she couldn't seem to stop it.

"I like to dance," she said quietly and immediately regretted it. She needed to put the rest of this aside and concentrate. She did not want to end up back at the asylum.

"Ballroom?" Francine asked.

"Yes and…and ballet—though I don't have much practice in it," she said. *Stop talking!* "Oh, my mother would be horrified." She looked down to her teacup, counting the leaves.

"I didn't know," Quinn said quietly, "you should have yourself a studio." It seemed he spoke only to her, and she focused on that, turned to him. Held his gaze.

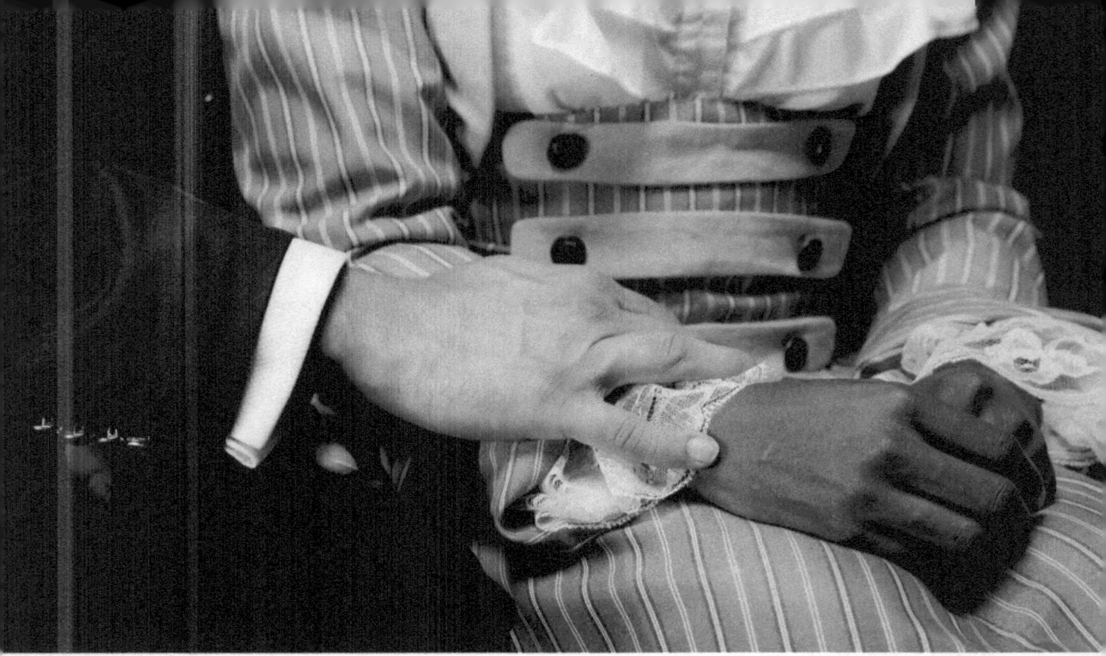

"Yes, well, once I marry, that will be entirely up to my husband, and no doubt a wife who dances ballet is beyond the pale in society," she said.

"This fucking place," Lulu said, and everyone looked at her. "Uhhh, sorry, I just can*not* get used to the blatant and pervasive misogyny of the Victorian era. It's really driving me crazy. It's simple enough to forget in Gray's home, but every damned day, there's some small reminder and I—" Lulu looked at Celeste and stopped. "Shit—crap—pardon…I mean, I beg your pardon. I'm so sorry. I think I should go… Gray will be looking for me anyway," Lulu said, and she stood, and Quinn popped up from his seat as Francine followed.

Was it true? Celeste couldn't take her gaze away from Lulu and Francine, but from the corner of her eye, she could see a sharp annoyance in Adeleine's countenance that dissolved completely when she looked to her.

"It's okay, Lulu. Give yourself time. Come on, I'll take you back," Francine said, and Lulu looked completely disheartened when Celeste turned to them. *It does take time. It takes about six months in an asylum with doctors telling you that you're insane and threatening all sorts of horrible things on your person if you don't stop talking about the future as if it's the past.* Celeste froze. She wanted to scream, she wanted to speak with them, she wanted to know more, but she was too terrified to say anything.

Lulu turned to Quinn. "A moment?" she said, and Lulu and Francine walked out to the entry. Celeste wanted to follow them from the house and ask so many questions, but her training and her fear made her keep her seat.

Quinn stood and squeezed her hand. "I'll be right back."

Take me with you.

He turned to his mother. "Behave," he said, waggling his finger at her.

Celeste set her teacup on the butler and twisted her fingers together.

"You impertinent boy, go!" She turned back to Celeste. "Well, we have a moment. How are you, truly? I only ask because I know the Season must be quite difficult without the support of your family."

"Oh, they fully support me, my lady—Adeleine, ma'am," Celeste said absentmindedly. *What are they talking about out there?* She tried very hard to concentrate on Quinn's mother.

"You know what I mean. I've heard your mother and father speak of you, and I simply could never speak of my child the way they have spoken of you."

"I suppose not," she said. She knew people noticed, but it hurt a bit more to have that thrown in her face. Celeste swallowed past the lump that had formed in her throat. She looked out the windows at the grayish day. This woman had defended a son who had gotten himself in some fairly serious trouble as of late, and yet she'd smiled when referring to him. She'd said she was proud of him, and she was, quite obviously, proud of him. They weren't just words. Celeste simply couldn't fathom that sort of love, and it cut deeply. She wanted so desperately to belong somewhere, and this woman was offering that, she knew she was. This woman would give her that if she married into her family.

Adeleine stood and moved to the settee next to her. "No matter what happens with you and my son, you now have the support of this family. Whatever you need, please don't hesitate to ask."

Celeste shook her head. "That's not—"

"Don't argue. If you need something, you'll let me know. Now, would you like another cup of tea? This blend is rather delicious. Lulu brought it with her, and I must say I need a second cup. You'll join me." The woman smiled at her, and it was so genuine and lovely that Celeste wanted to cry. These strange people were making her feel more welcome than anyone had in her life.

"Mother, I'm going to take Celeste to the galleries," Quinn said. His voice was tight, and Celeste looked over to him, only then realizing she'd been staring out the French doors to the back gardens. She hadn't even realized he'd returned from speaking with Lulu.

"I beg your pardon, Lady Cheshire—Adeleine, for my inattention. I don't know where my mind has run off to."

"Never you mind. Go with Quinn and enjoy the galleries. You'll both be staying for supper?" she asked, but it didn't sound much like a question.

"Oh, I don't know if—"

"She would love to," Quinn said. "Would you mind sending a note to her parents so they won't worry?"

Celeste knew he said it only out of some sort of propriety. Even so, the words cut a little.

"Not at all," Adeleine said. "Now, off with the two of you. You'll be called for supper."

Celeste couldn't concentrate on anything beyond Francine and Lulu. She didn't want to speak with them, but she wanted to be around them, to watch them. She wanted to *know*.

Quinn took her hand, and she thought about him and his mother. She wasn't familiar with the kind of managing she'd experienced today, because her family had never managed her in this way. Her family told her where to be or left her to herself. But this—when Lady Cheshire and Quinn told her what she was to do without question, it was different somehow…it made her feel warm inside. That frightened her, because once Quinn and Calder were together and she was back on her own…it was one of those things that would hurt because she'd know what she was missing.

Quinn

uinn took her to the gallery and let her wander, watching her reactions to the paintings and sculptures. They did have some lovely pieces. Nothing like their neighbor, the Viscount Mayjoy, but nothing to ignore either.

He watched as Celeste spotted the pieces he'd really brought her here for. She reached out toward a smaller marble statue of two people dancing. She turned to another—a single ballet dancer stretching as though she were on the floor of a studio, tying her ballet shoes. Both were presented on marble pedestals, bringing the work closer for examination. "Oh, Quinn, these are lovely," she said.

"I thought you might appreciate them. How is it you never told me of your interest in ballet?"

"It's not something proper society speaks on. Ballet is something society watches in opera houses, not something society partakes of."

"In France, it's more celebrated than that," he said.

"Well, that's France," she replied.

"Perhaps we can go to Paris someday, see the ballet there."

"I would love that," she said as she turned to him, and her entire face lit with excitement.

"Somehow," he said, "I will make that happen."

As he said it, her expression fell. "Or perhaps not. After all, you belong with someone else, and so do I."

"And who is it you belong with?" he asked.

"No one at the moment," she replied, and it squeezed his heart to hear her say such a thing. She was right, though. Lulu had asked his intentions for her before she'd left. He'd thought about it. He just wanted to take care of her. That wasn't something a man should do for a woman he wasn't somehow attached to, and it hurt.

"Certainly your future husband could take you to the ballet in Paris. Simply keep him blind to the purpose of it. All of society brags of trips to France," he said.

"Perhaps," she said as she turned back to the sculpture. She lifted her hand and looked back at him. "May I?"

"Of course you may," he said.

Her eyes widened, and her mouth dropped open the smallest bit as her finger reached out and slid the length of the woman's leg, clad in tights and tipped with ballet shoes. She had ribbons wrapped around her ankles, and she stretched toward her toes with both arms in a graceful arch, reaching, her head bowed to her knee. Celeste's delicate finger on the leg of this cold, hard, marble piece brought it to life, warming him and giving him a chill all in the same moment.

She reached over and smoothed the thick ribbon of marble that encircled the dancer's waist like the tail of a peacock, skimmed her finger down her arm and back to the shoes. "She's so beautiful," she said. "I wish I had ballet shoes like these, with the ribbons," she said as her thumb slid over the toe.

"You should if you're to dance," he said as he walked to her, needing to be closer.

"But I'm not to dance. It's not allowed."

"Have you ever?"

"My grandmother taught me a few things when I was quite young. She also hired an instructor for me from Paris. She was the most beautiful woman I'd ever seen. The way she moved…" Celeste turned toward him, holding her skirts in front of her, her toes pointed in opposite directions and her ankles crossed, and she tipped up onto her toes. She reached high above her with one curved arm, and Quinn lost his breath.

He reached out as he took that final step to her and wrapped his big hands around her ribs and held her as she reached for the sky with both arms, stretching high and leaning back as her hips pushed toward his.

Quinn watched her breasts strain the top of the corset beneath the dress, her nipples sliding free and hardening as they brushed the fabric of her shirtwaist.

She coughed roughly and came down, turned away from him, and put herself back to rights as he stood there, stunned. It was a side of her he'd never seen. Or perhaps he'd had glimpses of this sort of beauty on the ballroom floor, or last night in her room, but this had been the whole of her passion, and it was beautiful. No wonder he'd always been drawn to her. Her grace of movement was full and complete and undoubtedly came from her love and practice of ballet. He tried to swallow past his suddenly dry throat.

"Celeste, this is something you must pursue," he said.

She swung toward him, her skirts swirling around her ankles as she did so. "You know that to be impossible. Regardless, I'm too old to be of any good now. It's been much too long since I had a tutor."

"Why did that stop?" he asked.

"She died."

"The instructor?" Quinn asked.

"My grandmother," Celeste said as her hand reached up and played with the strand of pearls at her neck. "She died when I was quite young, and that was the end of…everything."

"What do you mean, everything?"

"Everything. Once she and Grandfather were gone and my father took the title, everything changed. I became the family pariah, and my life became one of extreme order in an attempt to appease them. Or to keep them from noticing me. Whichever it was."

He walked toward her, but she took a step back, her hand up between them so he'd stop. "I'm sorry that happened to you." She nodded, then she turned and stepped past the sculpture as she went to the wall of paintings.

"These portraits are lovely," she said.

"John Singer Sargent," he said absentmindedly. "He's a brilliant portraitist."

"Is he for hire?"

"What do you mean? Would you like to have your portrait done?" he asked.

"No, not me. Nobody wants to see me. I was thinking of you…and Calder. I would like to have something to remember you both," she said quietly.

"He is for hire, in fact, but I believe he would truly enjoy having you sit for him," he said. "He paints all sorts of people."

"What do you mean 'all sorts'?" she asked as she gazed up at the paintings.

"I mean he doesn't—he is an artist, he paints beauty, and if you're anything at all, Celeste, you are beauty. I believe he would love to paint you."

"That's ridiculous, Quinn. Nobody wants to see me, much less a re-creation of me." Quinn saw her breath catch and her skin flush just a bit right at the back of her neck. Her hair was up in a pile of curls atop her head, and the short fine hairs on the back of her neck arrowed down to her back. "You're wrong," she said on an unsteady breath.

No, he wasn't. It angered him that people, her people, *her family*, had led her to believe that she was ugly. She was possibly the most beautiful woman he'd ever known. "I'll commission a portrait, and you'll see," he said, and he meant it.

"I very much doubt that." She ran one hand up the gilded frame that held the portrait of a woman in a billowing white dress. "Your mother?" she asked.

"Yes." He moved slowly toward Celeste, unable to stop looking at the bare skin of her neck.

"She's beautiful."

"Yes," he said again. He reached out and slid one finger down the back of her neck. He felt her tense and shiver. "But not nearly as beautiful as you, Celeste," he said quietly. She started to shake her head, and he ran his hand to her cheek, stopping her. She turned to him.

"I don't understand what it is you see in me," she said, those big green eyes searching his.

"You, Celeste. I see you, and you are beautiful."

"The opinion of a single man," she said. She turned away and left him standing there, as if nothing had happened between them. "This is lovely as well. Who is she?"

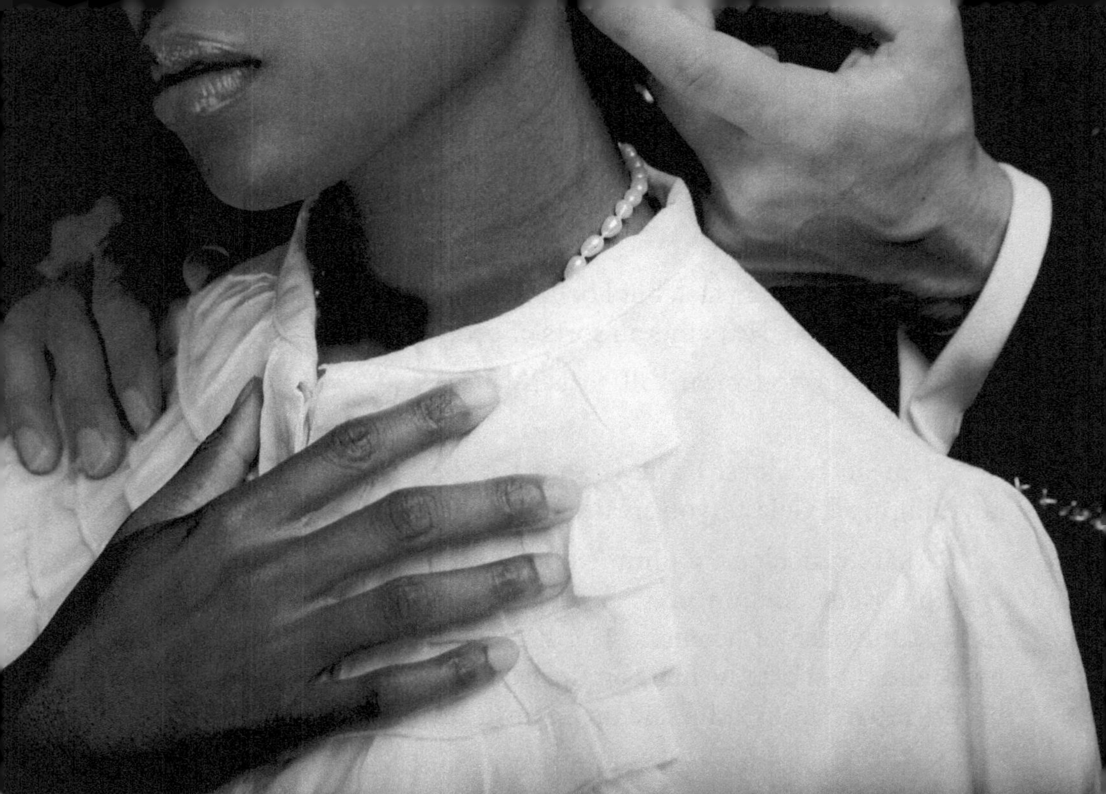

"Ah, that's Madame Gautreau, one of his favorite subjects." He walked over and swept his hand the length of her arm, like a caress that didn't quite meet her skin.

"She didn't want her portrait?"

"This is one of several. Madame Gautreau sits for him, not for herself. This he sold at the Salon."

"She's beautiful," she said.

"They're all beautiful."

"He's quite talented."

"It's more than talent," he replied.

"I think his appreciation for her comes through in this painting. It's more than a simple portrait. I think she's lovely."

"As do I," Quinn said, but he wasn't looking at the painting, not that Celeste would know that. Except that she trembled, so perhaps she did. "Celeste, what we spoke of earlier, what I asked you to consider…"

"Yes?" she asked as she turned to him, and what he saw stole his breath.

Whether she liked it or not, his words had done something to her. Her irises were wide, her cheeks flushed, and he could smell the want on her as though he were a predator. Perhaps in this he was. He supposed part of him was reaching out for the connection he would be missing while Calder was gone, but he'd never felt for a woman the way he felt for this woman, and against his better judgment, he wanted to explore that with her. "May I touch you?" he asked.

"You didn't ask the last time," she said, and her breath hitched in her chest.

"But I'm asking now. May I touch you?" He took a step toward her, and her chin came up so that her gaze remained on his face. Her head gave a quick little twitch as though her body and her mind were at war with the decision. "May I?" he said again, and his voice was deep and guttural, nearly unrecognizable to him.

Her mouth dropped open. The word didn't come. He took another step toward her, so close that their clothes did what their bodies would not. The edge of his jacket caught on the pleated fabric at her hip, and when she shifted, her skirts tangled about his feet. Quinn listened to the rustle of cotton and linen and silk and imagined it the softer, sweeter sound of skin and flesh. He could hardly draw a breath from the want of her.

"Yes."

He lifted his hand, placed it on her cheek, and absorbed the heat of her as his thumb coasted along the crest of it. "Celeste," he said quietly, "you like it when I touch you." He brought his other hand up and held her face so he could gaze at her, and her eyes fluttered shut, her breath coming in little puffs to his chin, her chest pressing quickly against his waistcoat as she breathed.

He ran his thumbs over her eyebrows. "You're simply beautiful," he said.

Her eyelids snapped open, and her gaze focused on him. "Calder," she said, and he dropped his hands and stepped away.

"I'll give you the room. If you need anything, simply ring the butler," Quinn said. He turned and walked away.

Celeste couldn't believe she'd done that to him. She'd thought of Sargent painting a portrait with Quinn and Calder, and the thought of the two of them portrayed with the intensity she saw in the portraits…but then Quinn had touched her and thought her reaction was to his touch. She didn't believe it was, so she'd stopped him in the only way she knew how to.

She'd cut deep, and it had been entirely uncalled for—that much was patently obvious. But she could not stand there and believe the words that came from his mouth. Because she wanted to believe. She desperately wanted to believe him. It would be so much easier if he were right. It wasn't fair to her. None of this was. Quinn would walk away from her one day, of that she was certain.

She turned back to the painting on the wall, floated her hand over the woman's arm much as Quinn had done with her, not making contact with the canvas. She needed to apologize. She picked up her skirts and ran to the doorway, sliding into the hall that made up the landing of the uppermost staircase. He was nowhere to be seen. She leaned over the high balustrade and swept her gaze around all three floors of landings. She didn't see him anywhere.

She turned back for the gallery and walked along the wall to avoid the dancers until she came to a painting so vibrant it shook her. The colors of spring surrounded the women in crinoline skirts, ballet shoes tied to their feet. They were posing—not quite dancing and not quite standing. Their posture a perfect showcase for their lithe bodies.

She looked back to the entry and saw no one, so she reached out and ran a finger down one spine. The bumps from the thick paint created shadows of the ridges in the dancer's spine and were reminiscent of actual bones. She did want to dance again, more than she'd ever wanted to. She couldn't. She wrung her hands together as she looked at the doorway again, probably hoping to find that Quinn had returned, forgiven her. He wasn't there. He hadn't forgiven her—he shouldn't. It was a horrible thing she'd done to call the ghost of Calder between them to protect herself. Horrible.

She walked over to the bench at the front windows of the house. It looked out over the park in the center of the square. People walked and smiled. Children laughed and played. Carriages swept up and down the road, their passengers also watching, also conversing out there between the happiness of the park and the solitude of the gallery. She hadn't felt so alone in some time, and she imagined that came from being so close to Quinn and his family. Something she'd never had and suddenly, impossibly…she did.

It also came from seeing Francine and Lulu. She was terrified and excited at the same time.

Grace. Her name had been Grace. It was a memory so buried in her mind, but it felt like it was being unzipped, and so many things rushed her.

She watched as the shadows moved across the park, and nobody in the house came looking for her. She wondered at that. Perhaps the household forgot she was here. Or perhaps they remembered and didn't care. Or perhaps Quinn had told the household to leave her be. She deserved that last.

Today had been a long day, and Quinn…she didn't like the idea of him giving up Calder to be with her, even if he had managed to stir certain feelings in her. It wouldn't be fair to Quinn, and it wouldn't be fair to Calder, perhaps above all because none of this was his doing. She felt guilty for spying on him and forcing his hand with Quinn.

She'd truly ruined everything. Was this what her family meant when they spoke of her? Was this what they thought of when they considered her to be bad luck?

She needed to help Calder and Quinn, somehow. She couldn't lose Quinn's friendship and refused to interfere in their relationship further.

"You shouldn't have done that," Quinn said, and she started, turning toward him. He stood not five feet away from her, his hands in his pockets, his face turned toward the windows. She stood and moved toward him, but he backed up a pace, and so she stayed herself.

"No, I shouldn't have, and I'm so very sorry, Quinn."

"Why did you do it?"

"I don't…" She looked down at her hands, twisting the pleating of her skirts. "You frighten me," she said.

"I do, I know I do. Learning new things about yourself that you never knew were there—that's terrifying. I believe these are things you should know, Celeste. I don't think you should close yourself off to the possibility of passion—physical or otherwise."

"It isn't your decision to make. This is my life, my body," she said. He tried to speak, and she waved him off. "You mean to show me what passion is…and what of me when I'm married off to some cold old man who has no intention of picking up where you left off? What then? I'll tell you what then. Then these things you've taught me will only damage my heart—serve to remind me for the rest of my life of what I don't have, what I won't have, what I can *never* have." Her voice shook, and she tried to steady it. Instead, it rose in volume. "Why can't you leave me to my illusions? Why must you show me these things?" she asked.

"It seems a bit self-serving when you put it that way."

"It does, doesn't it? You merely need someone to commiserate with you. I can do that without you pushing me to things I have no interest in. You touched me as if you wish me to belong to you, but you—you belong to someone else, and I—all I did was merely remind you of that. It was not well done of me, but it was the truth, was it not? You don't want me. You

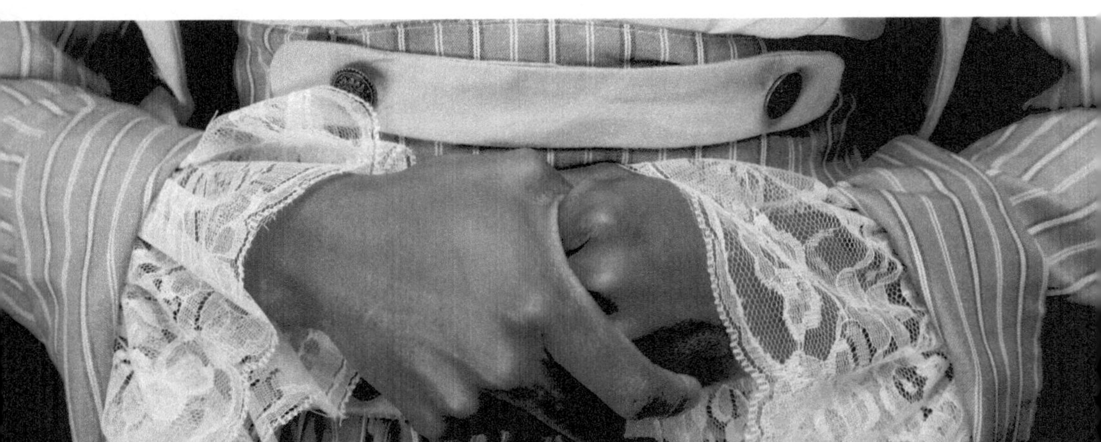

want him. You and I can never be." Celeste tried to calm herself. She twisted her hands together to stop their shaking, held them close to her belly to keep the tremble from turning her stomach.

"He may never return," Quinn said, and the sound of his resignation nearly gutted her, and she pushed into her belly with her fists as hard as she could.

"You don't know that. You can't know that. And even so, if he doesn't— what then? You intend to pine with me as your wife until you die lonely? Because you'll drive me away with the anger that finally takes hold. You know it will. You know at some point, if Calder doesn't return, that you will turn on me for forcing him away."

"No—"

"Yes. You will, as you should, because it was my fault he left. It was me, it was me!" And she knew it to be true in that moment. "I can't do that to you. I won't go there with you. Leave me be, Quinn. Let us be friends while we can be friends, and nothing more," she begged.

"I feel more for you than you seem to understand," he said.

"It's irrelevant because you will never feel for me what you feel for him. That's pure impossibility. I know it is because I've seen the two of you together. Need I remind you? What is required of a passion like the one you and Calder have is that it's shared, and you don't seem to understand that *we* do not share this. This is something you want, but I do not.

"Leave me to my illusions, Quinn, please. Leave me with the one gift you've truly given me, that I can manage myself, that I can remember the two of you, think on what I saw and…manage myself. That in itself was a gift and something I can keep. The rest of it—you need to leave me be, Quinn, please."

He turned toward the windows and stared at nothing, the sun falling quickly in the sky, the day coming to an end and dragging his intentions with it.

"I will leave you be, Celeste, as you wish, but I will not abandon you. I will help you find someone. I will make sure you marry a man who can do the things that I wish to do for you. You deserve that much, from me, from him, from someone. You deserve it."

"What *you* wish for me? What about what *I* wish for me? What I have now is enough. Why don't you understand?"

"I can't. I see so much possibility in you."

"That possibility is because of how *you* feel, not how *I* feel. You aren't listening to me."

"I can't understand why—"

"Stop trying and simply trust me. What you've given me is enough to carry me." She turned toward the window as the sun fell behind the houses across the square, and the bell rang for supper. "Perhaps I should go home," she said. She wasn't exactly hungry anyway.

"No, please stay. I need to know we will still be friends. Celeste, please. Don't leave like this."

"But you don't trust me to know myself."

"And you don't know what I saw that night. You coming off like that affected the whole of your body!"

"I know it did, Quinn! But it had naught to do with you. It was only me, and you were nothing but a vision in my head." Her voice rose, and heat flooded her face as she turned on him, and he shied. "I don't want anyone to touch me in that way. You need to trust me on this, or we cannot—"

"I will trust you," he cut in, his gaze frightened, his hands up like he approached a wild creature. "I will put aside my opinions, and I will trust you," he said as he tried to calm her. "I'm sorry, I didn't understand how determined… I'm sorry. I will trust you."

"I don't know if I believe you," she whispered. She felt completely wrought out and spent.

"I don't know that *I* believe me, but believe that I will try. I will do my very best, and I will try, Celeste, because I can't lose you." His voice hitched, and her breath stalled as she truly looked at him. "I may not love you like I do him, but I do love you."

Air rushed her lungs on a shocked breath, and the whole of Celeste's body trembled. She crossed her arms over her chest, her hands digging into her upper arms as she tried to hold herself together physically—if not emotionally—as she considered him. "Please believe I appreciate everything you've done for me. I'm not trying to be ungrateful. I may not know what's wrong with me—"

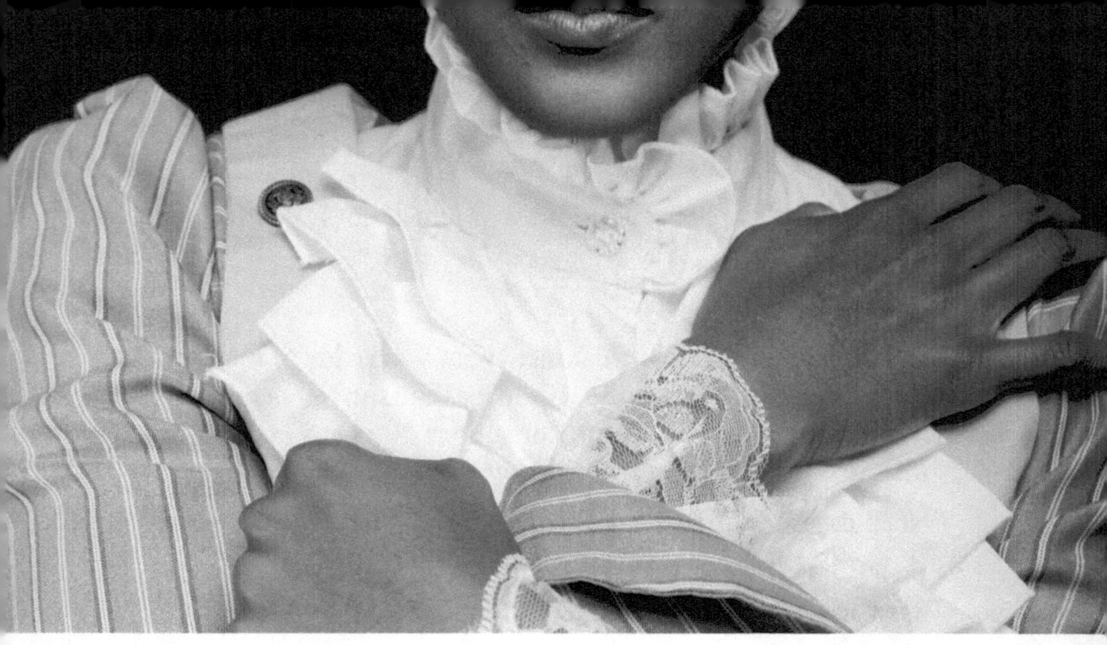

"There's nothing wrong—"

"Stop. I know I'm not like other people. I've listened to all of you people talk for years now. I don't feel that need for connection in the way you all seem to. That physical mashing of body parts. I don't want it."

Quinn shook his head to argue. Celeste hoped he wouldn't have her committed. "I really should go." She couldn't very well stay now, after all of this. What would happen? What would his family think of her demeanor?

His mother was going to know something was wrong with her. What would she do? The woman was a smart one. She'd probably go after her son for doing something ungentlemanly. She smiled at the sudden thought of Quinn being accosted by his mother for doing some unknown wrong.

"Why on earth do you smile?" he asked.

"Your mother. If nothing else, she'll most likely blame you for my odd mood," she said.

"You're quite right. A gentleman never sets a lady on edge. He should never, not ever, bring her mood down. A gentleman seeks only to elevate a lady's mood," he said, as if it were something he'd been forced to learn by rote memorization.

Celeste let out a great breath and dropped her arms. "There's nothing that I can say. I can't lie anymore, at least not to you. I have to be true to myself. I have to try to find a life in which I won't hurt anyone else. You have given me more than I can repay. You deserve more than this, and so do I. I deserve to be believed and to have my wishes honored."

"You do," he said. "And you have my dedicated and determined friendship, no matter what you decide to do."

"Well, then, let us go to supper so I can see your mother come after you. I think it might cheer us up."

"Us?" he said as he reached out to her with one hand. He started to pull it back, but she grabbed it.

"Yes, us. You've no cause to feel ambushed by your mother, because you already know what comes next. Besides, we probably deserve to be chided, the both of us, regardless that none of them will know the truth about why."

Quinn tilted his head to the side as he considered this. "I suppose that's true," he said, pulling her closer to him. "I'm sorry, for my part. You're right about one thing, I can't lose you either. I won't lose you," he said.

"Quit being an arse, and you have nothing to fear," she said, and his jaw dropped.

"Lady Alain, did you just call me an arse?"

"If the saddle fits."

"I would never attempt to saddle an arse, my lady. That sounds like dangerous business."

She laughed and looked up to him, and the clouds in her mind seemed to part when he returned the smile, his hands running up and down her arms, soothing her mood and her nerves. "This," he said, looking at his hands on her sleeves, "this is all right? This sort of touching?"

She nodded. "This sort of touching is welcome," she said, and he smiled. "Well, then, shall we?"

"I dare say we shall," he said. He placed her hand on his arm, and they went to supper.

His mother never did accost him, because Celeste's spirits had been lifted by the simple act of chatting with him—as happened with friends. Celeste hoped that it would continue, that he would agree to disagree and simply let her be ignorant of the things he believed a man could do for her. She feared, however, it was much too late for that. She feared he'd already gone too far, and the fact was it wasn't even his fault at all, but hers.

Because the moment she'd seen Calder and Quinn together, some piece of her broke and shifted, and there was no putting it back where it had been. She still didn't want to be party to what he had in mind. What she wanted, more than anything, was to see them together again. That certainly wasn't something she would tell him. And it certainly wasn't something that would ever happen again. She would have to live the rest of her life carried by that one memory.

Quinn

A week went by, and they readied to quit London for Westcreek. His mother had made the arrangements for them, quite happily, and Quinn looked forward to getting out of London to somewhere where there were fewer memories of Calder to drag him down. A mere week, and he could hardly stand it. Two months more of this, at the very least.

He and Celeste had spent the week riding, having dinners and tea with friends and family, basically pretending that there was nothing between them but friendship, while everyone who saw them assumed something more. He had promised, so he hadn't returned to her rooms, and he didn't meet with her alone, and he behaved as a gentleman should.

The moment Quinn agreed to returning their relationship to a superficial friendship, he knew it wouldn't be possible. Yet he'd agreed to it because the alternative was losing her entirely, and that he simply could not stand. Not when Calder was gone.

Quinn knew how he felt about Calder, but he didn't know how he felt about Celeste. The problem was, because of his feelings for Calder, there could be no Celeste, so returning to friendship really was the correct thing to do. It was difficult to stop that exploration before getting far, but he kept telling himself it was the right thing to do.

So he was honorable, and friendly, and definitely avoided looking at her for too long, and most definitely didn't touch her. Somehow he knew if he touched her again, just his skin against hers, just once, he would be permanently and irrevocably tied to her, and there would be nothing either of them could do about it.

The door to his bedroom opened, and his mother came in. "Quinn, dear, the carriage awaits, and Celeste has sent word that she is ready," she said.

"You could have sent the butler to let me know, Mother. You didn't have to come to my rooms yourself."

"I'm aware of what I can and can't do in my own home, Quinn, and I came to your rooms because I can." Her hand patted his shoulder, and he straightened, turning from the clothes he was sorting on his bed to look at her. "Just as you are aware that you have a valet available to you who can pack your things to be sure you don't forget something like…nightclothes." She winked.

"Truly, Mother?" he asked, and she laughed. He knew she was perfectly aware he hated wearing anything abed. He always had. He always managed to get tangled up in his sheets enough without the help of additional fabric. So, much to the consternation of the household governesses and valets, Quinn had always slept naked and refused to change. She stood beside him, and he put his arm around her waist and bussed her cheek. "I'll miss you, too," he said quietly, and she patted his chest.

"Well, now. Have you got this all managed?" she asked as she waved a hand over the clothing that covered his bed. "You know I would be of no help. I can't even dress your father in the morning, much less anyone else."

"I have this managed," he said as he waited for whatever was to come next.

"Quinn?"

"Yes, Mother?" He looked down at her. He knew she hadn't come all the way to his rooms for this inane chatter. Perhaps Jerrod had done something else. He kissed her temple. "Don't worry, Mother. Everything is going to be fine."

"You marry that girl, Quinn. You marry that girl, and *then* everything will be fine. Nobody will give any of the old rumors a second thought, and the two of you will have beautiful little children and be perfectly happy, and the past will truly be in the past. Do that for me," she said. Quinn tried to swallow past the lump in his throat as his arm fell away from her. She turned to him. "Marry that girl, Quinn."

This was the part that Calder didn't understand. The part where Quinn had to break his mother's heart and confirm her worst nightmares. That her perfect son wasn't so perfect. With Jerrod off destroying the family's reputation as quickly as he was able, Quinn was set to be the savior of them all, to wipe the board of the negative thoughts, to be the hero, to save the family name and all that. His mother wasn't yet aware that both of her sons were worthless fools with no future and no hope of carrying on the Cheshire legacy.

He turned back to the clothes on the bed.

"Quinn?"

"Yes, Mother. Of course, Mother," he said, because he did love her, even though she'd no idea who he was or what he wanted for his life.

"Well, then, that's settled. I'll see you off downstairs. Shall I send Bertie for your bags?"

"No, Mother, I can handle my things, thank you. I'll be down presently."

Quinn was left to finish his packing in solitude. He stood there an inordinate amount of time, staring at his clothing. He turned to the dressing table opposite his bed and swept it clean with both arms. A porcelain pitcher hit the wall and shattered with a satisfying crack. His shaving gear thudded to the floor next to it as the soap and water seeped into the heavy carpet under his feet. *Fuck it all.*

The last missive Warrick had sent fluttered to the floor.

Marseilles.

Nothing more. He picked it up. The ink had begun to run from the spilled water, and Quinn ran his thumb across it, smearing the word on the paper. He was safely in France. Calder. He'd lost Calder and, by tacit agreement with Celeste, had lost the possibility of her as well. Where did that leave him? He looked at the small mirror on the wall that he used for shaving, and he stopped lying to himself. He still lived in this room because this room was full of memories. Full of Calder. He could easily afford a home of his own anywhere in London. Anywhere in England, for that matter. He remained here.

How many years had it been since Calder had first entered his body, and they'd lost their innocence together in this very room, this very bed? He didn't even know, because there had never been a time for him without

Calder, not ever. Becoming lovers had simply been a natural progression to their relationship, one they had both fought and both surrendered to. Together. Everything they had done had been done together.

Neither of them wished for it. Why would anyone wish to be ostracized? When they were born, sodomy had still been a hanging offense. At least now the punishment was just life imprisonment. This wasn't something they chose. It simply was. They belonged together.

Calder.

He looked at the bed in the mirror.

"You're the devil," he'd said to Calder.

"What does that make you?" Calder had asked.

"If you're the devil, that makes me an angel."

"Perhaps a fallen angel," Calder said.

"Still an angel."

"And I brought you down to earth?"

"Or perhaps I raised you up," Quinn said.

"You're painting yourself in a much better light than you are me."

"Of course I am. I'm the good one. I'll always be the good one."

"Good what?" Calder asked.

"The good son, the good brother, the good cousin, the good man. The good everything," Quinn replied.

"I see," Calder said quietly. "And so I've ruined you."

"No, you haven't ruined me. I fell from grace a long time ago. I was simply waiting here for you."

"You're lucky I came," Calder said.

"I will wait forever for you."

"And I will always come."

Since that moment, Quinn had always waited, and Calder had always come. They'd been but boys. So young, just learning what life was.

Quinn's chest hitched a revolt against the pain, and he took a deep breath to fend off the tears. Someone had to be the good one so someone else could do whatever it was they wished. Someone had to pin the world back together at the edges when the ugly started to seep out. Because someone had to do it.

He was that someone. It hadn't been a choice, it had just been.

Quinn looked away from the mirror and picked up his shaving kit and other grooming tools and dumped them in his bag. He threw the portmanteau on the bed and tossed the clothes from the bed into it without looking. Whatever was there was what he would have. It would suffice. If he forgot something, he would borrow it from Perry. Just now he wasn't of a mood to sort through anything or consider something so inane as what clothes he needed to wear.

He latched the case and grabbed his boots and coat and left the room behind, hoping to never see it again.

Q

"Quinn?"

"Yes," he grumbled as he continued to look out the window at the passing countryside. This carriage ride with Celeste was turning into a lesson in patience.

"You're quiet," Celeste said.

He closed his eyes and rubbed them. He had been quiet. He'd had quite a bit to consider, and all of those consideration were weighing on his mind and eating away at his conscience. "I apologize. I've just…there's a lot going on," he said finally.

She reached out and tried to take his hand, but he pulled it away, so she twisted her fingers in her lap. He didn't think he could touch her just now. Not when they had the next hour together in the carriage.

"Celeste, I apologize. It isn't you. I'm simply exhausted."

"Perhaps I should return home?"

"No, I just need to sleep and clear my head. It's been a long week." Had it only been a fortnight since that ball? Just shy of it, if that. That ball. That night. Everything changed. Everything. He should have listened to Calder. He should have done what he said. He should have told everyone. What difference would that make now? None.

"Have you heard—"

"He's in France, on his way to India. That's all I know for certain. I only know that he's alive." He saw her nod from the corner of his eye, and he shifted in the seat. "Please believe me, Celeste, I simply need some sleep. It was a long day on top of a long week, and it really isn't you." He reached over and patted her hand, and one of her fingers reached out of the knot and twisted itself up with one of his, and he allowed it. Until the heat of her sank through both layers of gloves, and he had to release her.

Q

They arrived at Perry's Westcreek estate late. He asked that a tray be sent to her rooms because he wasn't of a mood to socialize, and he knew she wouldn't be either if he was absent. He made his apologies to Perry and showed Celeste to her rooms, which were in the opposite wing from his, thank God. He left her there at the door and felt her gaze on him as he walked the length of the hall to the other side of the manor. He didn't pause, and he didn't look back.

His room hadn't changed from the last time he'd been here with Calder. Perhaps this was a mistake as well. He tossed his coat to the chair by the bed and started to undress. It had been quite a long time since Quinn had felt this desolate. He crawled into the giant bed and stared at the moon shadows across the room as the light cast everything in shades of darkness.

All that week when he'd closed his eyes, Calder had been there. When he'd opened them, Celeste had been. He couldn't escape either and had no idea what he could do for either of them. Sleep apparently wasn't in the cards at the moment. He stood and pulled a robe from the wardrobe and skulked down the hallway and the back stairs to sneak into Perry's study. He poured three fingers of whiskey and sat in front of the banked fire, watching the embers as they tried so hard to burn.

"I thought you were for bed?" Perry said.

"I thought you'd still be at supper."

"With the girls visiting, it's too many women. I left them to their shenanigans."

"And what sorts of shenanigans can one expect from such a gaggle of women?" Quinn asked absentmindedly as Perry poured himself a brandy and came to sit with Quinn.

"Certainly some sort of nefarious knitting," Perry said.

"Nefarious—" Quinn laughed. "Nefarious knitting."

"Is there another kind?" Perry asked.

"Knitting? Noble. I imagine there to be some rather noble knitting."

"Ah, but noble knitting is not nearly as much fun as nefarious knitting."

Quinn looked over to Perry. "I've missed you since you married," he said.

"No doubt you have. Though I'm certain it isn't for lack of knitting prattle."

"No, not so very much."

"We had fun, and no doubt you still have fun, seeing as you're still unattached. Though I did receive an earful from your mother about ways to force you and Celeste to marriage."

"Force?"

"You know, the usual—find the two of you in some compromising situation and force your hand. That sort of thing."

God damn it all. Quinn shook his head.

"Don't worry, I would never attempt to arrange that sort of situation. And I wouldn't be party to forcing a marriage, unless it was absolutely necessary. We all know *you* would never do such a thing to a young lady, so—"

"Yes, of course. Good Quinn would not deign to ruin a girl, would he?" he said, swallowing the rest of his whiskey, letting it burn its way to his empty stomach. Probably a mistake, that.

"No, I don't think he would," Perry said carefully.

"Regardless, she doesn't want me."

"I find that surprising," Perry said.

"That she doesn't want me?"

"Yes, I mean, I assumed you weren't attached. However, by all accounts she's in need of a husband, and you are rather a catch."

Quinn grunted.

"What's got you?"

"My mother," Quinn said. He leaned forward with his elbows on his knees, and his dressing robe slipped open.

"Mind yourself, Quinn. I didn't come here for a show," Perry said with a laugh.

"Fuck's sake," he said, and he sat up and closed the robe again, tucking the edge carefully at his ribs and tying the band tighter. "It has been a while since we had any sort of inappropriate disrobement between us."

"Ahh, yes. We did have a few wild nights with some wild women once upon a time, did we not?"

"We did. Yes, something my family had no idea of." Quinn smiled for the first time in a while at the memories. He and Perry and Hugh had got themselves into quite a bit of trouble. Once upon a time.

"Listen, I know you said you came to Westcreek because you both just wanted some time away from London. Perhaps you'd want to go out with me to see the property, meet the tenants and such? Get away, out on the land, meet the sheep."

"Meet the sheep." Quinn laughed again. To think this man was the unruliest of cousins at one point.

"It's not a euphemism, by the by. I do actually have sheep that need attention on occasion," Perry said.

Quinn grunted as he thought about it for a moment. "What of Celeste?"

"Lilly and the girls will keep her busy. Whatever she's of a mind to, Lilly can see to it."

Quinn considered it. Perhaps they could use some time apart.

"It would get your mind of off…whatever," Perry said.

Quinn nodded. "When?"

"Tomorrow. We break our fast at dawn."

Quinn nodded. "See you, and your sheep, then."

$$Q$$

The next morning, after a cold shower to clear the webs formed from drinking whiskey on an empty stomach—well, that and a touch of the dog that bit him—Quinn met up with Perry. They breakfasted as the sun rose over the park, then headed out to meet the sheep.

"How long have you been here?" Quinn asked. "Five years?"

"Nearly that, yes. I took over the property in 1880, married Lilly, moved here."

"You don't make it to London often now."

"Not much, just for important debates in the House, Warrick's wedding, family whatnot."

"Whatnot," Quinn repeated. They walked their horses past the wide lawns at the back and finally came to the edge of the manor property.

Perry kicked his horse. "Come on, then!" he yelled.

Quinn leaned into his horse's neck and followed. God, but it felt good to ride like this. He'd needed it. The heat of the sun and the snap of the wind on his face. With nothing but the beat of the hooves and the heave of his horse's breath in the air, it quieted one's mind. It felt good. They cleared the rise, and Perry headed for a small border fence, jumping it easily.

Quinn followed. His horse balked at the last moment and came down in a mud bog as he stumbled. He managed to keep his seat and steer the horse back out. His clothes were a mess, his trousers wet through, his boots certainly ruined. "Damn it all!" he yelled as he let his horse walk it off. Perry pulled up short when he heard Quinn yell and turned back to meet him.

"Quinn, you're supposed to avoid the bogs," he said.

"Am I?" he asked. "I'd no idea."

Perry laughed and followed the fence line away from Quinn. "Hell and damn, the ditch gate is closed," he said. He jumped from his horse and tied him to the fence on the other side of the ditch, and Quinn followed suit, watching as Perry waded into the flooding ditch.

"Is this what happens when you're the master of an estate?" Quinn asked.

"Occasionally," he replied. "I do have a land steward, but…" Perry looked around the field, his eyes wide, then back to Quinn. "He doesn't seem to be here at the moment, and if I let the water continue, the ditch will be worthless. We haven't yet dug the second ditch, which will irrigate this field. The gate needs to be open to protect the work already done. Get over here and help me. Your boots are already ruined."

Quinn laughed and waded into the muck. At least this water was cleaner, since it was a bit deeper and flowed more freely.

"Here," Perry said, and Quinn took hold of the opposite side of the screw wheel, and they both pulled in opposite directions until it came loose and the gate raised, water rushing through to the ditch. "Looks like someone closed it. It's staying open now, at any rate," he said. "I'll let the steward know."

They rinsed their hands in the rushing water, and Perry helped yank Quinn back out of the ditch. "You haven't sold me on land management," Quinn said.

"No?" Perry asked with a laugh.

"No." Quinn looked down at his ruined clothes. "And I've yet to meet a sheep." His boots squelched mud as he walked. "Are we going to continue on to the sheep like this?"

"Sheep don't mind if you're a wreck, you know," Perry said with a grin.

"No? I assumed they would be much more fussy about appearances."

Perry laughed. "Of course you did. We should return now. I need to track down Jameson and let him know about the gate, so he can keep watch on it. The sheep will manage without us for the day."

"Are you quite certain?" Quinn asked.

"About the sheep? Quite. They may have to change their evening schedule. Tomorrow will be soon enough."

"Thank goodness," Quinn said as he stuck his book in the stirrup and groaned at the slip of mud.

They mounted their horses, but Perry didn't take off across the park. Instead, he walked them at the fence line, probably to check for other damage. "Are you at all interested in marriage to Celeste?" he asked.

"I had considered it. But I don't believe I would be good for her."

"I thought that very thing of Lilly," Perry said.

"Of course, but that's an entirely different situation. She was a maid and you a peer. Of course you were unworthy of her," Quinn said.

Perry laughed. "There was a bit more to it than all that," he said.

"Isn't there always a bit more to it?" That was the truth.

"Why do you believe yourself unworthy of Celeste?" he asked.

"Because I am…otherwise engaged."

"Calder?" Perry asked, and Quinn froze, his horse shifting uncomfortably, dancing sideways from his tension.

Quinn took a deep breath and loosened his grip on the rein and tried to relax so the horse would calm. "Am I delusional?" Quinn said. "Why does it seem that everyone in the family knows of something I thought nobody knew anything about?"

"Delusional, no question," Perry said. "Look, if it makes you feel better, the rumor has kept to family, and I don't think anyone but Rox and I know about the more current events. I believe most of the family have politely forgotten your younger escapades. Perhaps they thought you'd grown out of it. Most of the family has always known of Calder's preference. It matters not."

"The ball," Quinn cursed.

"Yes, the tension between the two of you did not go unnoticed by Rox. He spoke with me—and no one else. Considering how close the two of you have always been, it was no great step to consider. What does it matter?"

"Only my life, his life," Quinn said.

"Let's not get carried away. Certainly, if the two of you flaunt it and anger the wrong people— but that's not likely. I assume the two of you"—he cleared his throat—"for quite some time now, without issue."

"Yes…this doesn't bother you?" he asked.

"Why would it bother me? What you and Calder do quietly doesn't affect me in any way. Unless, of course, you get in trouble, then I would be concerned for your safety."

"And the rest of the family?"

"I don't think they care what Calder does, except that he's expected to succeed his father as St. Cyr. He can't give an heir to the title if he doesn't have a wife." Perry shrugged.

"Yes, queen and country," Quinn said. "I love how all of these things have been considered without our involvement."

"Of course they have. A family history like ours? Every damned one of us is scrutinized. You should be aware of that by now."

"Regardless, it's over now, so it matters not."

"Why is that?"

"Calder is unhappy with me after—"

"The ball."

"Celeste," Quinn said.

"And here you've brought her to my house," Perry said sarcastically.

"Calder has left England. What does that matter?"

"Again?"

"Yes, again, and I've promised to protect Celeste, even if I can't continue that protection in the future."

"Because she needs to marry for her family."

"Yes."

"And she's refused you?"

"Yes."

"So you're hiding here," Perry said.

"We needed to be away from society, from family, from those who attempt to push us together against our wishes."

"Is it truly against your wishes?"

"I care for her, but I cannot in good conscience give her what she should have by right."

"A husband who loves her?"

"Not exactly."

"A husband who will give her sons."

"Of a fashion."

"You don't care for her?"

"I do care for her. That's not at issue. I do care for her, perhaps too much. The problem is with—"

"Calder."

Quinn nodded. "Yes," he said, and he felt a wash of tension through his body, as though he released it all at once. Though it had been difficult to speak on, Quinn felt relieved to do so, especially with Perry because he was so very easy to talk to.

"I see. What has this to do with you and Celeste?"

"We can't be together. It wouldn't be fair to Celeste. Or to myself. Or to Calder, for that matter. How would that work—you only just said he must provide an heir for the St. Cyr title."

"Well, there is must, and then there are options," Perry said.

"There are no options."

Perry laughed at him. *At him.* "Who are you talking to? What do you mean, there are no options? Someone telling you there are no other options is merely someone attempting to control your choices. There are *always* options, particularly when something is that important. I was set to give up everything for Lilly. She was that important to me, so don't talk to me of options—or Rox, for that matter. Fuck's sake, we all know what his options were. You know of Ender as well, and you tell me there are no options for you? Well, aren't you the most delicate human in history that for you, and only you, there are no options?" Perry grumbled at him, clearly annoyed. "There are options, Quinn. You just don't *like* the options."

Well, then.

Celeste

eleste stood at the window of her room in complete and total shock at the world before her eyes. It was like a waking dream, the sunrise beyond beautiful. The colors of the sky over the horizon that brought all these new colors to the world? She'd never seen its equal. Without the black fog of London, the air was bright and fresh, and it didn't force its way into her lungs whenever she opened her mouth. She welcomed it. It even tasted good. And the colors…the green of the lawn was a true vibrant green, and the flowers, she couldn't believe the flowers. It was as if she'd spent the whole of her life with a gray veil over her eyes.

When Quinn walked out to the stables, she was still lost to the beauty of the countryside, even as she was saddened by the loss of him. Celeste watched from the window of her room as Quinn mounted the horse, and he and Perry took off with the sun rising over the far horizon. Beautiful picture, really. If she could have, she would have painted something much like it. But then, everything in the country seemed to be beautiful.

She ran one finger down her neck, sending chills through her body, just as he'd done in the gallery. The gallery—he'd been different with her ever since the gallery. He wasn't rude or careless. He was simply indifferent. He didn't laugh as though he cared. He didn't smile as though interested in what she said. His eyes didn't shine. They were—indifferent was the perfect description, really. Maybe she'd gone too far. She'd railed at him, and she'd told him the truth, and now—indifference.

He'd done exactly what she asked of him. He'd brought his guard up and looked at her differently, spoken with her differently. He'd taken her riding, brought her to tea and supper with his mother, even accompanied her to the Royal Gardens. He had not attempted to woo her. He had not climbed her trellis. He had not touched her—and her skin, it was pained from the want of his touch. All of the endearing things about him had been stifled, and she regretted that with a sharp clarity.

Then yesterday in the carriage, he hadn't even been indifferent. He'd been distant and cold and disconsolate. He'd said he was just exhausted, and he did have every right to feel exhausted, but Celeste couldn't help but feel that part of that exhaustion was with her.

When she'd tried to touch him, he'd pulled away. When he'd finally allowed her that one finger…it had been gone much too soon, and when they'd arrived in time for supper, he'd taken her to her rooms and left her there. It was what she'd asked of him. It hurt very much.

What Quinn didn't know was how very badly she wanted to take it all back. She wanted the warmth of his skin against hers, his fingers on her neck, his hands on hers. She wanted that ping of warmth when their bodies touched, no matter how incidentally. She wanted him to disobey her for once. But that wasn't in Quinn, and she knew it.

She understood the distance. She needed it, had asked for it, and her regret was her own. She didn't want everything from him. She just wanted so much…and he deserved everything, something she didn't have to give, whether or not Calder was involved. And now she didn't know how she would be around him, because he wasn't the person she'd come to know and care quite a lot about. He was quiet, he was sad, and he was…distant, and that was entirely her fault.

At least he would be gone for the day. Celeste was happy to wander the property on her own, perhaps read. She left her bedroom in search of breakfast, which was as simple as following the savory aroma that wafted throughout the house. She found the breakfast room with three young women at the table. The eldest stood and walked over to her.

"You must be Celeste," she said. "I'm Lilly. This is Amélie, and this is Maryse. They're Francine's sisters. They're visiting us from Eildon since everyone is in town. We thought it would be nice to have them here since they can't go into London quite yet. Rox and Perry won't allow it," she whispered dramatically.

"Which is ridiculous!" Amélie said in a French accent. "I am old enough to come out to society."

"So am I," said Maryse.

"Society is not as much fun as you may think it is," Celeste said.

Lilly started to say something, but someone else entered the room, distracting her. "And this is Ms. Faversham, their governess."

"Lovely to meet you, my lady," she said with a curtsey, and Celeste returned it.

"Celeste, please," she said.

Lilly pulled her to sit next to her as the girls talked about how lovely it would be to start the Season next year. How exciting it would be for them to find husbands and fall in love. Celeste decided to leave them to their opinions. It was interesting to listen to a perspective that she'd never really had. Though she was a bit surprised, considering they lived with Francine, and Francine seemed to have quite a healthy disregard for the Season and all of its trappings.

Celeste finished breakfast and begged off of doing anything with the group, saying she wanted to go for a walk. Lilly showed her to the library so she could choose a book and pointed her to the back of the house that looked out over the large green lawn.

She spent the next few hours walking the grounds and thinking about Quinn. She'd tried to sit and read, but her mind wandered to him every single time. She reread the opening pages of *A Tale of Two Cities* a thousand times. *It was the best of times, it was the worst of times.* Got it. Living it. Thank you, Mr. Dickens.

This wasn't going to be easy. Apparently, telling him to leave her be had much the opposite effect on her—she could do nothing but think about him and his touch. It warmed her as though she'd been trained in response to his name, no matter how she tried to quell it.

When she thought about that one finger that had swept the length of her neck in the gallery, she wanted to cry for the loss of it. Her nipples would harden to small points of sensation against the inside of her corset, making her shift and stumble. Any breeze that came across her shoulder did much the same as his hand.

Being awakened to these sorts of things—to the possibilities of them—was maddening. Because in her heart she knew, somehow, that being touched like that wasn't what she wanted. She was simply bereft of something she had never thought to have, she hadn't realized she'd miss, and she wanted in a way that wasn't welcome.

A light breeze blew one of her curls off her shoulder and swept it the length of her cheek, just as Quinn was fond of doing, and she stopped in her tracks, looked at the sky, and screamed.

That was enough of that. She scrubbed her hand against her cheek to rid her nerves of the feel of his hand. She found a small tree at the top of a small hill and sat down, leaning up against the trunk of it, soaking in the dappled light of the sun through its leaves as she let her eyes close on her tears.

She wished she could understand herself. She'd thought she merely didn't know and thus couldn't relate to all the talk of intimacy and sex, but that wasn't it, and she knew that now, and she still didn't want to be close to anyone in that way. Why, why, *why* did she have to be so very different? She leaned over the large root of the tree, pillowing her cheek on her arm, letting the tears soak the fabric of her sleeve.

She hadn't even realized she'd fallen asleep until another breeze pushed against her cheek. She flipped her hand at it to drive it away.

"Celeste," Quinn said.

"Quinn. Quinn?" Her eyes popped open to find him looming over her, his gloved hand sweeping the length of her jaw. Because of course he was. Of course he found her.

"What are you doing out here on your own?" he asked.

"I went for a walk. I was—I couldn't—I just—" She closed her mouth until she had her words under better control. "I was enjoying the sun and the colors and the air and…I tried to read," she said as she sat up and scanned the ground for the book. It was half wedged under her backside, and she picked it up and shoved it toward him as though she had to prove herself, then set it back down so she could shade her eyes with her hand as she looked up to him. "And now here you are."

His eyes narrowed, and she knew he wondered at her tone. It had been a bit rude, but she'd only *just* been trying to rid her mind of this man, and here he was, yet again. "Here I am," he said as he stood tall, swinging his hands behind his back as though to keep them from touching her again.

"You should return to the manor house with us because it's getting on in the day," he said. "You can ride with me." Celeste looked past him to his horse and frowned. "It's fine," he said. "I've done this before. All you'll need do is hold on."

She looked back up to him. He refused to meet her eyes.

"Must I?" she asked, and he nodded once.

"If you insist," she said.

"I do insist. I would prefer to not leave you here alone."

Such a gentleman. She was certain he didn't realize what she was going to have to hold on to. She reached down to pick up the book she'd set down and noticed his muddy boots. As she stood, her eyes drew up his body, every muscle in his legs cast in stark relief against the sun, every damned nook and cranny. It was as though his riding breeches had been painted on, and her heart started to race.

"Are you…are you wet?" she asked, unable to look away from his… equipage.

Quinn coughed, drawing her attention back to his face, which looked hard and a bit angry. "Yes, we had a moment with a stuck ditch gate that needed fixing. That's actually why we're returning." He shifted as though his wet breeches were becoming more uncomfortable, then he turned suddenly and walked to his horse.

She greeted Perry as Quinn mounted the beast, and she attempted to avoid staring at his arse in the tight, wet, no-longer-very-white riding breeches. Because, good God, those breeches were tight. And quite wet, and a bit like parchment, so thin they seemed. And they ended in those tall black leather boots that were very…boot-like.

She swallowed. She hadn't realized boots and breeches could be so thought-provoking. Correction—*muddy* boots and *wet* breeches. What the devil? What did her body want? What did her mind want? Why was seeing him like this so very arousing to her? She turned away as though to walk on.

"Celeste."

She stopped and turned back, refused to look up to him. "Pull your skirts up from the back, tuck the tail in the front at your waist," he said.

She stared at him for a moment, because she couldn't seem to catch her breath. She heard Perry laugh from not far away.

"So you can straddle the horse, Celeste. Pull your skirts up so you can straddle the horse," Quinn said.

"Oh," she said. "Yes, of course." She stared down at her skirts. *Tuck the tail*, she thought, *and what?* She shook her head, and he explained again, slower, as though she were an imbecile, which suited her at the moment, because she felt like she needed chastising. She pulled her skirts up and tucked them as instructed, then took a deep breath to steady herself before he touched her.

She smelled the wet of the mud, the leather of the boots and the saddle, the sweat of the horse and its rider, and Celeste truly wasn't sure she could do this now that she'd agreed to it. What she wanted to do was tuck tail and—she looked down. Tail was already sufficiently tucked. She wanted to cry because, sometimes, when you didn't know what the hell was wrong with you, a good damned cry was all you needed to clear your head and reset your mind.

Quinn startled her when he reached down and took her by the wrist and pulled her arm over his. "Take my shoulder and put your foot in my stirrup for a moment," he said. She did so, and he pulled, and she was flung behind him to the back of the saddle.

Then she was on the arse end of the horse with her arms wrapped around Quinn's middle and her cheek tucked against his back.

"Hold on," he said, and her hands scraped at his abdomen, finally clenching on some loose fabric at the front of him that allowed the bit of give she needed in order to fist it. His muscles tensed within the circle of her arms, and she realized just how hard a man's body was. Nothing like hers. There was nothing soft about him.

He leaned forward and clicked his tongue, and the sway of the horse only made her hold tighter, as it felt like her seat dropped from beneath her, one side at a time.

Quinn was all steel wrapped in wet linen and leather, and on top of it all, he smelled whole and wonderful—if a bit muddy and mossy. Even so, she wanted to rub herself all over him and absorb the scent and the feel of him, and she didn't exactly know why. She wasn't sure if it was because she missed his friendship and wanted anything she could get, or if her feelings for him had changed. She closed her eyes and tried to separate it out, but thinking about him like this while holding him so close was only making more of a muddle.

Celeste realized, rather abruptly, that she was holding him rather tight, and possibly exploring his abdomen with her hands a bit more than was seemly. She released him and jerked back and slid from the back of the horse, landing on her arse in the grass. She coughed and fell to her back.

"Oof."

"Celeste!" Quinn turned the horse and jumped down and ran to her. She was horrified, but she was in one piece. She supposed it could have been worse, but this wasn't much better than sitting the arse end of him and his horse.

"Are you hurt?" he asked.

Was she? She hiccuped and realized she was on the verge of tears.

"My pride has been very soundly damaged, I fear. Beyond that, I believe I'm hale and whole, even if I happen to be just shy of completely mortified." She looked toward her feet sprawled in the grass to find her skirt untucked and flapping in the breeze, and she felt the frown pulling at her face. "Let's just make that fully and completely mortified," she said as she gathered her skirts in front of her.

Without so much as a by-your-leave, he lifted her to her feet. She refused to touch him to keep from falling, which only worked to make her more dizzy, so she swooned a bit, and he caught her up against him. All of him, but from the front this time, not that it made a bit of difference, because he was still hard stem to stern…everywhere—*oh*.

Her hands wrapped around his lapels as she attempted to steady herself on her feet so she could *just—stop—touching* him, because she understood now how dangerous the touching had been. So very, very dangerous. Particularly after so many days of the not touching of him.

She closed her eyes and took a few deep breaths and pushed against him. His hands fell away as she took a step back. "Ouch," she cried, rubbing her lower back. She started to teeter on her legs, and Quinn swept her up into his arms before she hit the ground again. She closed her eyes and allowed for it. She was just going to have to suffer his attentions. Suffer. As best she could. Until she was back at the house and could hide in her rooms until everyone forgot she existed and she simply wasted away to dust.

She opened her eyes for a moment and saw Quinn look up to Perry, who appeared to be laughing at them. Because, of course he was. So she closed her eyes again. It was enough to have to breathe him in. She didn't need to see the rough edge of his jaw, the way his muscle there ticked from tension.

"I've got the horse," Perry said, and she opened her eyes, realizing Quinn meant to carry her the rest of the way to the house, which was not far. It was merely the size of her palm on the far horizon.

She buried her face in his neck to stop looking at him and was immediately repentant, because here he smelled only of fresh air and Quinn. Damn it all, but she was a wreck.

"I miss you," she whispered to his neck, hopeful he couldn't hear her. She felt his jaw tense and knew he had. "I'm sorry," she said through a hitch in her voice.

"For?" His voice was rough and forced and made her heart ache.

"Everything."

"You really need to stop apologizing."

"Not until I have nothing left to apologize for," she said, and he stopped. His breathing was heavy and loud against her ear. She felt her tears grow warm between them. "Let me down. I can walk."

"No," he said stiffly and started moving again.

Against all of her better judgment, she took advantage of him. She knew it was wholly inappropriate, but her senses were full of him. She couldn't escape it. She was entirely surrounded and filled by him. Touch, smell, sound, feel. She kissed his neck, darting her tongue out just at the edge of his jaw. *Taste.*

"Stop, Celeste, you know not what you do."

She knew she didn't, but he tasted salty and savory. It was beyond the pale, but at the moment, she didn't particularly care. She felt perfectly insane, because having him overloading her senses calmed her to some extent, but she still wanted away from him.

When they got back to the house, he took her to the front parlor and dropped her onto the settee next to Lilly.

"She fell from the horse. She should rest." He walked away.

Lilly watched him go, astonished, and turned to her. "Are you quite well?" she asked.

"No, I'm, well, I'm well, yes. I mean, I don't think I'm hurt—injured, I mean." Celeste shook her head and closed her eyes and wished she were anywhere but right here. She felt a warm hand wrap around hers, and she opened her eyes and looked at it.

"It's okay to be flustered. These men do that. It's something they do quite well, that blustery, menacing angriness. It runs in the family, I think," Lilly said. "Usually means they like you quite a lot, actually."

Celeste was certain that wasn't quite what it meant in their case. In their case, she was rather certain it meant Quinn was blustery because he *was* angry. Lilly wrapped her arms around her shoulders and squeezed her tight, and Celeste just closed her eyes and soaked it in. If she couldn't find some semblance of care in Quinn anymore, she would take it where she could get it.

Her arms went around Lilly's waist, and she held on. Once again, she relaxed. This was what she missed from Quinn. Just this, nothing more. She realized rather quickly that this was all she needed from him, but she had no idea how to let him know that.

Quinn

diotic, callous, horrid, insensitive, brutish jackass.

That's what he was. Celeste had fallen from the back of his horse, and all he could think of was how good she'd felt in his arms. She'd fallen from the back of his horse because he hadn't wanted to hold on to her arms around his waist.

He hadn't wanted to touch her any more than was absolutely necessary, so he'd told himself she was safe enough, that she held him and wouldn't let go. Even though she was acting terribly odd, he told himself she would be fine. Of course, he'd been wrong, and that's what made him an idiotic, callous, horrid, insensitive, brutish jackass.

He'd carried her to the house and left her with Lilly, because he'd had to get to his rooms and get changed and get himself under control before he frightened someone. Because Celeste had wiggled and twitched and made his goddamned cock rise in his breeches, which had made him stumble and have to shift her so he could adjust himself without her noticing that he needed adjusting. Which he had done.

Then she had licked him.

She had licked him, and it had taken everything he was to bring her to Lilly and not take her straight to his rooms. Because that's what he'd wanted to do. He'd wanted to show her what she did to him. The whole thing was so beyond the bounds of propriety and function as to be ridiculous. Truly. If he hadn't been so frustrated at the moment, he would probably have been laughing, just as Perry had.

There wasn't a single goddamned thing about this situation that was funny. The entire thing was a sodding mess, just like his boots and his breeches. He ran up the stairs and slammed the door to his room behind him before he thought better of it. It had felt good, though, to make that noise, to hear the wood complain about its ill treatment by him. Fuck all, if he couldn't behave badly toward a human, he would damage whatever inanimate objects crossed his path.

He shoved his boots down and wrenched them from his feet. They were probably a lost cause. He set them by the door nonetheless. He tossed his coat, waistcoat, and shirt to the floor. Grumbled. Shouted a bit. He peeled his breeches down his body and threw them at the door, where they hit with a loud, wet thwack and slid to the floor. Perry was going to hide his arse when he saw the state of this room.

He heard someone cough in the water closet and stomped over. Perry's valet stood there with a stack of towels.

"My lord, I was told you would be in need of a hot bath and additional towels."

Quinn didn't answer, just stood in the doorway buck naked and angry as all hell. Thank God the cold of his breeches had deflated his cock after he left Celeste with Lilly. The valet nodded to him and set the towels on the radiator and shut the water off to the bath. "If it pleases you, sir, I will see to your clothes?"

Quinn gave him a stiff nod, and the valet walked past him. Quinn heard him gathering the clothes, and he shut the door to the bathing room and walked to the bath, stepped in, and sank. The water flooded the floor a bit as he did so, but it didn't matter, because Perry knew how to design a worthy bath. The tub sat in a tiled area with a drain just for this purpose. It was heaven. He thought of the last time he'd enjoyed a bath. It had been a while because showers were becoming all the rage now, much to his consternation.

He wasn't kidding when he told Calder he preferred the bath. He thought he could find purpose with that shower. He imagined the metal ribs would be useful for holding on while fucking, or getting fucked. He had yet to get that far in one. Maybe he never would. He sank below the water, then reached for the soap next to the tub and lathered himself up.

Calder. Celeste. Celeste. Calder.

She licked me.

This had to stop. Something had to give, or he wasn't going to survive this. He had to be honest with himself. Was he just playing with Celeste because Calder was gone? When Calder returned, would he be able to give her up? No, he wouldn't. Not if it went any further with her. He was already in too deep with her. It hurt to be so distant with her, and when he'd helped her this afternoon… He closed his eyes as his cock rose in the warm water, and he smoothed over it with the soap in his palm.

This wasn't going to end well. None of this was going to end well. He loved Calder. That one was easy. That was never going to change. He was falling for Celeste as well, and that was trouble, because he could never give up Calder, he could not. It wasn't a choice, it was that simple.

Fuck. He sat up in the tub, sloshing more water to the floor. Perry was right. There wasn't a choice to be made at all. Quinn didn't like the options, but there were options. He needed to get a message to Calder. He'd send it to Warrick and hope he would forward it. Because living without Calder was not an option. The world was just going to have to get used to that. Now he only needed to figure out what to do about Celeste.

Q

For the next few days, Celeste and Quinn, by some unspoken agreement, managed to stay away from each other. She had to know it was a bad idea to come anywhere near him, or perhaps she'd realized what she'd done and remembered what she wanted and that this—what they had between them—could not happen.

He went out with Perry most mornings, finally met the sheep, wasn't terribly impressed with them. Didn't believe the sheep were very impressed with him either. He volunteered to help Jameson repair the flood damage from the gate, and it had been good to get his hands dirty and his muscles sore every day. He actually slept at night. He didn't care if it was from pure exhaustion, it was sleep, and it felt damned good, and his mind started to clear.

He sent a missive to Grayson, asked him to get it to Calder if at all possible. Grayson had written back, letting him know he would do what he was able, but it would be several days before the steamer would come to dock again. In the meantime, Quinn had invited his mother to Westcreek because he had to tell her what was to happen. She made arrangements to come up the following weekend. In *that* meantime, he needed to tell Celeste about his decision.

That was the part he dreaded most of all because he cared a great deal about her. He couldn't marry her and bring her into the mess he was about to create by chasing after Calder. None of it truly mattered. He was hurting her by staying away, and he would hurt her when he told her.

He'd set the deadline with his mother because he needed to force himself to talk to Celeste. Right now, he still had several days to do it, so he would wait, because she had thrived out here in the country.

She had blossomed in the fresh air whilst she ignored him. Here in the country, away from her family and society, she had come into her own, and it was a beautiful thing to bear witness to. So he kept his distance and hoped she would understand when the time came to tell her. He had put them in this difficult situation, and that made it his responsibility to repair the damage he had done.

Celeste

Celeste rolled the ball as hard as she could and squealed with delight when it knocked down all the skittles. No—all but one. That brought her score to forty-one. She was getting better at this game. Maryse set the penguin-painted skittles back up for Lilly's turn, and Celeste sat down on the rug next to Amélie.

"Well done," Amélie said.

Celeste smiled. "Thank you." She watched as Lilly bowled her hand—seven pins down, two standing, bringing her score to thirty-five—and Maryse reset the skittles again. Ms. Faversham stood for her hand, and Lilly came to sit with her.

"I think you're enjoying your stay at Westcreek quite a bit now," she said.

"I am. It took a few days to settle in, but now that I have, I am quite enjoying the country," Celeste said. "Thank you for having me. I truly appreciate it."

"Of course, any friend of Quinn's. Have you spoken with him since the—er—incident?" she whispered dramatically.

The incident.

Celeste preferred to forget *the incident*, but it had been rather a shared experience with Lilly, so there wasn't much to be done about it.

"No, but we seem to have a reasonable agreement at the moment to avoid each other. That seems to be going well, so I'm not going to push it. Perhaps one day we'll even have conversation again. Who knows?" She grinned, and Lilly laughed. It was strange not speaking with Quinn. She hardly saw him, and yet it wasn't only that, but that they needed some space, the both of them. She hadn't felt that needy again, but she'd also become much closer to Lilly, and she loved having another woman as a friend.

They commiserated. They talked of the men. They talked of all sorts of things. Of course, Celeste didn't talk about the truth of her relationship with Quinn, but the rest…it was something Celeste had never had. She hoped she and Lilly would remain friends beyond whatever the future held.

That first day here had been inordinately difficult because they'd been living in a house of cards for nearly a week, and the slightest breeze was all it had taken to knock it down. Now they would rebuild, hopefully with some stronger stuff. It felt like starting over for her, and that was fine, because she hadn't lost him, which was all that mattered.

"Are you looking forward to the visit from his parents next weekend?" she asked.

Was she? She considered it. Perry had let it slip that Quinn's mother had requested he do whatever he could to force Quinn's hand, so while she *had* really liked Adeleine, Celeste wasn't so sure about her at the moment. Her feelings all hinged on motives. Until she knew what Adeleine had been thinking, Celeste was going to reserve judgment.

"I have questions for her," Celeste said, and Lilly's eyes went a bit wide. Celeste laughed. "Don't worry. I just want to know why she would request such a horrible thing. I'm certain she has good reason to put the two of you in such an awkward position." She nodded. She also supposed that everything going awry out in the country and away from society was a good thing.

"Your hand," Ms. Faversham said as she sat back down on the rug next to Lilly.

"What did you get?" she asked.

"Three. I'm afraid this isn't my game. Though perhaps we could play some croquet? I'm much better with a mallet."

Celeste could imagine that. Ms. Faversham wielded a simple pencil with menace, so giving the woman a mallet might actually be dangerous. "I'd love to play croquet. Perhaps a tournament tomorrow?" She stood and picked up the ball and squared up against the skittles as she concentrated. Their little penguin faces looked terrified. *I've got you now.* She took a step and rolled the ball toward them. "That's nine! I've done it. Fifty points total for me," Celeste said, and she gave a little jump as everyone congratulated her.

"I don't think any of us can catch you with the remainder of the hand, Celeste," Lilly said.

"No, I suppose not." Celeste grinned. She hadn't ever won at anything. Maybe she could just move in with Perry and Lilly. The house was big enough they might not even notice. She'd never have to return to London, and how lovely would that be? Perfectly lovely.

"Tea should be ready," Lilly said. "I had them set it on the back landing."

"I am a bit famished," Ms. Faversham said. "Come, girls," she said as she stood and brushed the grass from her skirts.

Celeste stayed behind, collecting the penguin-painted skittles and balls and putting them back in the basket next to the rug. She really wouldn't mind living here, or somewhere like here, but the possibility of that was rather slim if she didn't find a husband with a country estate. Perhaps that's what she could do, find an old man with a country house. He could stay in London, and she would keep their country home. She supposed she would have to give him a son to earn her keep, but she supposed she wouldn't mind the company of a child either.

Q

The third day of their grand croquet tournament had been the best yet. Celeste was leading the lot of them with only two games to go, and she couldn't contain her excitement. Even Perry had joined the games. She was winning against a man. She looked at him as she wondered if he played badly on purpose.

He squared up in front of a wicket, and Lilly came up behind him, holding her mallet by the wrong end. At the moment Perry swung, she ran the stick of the mallet up the back of his thigh, and he jumped, his ball going awry. So he wasn't cheating. Lilly was.

Perry turned on Lilly. He dropped his mallet and took her up in his arms, swinging her around in a large circle as he accosted her, and she laughed toward the sky, and Celeste wanted for that sort of closeness, companionship, and joy with another person. Lilly took his face between her hands and kissed him, and Perry stopped spinning and allowed her to find her feet. He didn't stop the kiss for an entirely unseemly amount of time.

There wasn't much Celeste could do about the cheating except watch—and it had been fairly adorable. The girls giggled, and Ms. Faversham turned them away, but Celeste simply couldn't take her eyes from the display. What would it feel like to be kissed like that? She tried to imagine herself kissing Quinn like that. She found no pleasure in the imagining. While the other display was enough, this was too much.

The sun was behind Perry and Lilly, their bodies cast in stark silhouette. She watched as his mouth opened, then hers as they shared breath between them, but when his tongue licked into her, Celeste winced. She didn't want anyone's tongue in her mouth. She slapped her hand over her eyes, winced again from the smack.

"Are you quite all right, Celeste?"

"Pardon? Yes, I—" She peeked out between her fingers to find everyone looking over at her. "I'm fine," she said, but she was confused. Why was this so different from watching Calder and Quinn?

"You've a handprint on your forehead," Perry said with a crease in his brow.

"A bug. A bug flew at me," she said absentmindedly. Celeste had felt nothing in watching Perry and Lilly's intimacy, beyond the want of companionship.

"All right, then," Lilly said as she patted Perry's lapels and turned him back toward the balls and wickets. Celeste took a deep breath. Perry really was a striking man, tall and broad and joyful. He was different from his brother Rox and cousin Warrick in that. He was more like the Calder she used to know, the one she really didn't know. The Calder who was apparently only suitable for public consumption, because the Calder in private was much more powerful and dark, like Rox and Warrick.

Calder…

Celeste felt a bit lightheaded as the thought of Quinn and Calder once again assailed her. She sat in one of the chairs next to the playing ground as she wondered where Quinn was off to today. He'd been off every day, mostly with Perry, but since Perry was playing croquet with them… Her skin prickled, and she glanced around the lawn. She saw no signs of him, so she looked up to the windows at the back of the house. She put a hand up to block the beam of sun against the windows, but could see nothing but the bright sky reflected in them.

"Celeste!" Perry yelled for her, and she turned around. "Your ball," he said.

"Oh, yes! Thank you." She smiled brightly to cover the fact that what she wanted to do was run off to her room to manage herself. She positioned herself at her ball—which nobody had succeeded in hitting away from the winning wicket.

For the game.

The past couple of weeks had been a much more lazy sort of life, even if it was only a day's ride from the bustle of London. Walking, riding, lawn games, grand dinners and suppers. Late evenings followed by later mornings. The peace of it was driving Quinn crazy. Avoiding Celeste was driving him to madness.

He stood from the desk in the library and looked out to the lawns where everyone enjoyed their croquet tournament. Perhaps he could join them. Perhaps the two of them had calmed down enough to attempt friendship again—or at least a cordiality. They'd managed it at suppers anyway, with the massive wood dining table and a few candelabra between them.

He walked out to the back lawn where she played croquet with Perry and Lilly, the two girls, and the governess. He sat at the edge of the patio to watch for a while. Celeste was welcome here. She was happy, she was relaxed, and…and he was a goddamned mess. Just being near her when she was this excited was yet a trial.

She laughed, and the world seemed brighter and infinitely smaller. It had taken several days for her to realize she was safe here. Once she did, she bloomed like the headiest rose in Christendom.

God, he loved her in a way he didn't understand. He loved everything about her, and for that he was damned, because he was already in love with someone else. He missed Calder as if he'd borrowed one of his lungs before he left. He felt the loss of him like a tangible thing, bright and painful whenever he looked up to the sky.

He heard her laugh and looked back to her, watching. Now that he knew of her passion for dance, he could see it in the way she moved, the grace of her long limbs, which would be unwieldy for so many. Everything she did, every time she moved, it was her own personal ballet, as though she lived with music in her head and moved according to it.

It stole his breath and made him feel so sickeningly guilty he couldn't stand himself, because Calder had always been his everything, and he simply didn't know how to manage this. He was doubly guilty because he knew his feelings affected Celeste, and as much as he tried, he simply could not ignore what he felt for her so naturally—albeit differently from how he felt for Calder.

If Calder was the hard core of the earth, the volcanoes, the quaking land, the heat, and the passion, Celeste was the lakes and rivers, the rain and the snow, the cool, soothing care of it. He felt differently and the same for both of them. But Calder—he was just so much a part of who Quinn was as a person that excising him from his life would be a simple impossibility.

That wasn't necessarily accurate, because the want of Calder was so strong that Quinn wouldn't even try if he had to. He would die before walking away from Calder. They might have had other people in their lives at times, but at the core of it, it had always been the two of them, and it would be again. Quinn was determined to that end. He only had to tell Celeste.

His feelings for her, however, had not lessened in any way since making that decision—if anything, they'd grown inconceivably stronger, which was why he had yet to speak with her. He was having a hard time controlling the want of her.

He couldn't stop thinking about either of them for more than ten minutes. Maybe fifteen. Even as he slept, he dreamed of the both of them. Sometimes alternating, sometimes together, sometimes the two of them managing themselves as he watched. He'd woken up with more cockstands than any man had a right to, and his hand began to chafe from use. It was a frustration he wasn't terribly fond of.

Quinn's conscience, though, wouldn't allow him to find a mistress this time, not with Celeste so close and so much a part of his life. For him, it had come to feel the same as it did with Calder. When Calder was in London, there was no other. This arrangement with her was an entirely different kind of torture, the following of her wishes and keeping to friendship—and Calder hadn't even been gone a month.

Grayson was keeping him abreast of the situation, which most days meant sending word that there was no word to send. At least Calder was alive and well, albeit in a different country, but Quinn didn't think he could survive an entire year if it came to that. He was having a hard enough time reconciling the two months he was certain of.

Perhaps if he knew…had some idea of how long it would be ultimately—but he didn't. Calder could turn around tomorrow, or he could return never. Quinn knew in his bones he would return eventually—but part of him was more frightened than he'd ever been. Because forever was a terrible amount of time to plan for. Forever required mourning, and he felt it like a keening in his soul. So Quinn avoided thinking on it.

When his thoughts turned to Calder, he would sway them to the physical to avoid the practical, and as always, with thoughts of the physical with Calder, Quinn was a walking state of arousal, and because Calder was not here, he was forced to take care of his own needs.

So he thought of Calder as he came off in his hand. In the shower. In the forest, like a lunatic. In the freezing lake where he'd tried to cool his blood. He was mad as a hatter. Watching Celeste being lovely and thinking of nothing but being smothered by Calder's heavy body, his body invaded by his thick cock, dreaming of the both of them nightly and not having some sort of outlet for this…he was losing his wits. Rapidly.

As for his want of Celeste, he didn't think it was simply because he wanted her to understand passion—of that she'd been absolutely correct. He was selfish. He'd watched as she came off for the first time in her life, and it had been so intensely alluring he wanted to live that moment again, and again. And again. He couldn't approach her with that sort of want so blatantly obvious in his eyes, so he'd avoided her entirely. Because he'd promised. So he couldn't touch her, and he wouldn't touch someone else because of her. It was a sticky wicket, that, and in the meantime, his cock was raw, but it wasn't yet exhausted.

She made him want to bury himself in his hand or in Calder while she watched.

Celeste strutted over to her ball, swinging her mallet gracefully beside her. Her shoulders back, her neck long, and her chin raised with such a profound confidence it made him shudder and want more. She positioned herself behind the ball, and he watched as she wiggled her arse in his general direction, certainly with no malice of forethought—still. There it was again, that precious little wiggle.

Wiggle wiggle wiggle.

He narrowed his eyes as blood rushed his cock, and he attempted to control his breathing. He closed his eyes and pressed the heels of his hands to them.

He heard the crack of her mallet against the ball, and he felt the hit in his pained bollocks. He winced when she yelled as it went through the wicket and hit the stick. He looked. She'd won. She started jumping in celebration, and Quinn simply had to leave. This bouncing woman was more than he could stand just now.

He turned away—hopefully before she caught sight of him—and ran up the steps to the back entry and through the house to his rooms. His shirt and waistcoat were pulled from his trousers before he even got to his bedroom. He shut the door and turned to the bed, toeing off his shoes and releasing the buttons of his trousers as he shoved them down his hips.

He poured the oil he now kept readily at his bedside and took himself in hand. That first glance of his palm against his rigid shaft was enough to double him over the bed, his face buried in the pillows as he yelled his frustration into their softness, and his knees gave out against the side of the mattress.

He pulled hard, then stroked himself gently for a moment, until his need subsided enough that he could stand and remove the rest of his clothing so as to keep from soiling it. He didn't need to call attention to the amount of laundry he had.

He pulled his shirt off, avoiding his slicked palm and cock, and turned to toss it across the chair. His arm went limp and his clothes fell to the floor when he saw Celeste standing in the doorway, staring at his penis jutting from the fall of his trousers, her hand a white clench on the edge of the door.

"What are you doing here?"

"I won the game. I—" She shook her head. "I followed you inside."

"Shut—the door," he said gruffly, and her eyes snapped up to his. She didn't move. He could see the want, could feel it all the way to the tip of his—now much more painfully hard—cock that stood out from his belly like a flag of surrender in the wind. "Celeste," he groaned, and her name sounded so hard it didn't even sound like him. "In or out, but *shut* the door." *Please.*

He closed his eyes and listened as the fabric of her skirt rustled, and all the air was sucked from the room with the sturdy click of the latch, and he was left with a damning stillness. He heard himself whimper on an exhale and opened his eyes to find her standing on his side of the door. All the air returned and with it the scent of the lavender on her skirts from being in the fields.

Quinn wasn't entirely sure what to do next, faced with something he'd never thought to be facing. Something he'd been actively attempting to avoid. He took a deep breath, scooped his shirt and waistcoat up from the floor, and shook them out, throwing them across the chair to try to keep them clean as he'd first intended. He turned directly toward her and pushed his trousers the rest of the way off, kicking them aside.

Completely naked, he took one step toward her. She shook her head again, raised her hand, and left him standing there wondering at her as she moved toward the chair. No, she didn't just move to the chair—she swayed to the chair, the swing of her skirts filling his head with that heavy scent of purple.

She picked up his clothes, dropped them to the floor, and sat down. She fisted her hands in the cotton of her skirts and pulled them up until he could see her glistening pussy.

Quinn hadn't had the pleasure of seeing this much of her in the reflection that night, and it *was* a pleasure to see her now, because she was beautiful. The opening of her drawers framed her perfectly, the white linen

against her brown skin and the pink of her cunt right in the center, like a rosebud waiting to bloom. Good God, he nearly came off just looking at her.

She flicked her hand at him. "Carry on," she whispered.

Fuck me. Fucking fuck everything, he thought. This was not his sweet Celeste. Every muscle Quinn had—including some he'd never known existed—tightened on his frame to the point of pain. He took a step backward toward the bed, not daring to look away for fear she was some sort of apparition that would dissipate as soon as he did. If he'd truly gone insane, he was going to enjoy it while it lasted. The backs of his knees hit the edge of the bed first, and he scooted back into the pillows, poured more oil in his palm, and took himself in hand again.

His hand skimmed down the length of his cock, flipped over, and cupped his bollocks, while the tips of his fingers ran the length of that seam of flesh and teased his arse. He stayed like that for a moment—watching her watching him so intently. He slid his hand back up, and she slid one of her hands down to that warm place between her thighs. That warm space that most men wanted to return to from the moment they were evacuated from it at birth.

Her finger skimmed carefully the length of her pussy, slick and wet, and he couldn't bring himself to move as he watched… She stopped, and he looked up to her face. She lifted one eyebrow in question, and he met her demand by wrapping his hand around his cock once again and moving the skin against the hard length of himself all the way up over the head of his cock, gathering all that slick mettle before sliding back down again. She flung one leg over the arm of the chair, spreading herself wide for him, and his heart picked up, nearly choking him.

He played with his foreskin, slipping it up and down the crown of his cock until her eyes grew dark and her breathing stilted. He used one finger from his other hand, swept more fluid from the head, and skimmed past his cock, past his bollocks, down that seam that led to his arse, and he stopped there, massaging gently as he pulled with his other hand.

"Are you watching, Celeste?" She nodded. "Tell me."

"Yes…I'm watching," she said, and her voice was light as air, as if there was no force behind it, the opposite of his own, the opposite of Calder's when he was fucking, too. Quinn closed his eyes to her as the thought of

Calder's voice—how it would grow heavy and thick, as if his body couldn't contain the sound of it, how it would reverberate from him, become a tangible thing—hit him square in the chest. Quinn pictured him, his smug smile, his beautifully hard body, and he nearly lost himself to it.

He groaned, and when he heard her breath catch, he opened his eyes in time to see her push that slender middle finger into her cunt as the others framed it like it was the most priceless of artwork, and Quinn decided to follow suit. He lifted one hip and smoothed his hand around his leg and teased his arse before he pushed that finger past the tight barrier as he watched her and she watched him, and it was simply too much too much too much.

"Don't look away," he grunted as he shifted more to his side, his finger massaging slowly while his other hand pulled and pulled, demanded he come, but his finger wouldn't follow directions. It waited. It didn't push into that spot he wanted it to. It just pulsed slowly, pushing him higher and higher, waiting until he simply could not hold on anymore.

Celeste screamed, she knew she did, so she shoved the wad of skirts she held into her mouth to muffle it, because she sure as hell wasn't stopping this, not even if someone walked in. Well, perhaps if someone walked in. She truly hoped nobody would walk in, and so she bit down on the wad of cotton petticoats between her teeth, and she added a second finger to the first as she slid and she played and she watched, and she couldn't believe what they were doing.

The way he slipped the skin over the head of his penis, the way he alternately caressed it then pulled on it—it was almost a love-hate thing the way he moved against himself. But when he pushed his finger into his arse, Celeste was done for. Her skin was hot and slick with sweat, which sent a chill across her chest and up the back of her neck. She couldn't breathe. All she could do was grind the heel of her hand against that sharp ache at her mons to attempt a momentary appeasement.

Quinn writhed and grunted and twisted on the bed. He jerked his hand faster and faster, pushed his finger in farther, and his foot came down on the mattress and pushed, and he arched off the bed with a deep guttural growl as he came off across his chest. Thick, milky white ropes of him.

The first hit his chest and neck and shoulder, and she stopped moving to watch the rest of it, her skirts slipping from her mouth as her jaw hung there in awe.

Every pull brought another spurt from his cock, each one slightly less than the first, until he collapsed back to the bed, both of his hands on his cock and bollocks, soothing himself. It filled her with pride that she understood that feeling.

Quinn opened his eyes, looked down to his cock, squeezing the last of his seed from the tip and smoothing it across his abdomen, and Celeste nearly choked.

He looked up at the sound and rolled slowly toward her until he was on his belly, one arm hanging off the bed close to her foot, the other tucked under his chin, his hips pushing slowly against the sheets as if his penis yet needed soothing.

She watched the half-moon shape of the muscles of his arse come and go in sharp relief as he moved, but she couldn't keep herself from his eyes for long. The sleepy contentedness of them held a fire deep within, and he caught her gaze and held it. "I'm waiting," he whispered.

A chill broke across her skin, crawling from her knees to her neck and making her shudder. "For?" she asked. Even she could barely hear the word.

His finger danced across the toe of her slipper, and she felt it all the way to the center of her, and her hand slid down without her ever having decided what for.

Could she do this? She had done this, she had only *just* done this, but he had been distracted then, and now—now he wasn't distracted at all. Every bit of his attention was on her. Every flick of her wrist, every flinch brought his gaze. It traveled her body like a road map, stopping at different points along the way, and the zing of her nerves seemed to follow along.

Fluid pooled in her hand and dripped to the seat of the chair. She was shocked at how much came from her, and she pushed her fingers back into her pussy, one of her legs still flung over the arm of the chair. She dared not move the one on the floor and break that single bit of solid contact with him.

She had the feeling if she did, he would come after her, touch her in a more tangible way. So it held her to the spot, kept her from moving, prevented her from straightening herself, putting herself back together, and walking out of this room that smelled so strongly of sex and need. And she allowed it. As long as he stayed himself, she would remain.

She grunted at that thought, then inhaled and caught the slightly sharp scent of what must be him, which, she only just realized, he had not cleaned from his chest. He lay on it now, as if it were nothing. She could still see some of it on his shoulder, his neck. She wanted to know what it felt like. Did it feel like the fluid that came from her? Was it hot because it came from his body? Did it cool quickly or retain his heat? It reminded her of the simple powdered sugar glacé from a cinnamon bun—was it sweet?

Her other hand went to the neck of her shirtwaist, and her fingers tangled in the placket as she released the buttons, and all he did was watch. She pushed it aside and arched her back, bringing her breasts up until she could easily slide them free of the corset, and his eyes, oh God, his eyes and how they bored into her now.

She shook her head, losing nerve, and his hand wrapped around her ankle and squeezed. She closed her eyes and concentrated on breathing, but calming her racing heart seemed a bit counterproductive. She wanted it to race. She wanted to chase it, to fling herself from the cliff after it like a bird taking flight.

"Celeste," he whispered, and it sounded like a prayer.

His thumb circled the small bone on the side of her ankle, bringing her back to the chair, to his room, to the sensation of this naked man caressing her stockinged ankle with his warm bare hand. He squeezed her ankle again gently, and she opened her eyes to him as he swirled his thumb around that bone again and again and cocked one eyebrow in challenge. She smiled at his audacity. It stretched her cheeks and burned. She followed his lead.

She took her breast in her hand and did exactly as he did. She squeezed. His thumb coasted along the inner arch of her foot, and she followed him, skimming the soft underside of her breast as she melted. His hand went across the top of her foot, and she skimmed over the top of her breast, making her nipple peak, and his eyes went black. He squeezed again, and so did she. Two of his fingers circled and then pinched the small bone of her ankle, and she circled and then squeezed her nipple, jerking at the sharp bite of it, reveling in the sound he made when she did.

Quinn nodded—a hard, jerky sort of uncontrollable thing—and she kept going, working her breasts one at a time just like that as his jaw went slack, his tongue darting out to lick his lip.

He shifted, and the loss of his heat on her ankle saddened her. His hand came up between her legs so very slowly, but he didn't touch her. She shivered at the fear that he would touch her, and he seemed to know it. He pressed two fingers to the wedge of chair between her legs where her arousal had pooled.

Quinn brought his hand up and smelled her on his fingers before he brought them to his mouth, his tongue coming out to flick them, and *oh God, it was obscene.*

Those two fingers slid in and out along his tongue, and she very nearly lost her wits. Her heart jumped against her rib cage, reminding her of how alive she was in this moment. In and out, in and out, then a flick of his tongue between them. She tried to force the breath through her lungs and failed with a miserable whimper.

He paused, raised that devil of an eyebrow, and waited. The whole of her body exhaled, and with her next breath, she did just as he instructed. She slid two fingers the length of her pussy. She pushed inside, slid and pushed.

Her pulse hitched, and her breath caught, and she moved in the chair, pinioning herself between the arm and the back and the floor as she leveraged for more pressure in her pelvis, fighting the slipping sensations as they came and faded over and over until the entirety of her body tensed, and she cried out, losing herself to it, to him, and to the great deep of his eyes.

Oh God, but what were they to do about this now? Celeste started to fade from exhaustion. She sank into the chair, her hands cradling her breasts and her mons, her chin against her chest as her corset bit into the sensitive flesh beneath her breasts and she winced.

Quinn pulled himself from the bed and brought her to standing in front of him. He released the busk of her corset without touching her skin, loosened her skirts, and let them fall. He turned her and put her to bed beneath the quilt. He seemed to avoid any sort of direct skin-to-skin contact with her, but right now that he was helping her was enough.

Quinn went around to the other side of the bed and crawled under the quilt, facing her, and they lay there for a while just considering each other. It seemed neither of them was prepared to talk, but neither of them was prepared to leave either. After what felt a very long time, his hand slid from beneath the quilt and skimmed across her cheek, and every bit of tension she still held dissipated with that single touch of his skin on hers.

"You are the most beautiful creature I have ever seen in my life," he said, "but I've decided I cannot live my life without Calder."

Impossibly, Celeste felt the most peace she ever had with those words. Celeste closed her eyes on those words and let herself drift to sleep.

Calder

alder pulled on his cock, but the sensation waned, his arousal quitting before his need was met. But he simply couldn't get there. Even though he'd woken from the dream of Quinn with a heavy cockstand, the reality of his current situation overrode everything he had felt before. Everything he had built up simply vanished and left him there, more wanting than he'd ever been.

A knock at the door to his berth startled him, and he flung the blankets over his naked body. "Come," he said.

"My lord."

"Rakshan."

"We will arrive in Marseilles within the hour. The steamer will not depart for Alexandria for two days. We missed the other ship."

"Thank you, Rakshan."

Marseilles wasn't a bad place to be. At least it was away from London and Quinn and Celeste. Celeste. He didn't *want* her, but he couldn't seem to keep his mind from her, and it was driving him to insanity. He had been passing it off as a sort of jealousy born from his want of Quinn, but…Quinn had danced with women all their lives. It was this woman who drove him to the brink, and this woman alone, and he could not fathom why.

"Will there be anything else, my lord?"

"No, Rakshan, thank you. I'll be ready shortly. Do we have a hotel?"

"Not that I'm yet aware. I sent telegrams at the last stop. Hopefully, we'll have word once we arrive."

"Good, then."

Rakshan left, pulling the door closed behind him, and once again Calder was left alone with his thoughts and his want and his unattainable desire to come off.

He wished it would all simply go away.

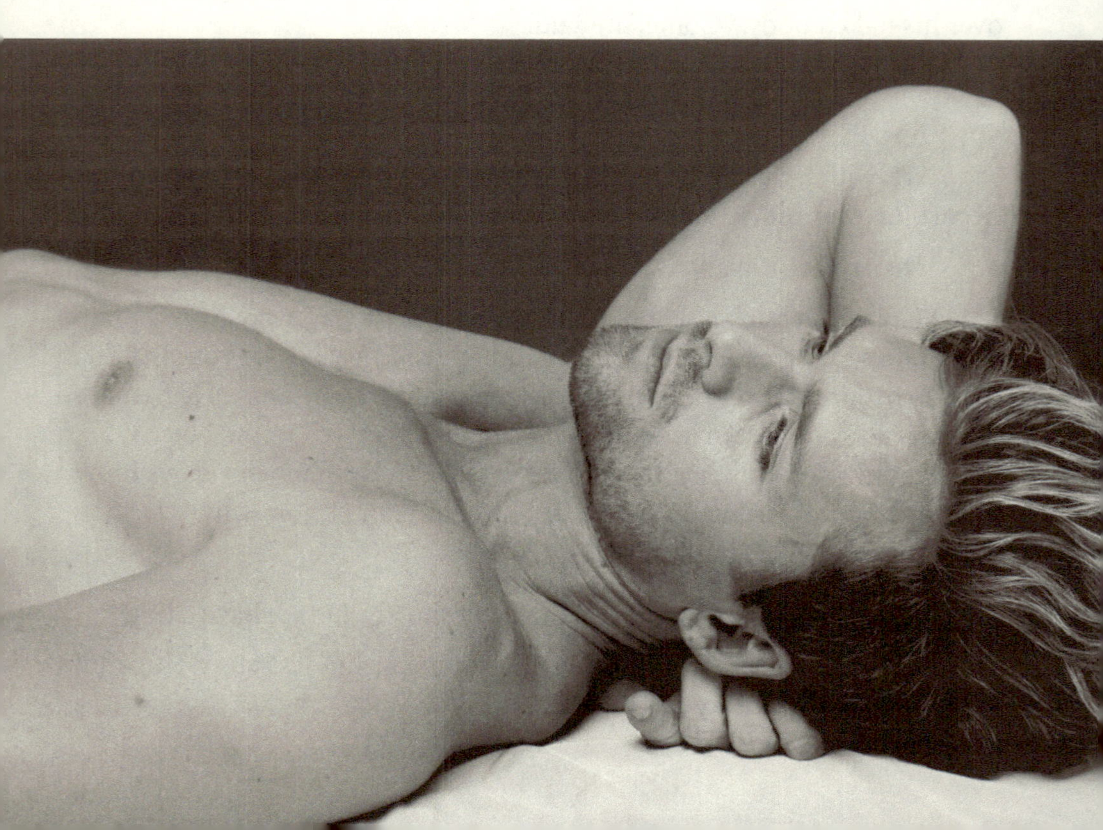

Quinn

A soft sound woke Quinn in the dead of night, and he opened his eyes and stared into the moonlit room, attempting to discern where it came from. He closed his eyes, listening, trying to remember…*Celeste.* He opened his eyes again and leaned up on one elbow, reaching toward the shadowed side of his bed. Her shoulder twitched when he touched it. He smoothed gently to her cheek, wet with tears.

Quinn shifted in the bed until he was closer, being careful to keep some of the bedding between them. "Celeste," he whispered as he leaned toward her. He felt a little puff of air against his chin. He ran his thumb over her eyebrow. Her eyelashes didn't flutter against it. "Celeste?" Still nothing. She had to be dreaming. He lay back down on the pillow, their foreheads almost touching, his legs bent beneath hers where her knees were drawn up toward her chest, and he held her cheek and ran his thumb across her eyebrow.

Slowly, she settled. Her breathing became the long drawn-out breaths of a deep sleep, and she sank into the bedding as her body once again relaxed. Quinn pulled his arm back to his chest, but he stayed close, just a breath away from her in the dark.

Q

The next morning, Quinn awoke to beauty and wished then that it wouldn't be the last time. The day before should never have happened, and they both knew it. He would only hurt her more if they continued on this path.

Celeste's eyes fluttered like the new wings of a butterfly, and her hands came up to rub the sleep from them. She gazed back at him. "That's as it should be," she said, as if they'd just continued their conversation after so much sleep.

"I'm sorry. We shouldn't have—"

"No, we shouldn't have. I shouldn't have followed you. I should have given you the space you clearly needed."

"I should have told you to leave."

"I should have closed the door behind me, from the hallway."

"I shouldn't have given you the choice."

"I shouldn't have accepted the challenge."

"I should have known better."

"*I* should have known better."

"I should have stopped you."

"I should have stopped myself."

"I should have told you sooner."

"I wouldn't change it for the world," she whispered.

"Nor would I," he replied.

Quinn pushed her tangled hair from her face, smoothing it behind her ear as he touched her cheek. He had to touch her, somehow. He had to show her how important she was to him, that because they couldn't be together did not mean that he didn't care for her. Because he did. Probably much more than one single ounce worth, in fact. He could no longer not touch her. He wouldn't touch her in ways he shouldn't. He would touch her to show her how very much he cared for her.

"I should go," she said.

"Unfortunately, yes. I'll ready so I can be sure that nobody will see you returning to your rooms," he said—he didn't move. He kissed her eyelids, savored the stilted breath against his neck, and breathed deeply of the scent of her that he would miss so very much. "I'll never abandon you, Celeste. I will protect you no matter what comes of us."

Her hand came up and wrapped around his wrist and squeezed, and he looked down to find her bright, shiny gaze on him. "I know."

Quinn leaned into her and placed a kiss on her delicate nose as her eyes fluttered shut, and he pressed a kiss to her cheek.

The door to his bedroom swung wide, banging against the wall, and Quinn sat up, pulling the bedding over Celeste as she curled into a ball. As if covering her from prying eyes would do anything to protect her. He was ready to scold the valet for entering without permission, but was stopped by the loud swirl of satin skirts and petticoats.

"I told you my son was still abed. Certainly your Celeste is in her rooms as well," his mother said cheerfully.

No, Quinn thought. *No*. They weren't due here for several days. *No*. He stood and held a pillow at his waist because he refused to pull the linens off of Celeste. His body hummed with energy he had no expenditure for, and his mind raced as he tried to find a solution.

He rushed forward, putting himself between his mother and his bed. "Mother!" he yelled at her, and he had never yelled at her, but why—she shouldn't be in his rooms. She didn't do such things. This wasn't at all like her. This feeling…he didn't have a name for it, but it was horrible. He felt cold and hot at once, and a chill rushed his skin.

"Quinn, my dear, we've come early and brought a surprise with us. Celeste's parents." She smiled and blinked at him as if he weren't standing in his bedroom full naked in front of his mother and her *guest*. Her smile grew wider, and she shrieked, "Quinn, is that Celeste?" She pointed beyond him to the bed, barely hiding her delight as she clearly feigned her horror.

Of course. Quinn watched it all happen as he stood there, completely helpless. As if he were watching a play, as though this wasn't actually his life. It was so incredibly, ridiculously perfect.

"Well, the butler said he hadn't seen the two of you since yesterday afternoon, but I *never*—"

Never? he thought. She flapped a hand at her face as though this was entirely too distressing for her. *For her.* His mother probably had no idea her plan to show up and trap them was going to work out so soon and so perfectly.

Celeste's mother came forward before he could block her, and she swept the sheets down, uncovering Celeste as she huddled in a ball, shaking.

The sight of her cowering snapped Quinn back to reality. "Get out. All of you, get out," Quinn said.

Her mother turned to him. "Her father will know of this and demand satisfaction from you, Lord Wyntor," she said in a cold voice. She turned back to Celeste, "You come with me." She took Celeste's wrist and started to pull her from the bed, and Quinn could not stay himself. He dropped the pillow and put himself between them. He took her mother's shoulders in his hands and forced her back toward the door. She sputtered and held her hands in front of her eyes to avoid looking at him.

"I said, get out." He pushed her, tripping, into the hallway before he turned on his mother, who was also comically trying to avoid looking at Quinn's penis. "Get out, Mother."

To her credit, she didn't say another word as she left. To her detriment, she turned once she was in the hallway and did speak. "Now you must marry that girl, Quinn." And then she smiled. His mother had destroyed their lives, and she smiled whilst doing it. He didn't understand.

Quinn took the door in his hand and slammed it as hard as he could before staring at the back of it. Ruined. Celeste was ruined. He'd ruined her and in the process destroyed whatever chance he had of a life with Devil. He'd done this because he couldn't control himself when faced with this woman. This beautiful, amazing, ruined woman. He turned back toward the bed. "Celeste?"

She'd pushed herself up against his headboard and pulled the sheets up to her chest. Her head moved back and forth slowly in disbelief. She turned to him. "Quinn, I—"

"Do not apologize. This is not your fault. It isn't even close. This is my fault entirely. The machinations of my mother have reached a new level of insanity. My brother must have done something so incredibly idiotic that she needs to sweep it under the carpet of a wedding—*our* wedding. I never thought her capable of something like this."

He heard voices in the hallway and turned back toward the door. Perry spoke, followed by Quinn's father. Quinn placed his hands on the door and leaned into it, both to keep it closed and to listen.

"How dare you, madam," Perry said. "How dare you come here and create such a disturbance? How dare you invite strangers to my home without my permission? How very dare you!" he said.

Oh…Perry was angry. Quinn hadn't heard this sort of seething anger from him in years.

"Adeleine," his father said, "if I'd had any idea—God's sake, woman, get downstairs. What do you mean by managing this? I don't even know you! Get downstairs, now. And you, madam, your husband is downstairs in the parlor, like a respectful guest. I cannot fathom this behavior. Leading a perfect stranger through the private rooms of Peregrine's home. What have you done, Adeleine?"

Quinn heard a scuffle of shoes and fabrics as people shifted, and his mother spoke. "My lord, I beg your pardon. I meant nothing—"

"Hold your tongue!" Perry boomed from just outside the door, and Quinn stood straight from the force of it. "Do not lie baldly to me, madam. *Do not.* I was raised to respect you, but you have diminished that respect entirely with this egregious act. Get out of my sight."

The hallway stilled to the point that Quinn couldn't even hear the shuffle of feet or the shift of fabric. He waited. A knock sounded.

"Are you decent?" Perry asked.

"A moment," Quinn said as he turned to Celeste. "Come now," he said.

He pulled his dressing robe from the end of his bed and helped her into it. She crawled back into the bed. He pulled his trousers off the floor and stepped into them, buttoning the fall as he walked back to the door and opened it a mere crack.

"Quinn." Perry had his hand against the doorjamb, and he leaned heavily, his other hand on his hip. Perry's expression said everything Quinn felt. The desperation, the shock, the desolation. Quinn opened the door, and Perry walked in.

His father was behind him. "Son," was all he said.

Quinn looked down and stepped aside so his father could follow Perry into the room. "Sir."

His father's hands squeezed his shoulders. "Quinn," he said. "Look at me." Quinn lifted his chin to meet his father's eyes. "I had no idea of her intention. Your mother led me to believe you had invited the four of us here for an announcement. I would not have stood for this sort of unwitting design upon your life."

Quinn nodded once and left the door open as he walked back to the bed, sitting at Celeste's feet. Perry paced at the end of it.

"Quinn, I—" Perry started.

Quinn waved him off. There wasn't anything to do now. It was done. He looked over to see Celeste, her forehead on her knees, her arms wrapped tightly around them. Her shoulders shook, and Quinn slid one hand down her leg to her foot and squeezed it.

"I will not abandon her. I will not be her ruination. I know what comes next, and it may not be what we wanted, either of us, but I will not let her be shamed further in public by her family or mine. I will take her to wife."

"No, Quinn, no," Celeste sobbed. She looked up to his father and stretched her arms toward him as she pleaded. "Please, my lord, don't make him do this. Please, this isn't what I want. I know what it looks like, but it simply isn't. You don't understand—nobody understands. This isn't what we want, either of us."

Quinn's father came to stand by the bed. She took his hand, and he squeezed hers, then released them. "Celeste, you came to be part of our family over the past few weeks. You were a natural fit, and if Quinn had chosen you, I would have been happy to make you a lawful and permanent part of our family. I would have been pleased to have my son offer you my name and our protection. I did not expect that would happen, even as my wife demanded it. I must apologize for her behavior. I can make no valid excuse for her. Her actions in this have been horrendous. I beg your forgiveness."

Celeste was silent, and Quinn looked up at his father. A chill ran his spine. "Father, I—"

"Son, you will do what you must. I know you will. Just know that I only wish I could have seen this coming and avoided it. Your mother…she can be difficult, but I have never seen her deliberately harm one of her family. Whatever comes next, you have my full support."

Quinn shook his head, unable to find any words. He nodded once, and his father turned to Perry.

"Peregrine, you've been nothing but a good man these past years, and you did not deserve to have this sort of scandal brought to your doorstep. I am devastated at the choices my wife has made."

Quinn looked up as his father's voice shook, and Perry walked to him and took his hand. "Thank you, sir. I am only as good a man as those who led me as a child," Perry said, and Quinn's father clapped him on the shoulder and turned for the door.

He stopped just shy of it. "We are leaving forthwith. Hopefully, the carriage hasn't yet been unhitched. Judging from the amount of baggage that was tied to the back, I would hazard to say that it isn't even unloaded. A blessing, that. For once."

"Father," Quinn said.

"Quinn, you will do what is right, and you will send word to me directly. I trust you now as I always have, son. Peregrine, if you need anything—if they need anything—please let me know. I am truly sorry." With that, he turned down the hall and left.

"Quinn, we don't have to marry. We don't. Your father—"

Quinn stood. "That's not what he meant, Celeste. Perry, can you make arrangements? Invite no one. I mean *absolutely* no one. You, Lilly, the girls, fine. Nobody else is to have word of this until it's done."

"I will see to it," Perry said. He squeezed Quinn's shoulder. "This is not what I wanted for you." He pulled Quinn in and squeezed the back of his neck before he turned and left, closing the door gently behind him.

Celeste stood and went to the window, and Quinn followed. His shrieking mother and hers were loaded into the carriage as their husbands looked on. Though Quinn's father was the only one who looked truly disappointed. Her family was ruinous, and his mother… Celeste shook her head, and he wrapped one arm around her waist.

"This wasn't supposed to happen. None of this was supposed to happen," she said.

"No, but the decision has been taken from us. There's no taking it back. I can only hope that Grayson is able to explain to—" Quinn's heart seized in his chest, and he doubled over.

Calder.

He flung his hand out to the window seat and hung on as the world around him spun. "Oh God," he said. "That's it, then. That's done it."

And his world went black.

Calder

Calder walked into the suite on the steamer and fell into the chair by the porthole. Rakshan followed and directed the porters where to put the luggage. He had purchased a first-class suite so Rakshan could stay with him under the guise of being his valet. Since they would be on the ship for a bit less than a month, having separate bedrooms and a sitting room were luxuries he was happy to be able to afford.

He couldn't imagine the lower-class cabins in the bowels of the paddle steamer. Four berths to a cabin with barely any room to turn about between them. He shuddered. It was gratifying that he was able to do this. Men like Rakshan wouldn't have this sort of opportunity without him to provide for it. Rakshan would have been below, with no window and no space of his own, regardless of his service to the Crown. It frustrated Calder to no end.

"My lord, your things are in the larger of the berths. If you wish, I'll leave you to settle in," Rakshan said.

"That's unnecessary, as I have very little to settle. When is supper?"

"I made arrangements for you to dine in-room tonight. I thought that preferable."

"Yes, thank you. Now stop acting like my servant and see to yourself. I appreciate what you're doing, but I consider you my equal as much as any man in the peerage of England would be."

"This is not true, my lord, and we both know it. A nephew of the Raj is a servant until he has served enough, and until such a time, I will live to serve."

"When is enough?" Calder asked. They'd had this conversation many times, and the answer was always the same.

"Not yet, my lord."

"Yet you are Warrick's man, not mine."

"And His Grace has put me to your use. Therefore, I am here to be of service to you."

"Rakshan."

"My lord."

Calder rolled his eyes. Gray had the patience of a saint when it came to Rakshan. "Stop hovering," Calder said.

He took the chair across from Calder. "What do you run from?" Rakshan asked.

Calder let his head fall back against the chair. "Are we going to spend the next month doing this?" he asked.

"That is up to you, sir. We can spend the next hour discussing the true issue and then enjoy the following twenty-seven days in peace and quiet."

Right. "Perhaps not tonight, Rakshan. At least give me one day to settle in."

"You already said you have very little to settle," Rakshan replied.

"So I did," Calder said. Rakshan waited quietly, watching out the porthole. "Do you manage Gray like this?"

"There is no managing His Grace, my lord."

"Rakshan," Calder warned.

"My lord, it is simple, is it not? If we are not at peace in our minds, we cannot be at peace in our bodies. If your body is not at peace, you will never be able to rest. If you cannot rest, you will be of no use to me, because your mind will not be clear."

"Oh, I see, so this is more self-serving, is it?" Calder asked.

"No, my lord, this serves you above all else, but I do not wish to die simply because you have no interest in coming to peace with whatever it is that disturbs you."

"Point taken, yet we still have nearly four weeks until we arrive in Jodhpur—"

"And the sooner you are at peace, my lord—"

"Rakshan, I fear you will have to become familiar with my being unsettled. I don't see how I will ever be at peace again," Calder said, allowing the words to cut and sink into his gut. There—there it was, out for him to see and hear and digest and—

"Is it Quinn?"

"Pardon?" Calder leaned forward, elbows on his knees. Rakshan didn't flinch or look away, so Calder dropped his own gaze to the floor. "What do you know of Quinn?" Calder asked.

"The first time you came to India, you ran from him as well."

"Did I?" Calder asked. It was true, but he wasn't sure how Rakshan knew any of this.

"Yes, my lord, you were. There is something you refuse to face when it comes to him. But face it you must, if you are to ever come to peace."

"There's nothing to face, Rakshan. It's over. Whatever was between us is over."

"Pardon, my lord, but to me it does not look to be over. If it were, we would be discussing India from His Grace's study and not from this ship."

"While that may be partially true—"

"There is no partial to truth, my lord. It is true, or it is not."

Calder thought about that for a moment as he massaged his temple with his knuckle. Rakshan was right. He needed some peace, and he wasn't bound to get it any time soon. "Did you send the wire to Gray?" he asked.

"Of course, my lord. We can send the next from Alexandria, and he will forward any information for us to receive when we dock there."

"Good. In the meantime, while I appreciate your concern, I think tonight I'm going to try to sleep, if you don't mind. We can discuss these things another day."

"Yes, my lord. I have reserved the sparring lane for Monday, Wednesday, and Friday mornings at seven o'clock. The gym will be closed at the same time on the other days for your privacy."

"Good, then," Calder said.

"Breakfast will arrive at six," Rakshan said as he stood.

"Very well. I will see you tomorrow at six," Calder replied.

"Yes, sir. Until then, consider this: Whatever ill you perceive against you, halve that and consider it again. This is the truth of how you have been wronged. Whatever ill you perceive yourself to have caused, that you must double." Rakshan turned and walked from the suite without another word as Calder stared after him.

This was going to be a very long trip.

eleste stumbled to the floor with Quinn, trying to soften his fall. She only managed to fall under him, catching his head before it thumped against the wood. Damn her mother. Damn her family. They had no idea what they'd done.

"Perry!" she screamed. "Perry, come!" she yelled again against a heavy sob. She heard footsteps thunder up the stairs, skidding to a halt in the hall before he knocked at the door. "Come," she said again, and the door opened.

Perry rushed to her side, rolling Quinn off of her and to his back at least. He checked his heartbeat and his breathing and took her hand. She jerked at the shock of it, but he held her tight and forced her to look at him.

"He should be fine, but I will send for the doctor. Listen to me…" He leaned up on his knees and looked out the window at the front of the house, then back to her. "No more screaming, or we won't be rid of your parents."

Celeste plastered one hand over her mouth. She continued to sob, but she did so as quietly as possible.

"My lord?"

Celeste looked up to see that Perry's valet had followed him in.

"Send for Dr. Whittingbone. First, be sure they leave. Follow the carriage to the far edge of town if you must, but be certain they've gone. When you return, lock the gates."

"Yes, my lord," he said, and he bowed and rushed from the room.

"Celeste, can you help me?" Perry moved to Quinn's shoulder and lifted, and she stood and picked up his feet. She finally understood what the phrase *dead weight* truly meant. Quinn was heavy. Heavier than anything she could have imagined. So heavy, in fact, that now thinking about all the sweet, soft, and delicate touches he'd managed seemed a dramatic accomplishment. How could such a solid mass be so gentle?

She followed Perry to the bed, her half of Quinn basically dragging on the floor.

"I should have had my valet help before he left," Perry grunted, smiled, and winked at her. He lifted Quinn and settled the bulk of him on the bed as she lifted one leg and threw it up there, then the other. They managed to arrange him, and Celeste tucked him in and went to the water closet for a fresh bowl of water and a cloth for his forehead.

"So you're used to his—" She waved her hand over him since she couldn't remember the word Francine had used that day after the park.

"Yes, the whole of the family is aware of his episodes, and he should be just fine. He always has been. I've sent for the doctor only as a precaution," he said, then he stopped and seemed to inspect her. "Celeste, I'm certain he'll be fine." He nodded stiffly, and Celeste was suddenly just a bit more worried.

"Celeste," he said, and she looked up at him again. "I mean he'll be fine with the marriage. He'll make you a fine husband."

"But he shouldn't have to. It wasn't meant to be this way. We weren't meant to be…well."

His eyes narrowed a bit. "Calder," he said as he watched her.

She nodded slowly as she picked at some loose threads on the robe she wore. "Does his mother know? Is that why she's so desperate for him to marry?"

Perry sat on the chair next to the bed, and Celeste sat down next to Quinn, her hand on his thigh for a moment before she moved it to his knee and finally just wound her fingers together in her own lap.

"Quinn's mother might know. I'm unsure. I only know that she's never approved of Calder and his predispositions, which all of the family know of, for the most part. I'm aware there were rumors about Quinn. His parents quashed them rather soundly. I suppose if those rumors were stirred, she might become much more anxious for a marriage to prove them wrong."

"Marriage doesn't prove anything."

"With society it does. Marriage in society proves conformation, which is exactly what they want. Society wants the outward appearance of propriety. In fact, society loves those who only conform outwardly, because if they stray or behave badly, there's something they can do about it. It's quite simple, really. Society as a whole doesn't care what you do as long as you do it quietly and don't cross the wrong person. That, in point of fact, is the only hard and fast rule for society."

Celeste nodded and looked back to Quinn. She readjusted the cloth on his forehead. "I can marry him to rescue him from society's shame, but I refuse to come between him and Calder," she said.

"And what of you, Celeste? Don't you wish to be cared for in the same way?"

"No, I don't. I—" She stopped. If Quinn didn't understand her, then what good was there in attempting to explain it to Perry? "You sound like Quinn."

"Celeste, I believe the problem Quinn has right now is that he cares too deeply for you to leave you to chance. He can't be two men, but I certainly think he wishes he could."

Celeste nodded. That did sound rather like him, and she wondered how hard it was for him to be so torn between her and Calder.

"I need to make arrangements. The only way to get you married without fuss is to do it post-haste. Quinn will have to get a special license from the Archbishop of Canterbury, as this isn't either of your parishes, and we need to avoid the posting of the banns. That's just a matter of money—which he has in abundance, in case you were unaware."

"Isn't that a bit unseemly to discuss with him like this?" she said as she looked back at Quinn, who seemed to have lost all the tension and gone into a deep, restful sleep.

"Quinn won't mind. He's taking you to wife regardless. I've learned that wives should have the right to know certain things about their future husbands. If you have something against being well-off, you've been warned," Perry said. He winked again, and this time it actually put her at ease somewhat.

She smiled as he stood and walked to the door. "For what it's worth, Celeste, I do believe the two of you will suit. For whatever this situation holds and whatever troubles the two of you have, I can see how much you do care for each other. Most arranged marriages won't have that. In truth, most marriages, under any circumstance, don't have even that." He left.

They did suit, she and Quinn, perhaps a bit too well. But that had never been at issue—it was *the* issue. That they suited was irrelevant to the true issue at hand. That they suited only served to complicate things.

Quinn loved Calder, and that's where he belonged, not tied to a woman who cared for him but didn't want him to touch her. Taking that physicality out of Quinn's life would be the tragedy because, *damn her*, but he was beautiful when he… She closed her eyes against the memory as she felt heat rise through her skin. She stood and walked to the window. That was something she did not want with him, but Calder did, and they deserved to have it—to have each other.

Celeste watched as the carriage rolled through the far gates at the edge of the drive, dust kicking up as the cobbles ended and the ruts began. She could not live with herself if she allowed this marriage to come between Quinn and Calder.

Much to Celeste's dismay, they were married three days later by special license of the archbishop. The Vicar Thomas performed the service in the small church at Westcreek. There were no announcements—even to the village—of the pending nuptials. As such, nobody came but those invited. Roxleigh and Francine joined Perry and Lilly and the girls since they'd happened to arrive the day before the wedding to pick up Francine's sisters for the family's return to Eildon Hill. Celeste had been happy to have Francine and Lilly with her, because they were the closest she'd ever come to having friends, and Francine…she wanted more time with her.

Celeste wore a dress she already owned. Quinn wore a suit from his wardrobe. He picked some flowers for her from the field on the way to the church, which they walked to—and it was done. When Vicar Thomas pronounced them man and wife, Quinn had tears in his eyes, and so did she—both of them for the wrong reasons. The day was not joyful. The day was painful, and it was not the celebration most people preferred. The vicar was unhappy, but cooperated once convinced it was what everyone wanted—though it didn't at all seem that way.

They walked back to the house after the ceremony, and Quinn begged a moment in the study while the rest of the family went to the wedding breakfast. She watched as he walked away from her, and moments later she knew the sound of a heart breaking as his cries echoed through the halls. She could not bear witness, would not do that to him, so she followed the rest of the family to the breakfast room at the back of the house, closing the doors behind her.

Overall, a lovely if incredibly miserable day.

Quinn had made arrangements to go to Paris for their honeymoon, and they were set to depart three days after they wed. He'd arranged to have an entire wardrobe made for her at the House of Worth, and he'd already commissioned her wedding portrait be done by John Singer Sargent. He made so many beautiful promises to her before the wedding, and they all sounded like apologies, and every single one of them tore at her conscience just a little bit more.

That night, Quinn crawled into bed across from her, his knees drawn up just as hers were—as though they guarded themselves, each from the other. Quinn looked older, he looked tired, but worst of all he looked resigned. There wasn't really much either of them could say, since they'd both professed enough apologies in the past weeks to last a lifetime.

He reached toward her with one hand, slid it up her cheek, and caressed her eyebrow with his thumb.

"I'm searching for a house in the country. Somewhere like Westcreek where you can be safe and happy. Somewhere far enough away from the city that you won't have to worry about unwanted visitors. Somewhere as beautiful as you are."

"I would like that," she replied, and she wrapped her hand around his wrist and placed a kiss in his palm. "Thank you for caring for me," she said.

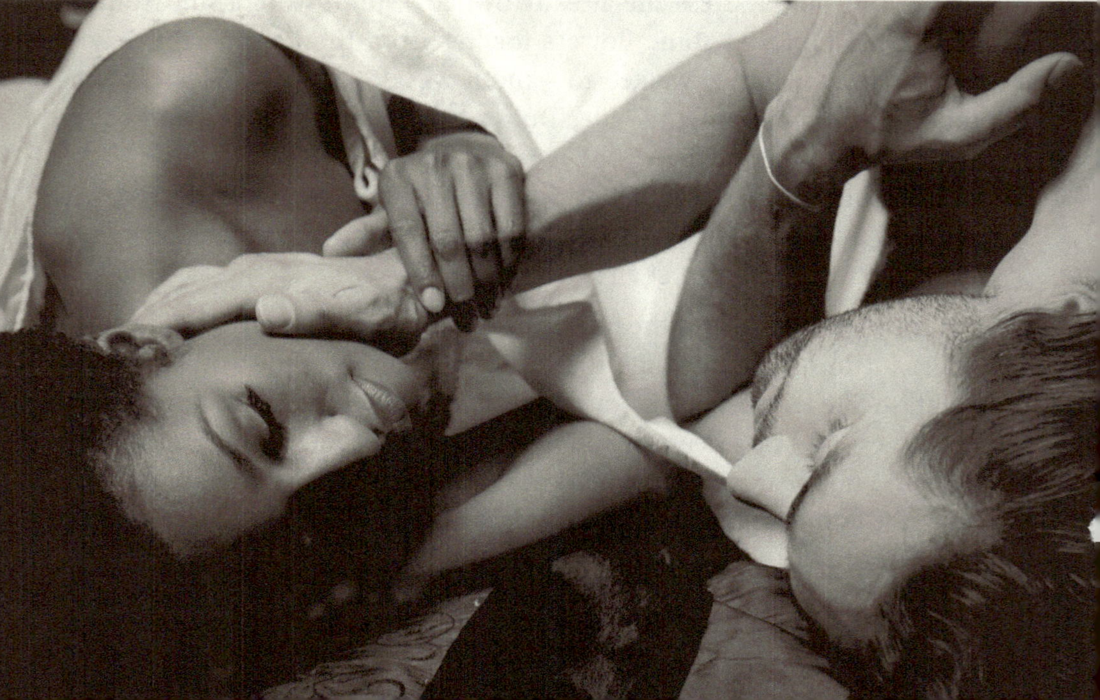

"Always."

Their first night as man and wife, they slept.

𝒞

Francine found her in the gardens. Celeste had gone out for a walk amongst the flowers, her hope that nobody would follow quashed but then swept aside when she realized who it was. She'd been afraid to truly approach Francine around the others, and when she did, she didn't say anything of importance.

Francine didn't say a word, simply walked up to Celeste and wrapped her in her arms and held her. She ran her hands down her back, squeezed her, and soothed her, and Celeste broke, allowing all the emotion loose as she hadn't before.

She wasn't sure why, but it simply felt like time to let it go, and Francine allowed it, encouraged it, didn't rush her to finish, as so many people did with ugly emotions. They tried to hurry them along and sweep them into the closet or under a rug so they could plaster a smile back on their faces and get on with the pretending.

Celeste's body calmed, the sobs subsiding, the shivers calming, the tears drying, and she leaned back, and Francine let her, but she didn't let her go. She held her arms and soothed her with her thumbs, spinning circles on her forearms, her expression open and accepting.

"This has been one of the most difficult weeks of your life, I think," she said. And Celeste could do naught but agree. "Come, there's a small folly on the lake. Nobody will be there, and we can sit and talk for a while." Francine took Celeste's arm and wrapped it with hers, her other arm going around Celeste's waist as she guided her along the edge of the gardens as she spoke.

"My wedding was the most beautiful day of my life. I think it was the day I finally accepted that this is where I belong. I wasn't born in the nineteenth century. I was born at the end of the twentieth century. Somehow, by some stroke of fate, I came to be here, and I believe it's because Gideon and I were born to be together…but time kept us apart. I know that may sound perfectly insane, but it is what I believe."

She pulled Celeste to a small bench in the center of the Roman columns that held up a circular arbor covered in vines so thick the sun couldn't even get through. They sat peacefully for a moment, and Francine held her hand.

"There are others," she said quietly. "Gideon's mother, for one. She was sent to Bedlam and never returned. I believe she and his father were also born to be together. His father tried to do everything he could for her. He loved her with a fierce passion, but the world being what it is, he believed sending her away was the best thing for her. He believed he was helping her. That's what they told him. That he was hurting her by keeping her. They told him he was helping her by sending her away. They both died with broken hearts, that much is true."

Celeste felt a chill rush her skin. "I was sent to Earlswood. They specialized in children. I—" Celeste pulled her hand from Francine's, twisting it in her skirts as she turned away.

"I'm not asking you to tell me anything you aren't comfortable with. I simply want you to know that I am here for you whenever you need to talk, whatever you have to say. I will not tell a soul. You are safe with me, and I will protect you with all that I am, and so will our family, now that you are one of us."

Celeste nodded, slowly turned back to Francine. "It's difficult to pull the past away from the before. I've been here for as long as I was there, and I think I had convinced myself that they were right about me. I had no idea." She looked up to Francine, who reached out and cupped her cheek, and Celeste sank into the warmth of her hand, holding it to her face as she closed her eyes and breathed of the reality of this woman.

"I have felt so very alone for all of my life. I found Quinn, and it felt as though he was calling to me, as though I had known him already, which was impossible. But I never wanted to marry him except to keep him in my life, and when I learned of Calder…I actually believed that might be a possibility. I thought my presence in their life together might help, and as I had no interest in a true marriage beyond society… But now, without Calder here, the way this happened, it's horrible." Celeste dropped Francine's hand and looked out over the lake.

Francine took Celeste's hands in her own once again. "It is horrible. I can only hope Calder will understand what truly happened," she said.

"He was so angry," Celeste said, then she shook her head, knowing she couldn't talk about those moments with anyone.

"Do you feel a connection to him as well?" Francine asked.

Did she? She had watched him more than any other peer. But she had steered clear of him because she'd had no intention of ending up the wife of a duke. That much attention was entirely too much attention. But she had loved to watch him whenever she saw him in society, because he was simply stunning. His clear, bright laughter, that cunning grin that spoke volumes on what he was keeping to himself, his strength and size, his possessive eyes.

"I don't know that I would call it a connection. I don't believe he ever noticed me, but I did notice him. Of any men in society, I noticed Calder and I noticed Quinn, and Quinn was accessible and pulled me to him like…" She shook her head again, unable to find the words to explain.

"I understand that feeling, believe me. I thought I had this whole process figured out, but then…you came along and blew it all away."

"What do you mean?" Celeste asked.

"Melisande, Gideon's mother, she left diaries, and from what I can tell, she was in an accident before she came here—incidentally, that's how I arrived here, because of a car accident. The first person she saw was Darius, and they were married not long after. With me, Gideon was the first man I saw, and I felt that—that something, like a thread that bound us together to the point that I could tell when he was in a room even if the door was closed between us. He fought it, of course," she said with a smile. "Boys."

"So that's…that's it? The two of you?"

"No, but until she's comfortable—"

"Lulu." Francine nodded. "I understand…I leave in a couple days for Paris, but I want to visit with you. I would like to try to sort out my past somehow, and I think you can help. I hope you can."

"I will do whatever I can. Have you told anyone else?"

"Oh, no. No, I have no idea what I would say."

"Look, I won't tell anyone without your permission, but just so you know, Gideon and Perry, Calder and Warrick, they all know the specifics about me. So if you're frightened, if you need someone and I'm not around for some reason, you can trust them. I know it's frightening, but you can trust any of them, with your life. I would. I have," she said.

"Calder knows?"

"He does."

Celeste turned away and considered that. She wondered if she should tell Quinn. "Not Quinn?"

"Not specifics. He knows I'm different somehow. He knows I'm not the Madeleine I'm supposed to be, if that makes sense, but he doesn't know the actual machinations of it. Though I don't think I would have a problem with him knowing. We just…we haven't really told all the family. It isn't quite necessary."

"Quinn should know. Eventually, I mean. I—well, we are married."

"But when you are ready, and if you need me—"

Celeste nodded. "Thank you. I'm frightened. Terrified, actually, to try to open my memories and remember the things I convinced myself were lies." She jerked her head as if to send the thoughts away. "I'm frightened."

"Don't push yourself. There's no rush. You're safe. We've got you now."

Celeste turned to her. She stared into those beautiful eyes and saw the most love and compassion and intelligence she had ever seen in another woman, and she couldn't help but start to cry again.

"Oh dear," Francine said, and Celeste laughed. "We've gone and done it again."

"I'll be puffy for a week. Perhaps I can blame it on allergies, all the flowers." She waved her hand about her head.

"Allergies…that's a word I haven't heard from someone else in quite some time," Francine said, and Celeste looked up as she wiped her eyes.

"What is it about Quinn?" Celeste asked then.

"You mean the episodes?" Francine asked and Celeste nodded.

"Panic attacks, I think. He has anxiety, and I'm not sure if it's from growing up in fear for so long because he didn't want to be discovered, or if it's something else."

"I was so young…I don't even know these things."

"Well, I studied business, so I don't know a whole lot either, just what was in the news at the time. Do you remember what year?"

"I was born…I think I was born in 1978."

"You're older than I am. I was born in 1993."

"That's…" Celeste let her vision go soft as she considered. It was too much. It was all too much. "Not yet," she whispered, and Francine reached out and hugged her.

"We have time," she said. "We have plenty of time."

C

The day before they departed for France, they both received missives from Adeleine. She professed her annoyance at not being invited to the wedding as she apologized in a very, she apologized in a very *so sorry, but everyone is happy now, so it's done and makes no difference sort of way. sort of way*. Not really much of an apology at all, and Celeste had thought Adeleine such a lovely person. She decided she would refuse all future letters, returning them.

Quinn didn't let many people in the family know of their travel plan. The only people who would know how to contact them for the next month would be Warrick and Perry. Celeste hadn't heard from, or spoken with, anyone from her family since the day Perry removed them from his home. She supposed that was for the better. She wasn't entirely sure what she would have to say to any of them.

Celeste watched out the window as they took tea in the small parlor at the front of the house. Francine and Lilly and the girls talked of London, of the coming babe, of returning to Eildon. Francine invited Celeste to the far estate to visit, and she nodded her agreement, but her mind was simply elsewhere. For days, she had done naught but think on how she could bring Calder back to Quinn, how they could manage this without ruining their family. Now her family.

She saw a cloud of dust kick up beyond the far gate and watched as a horse-drawn cart pulled onto the cobblestone drive. The cart was loaded with things, most of which were covered by a large tarp. The rough cables made the cart vibrate, and Celeste watched as the canvas slid and her desk chair was revealed. Her teacup slid from her hand and spilled down the front of her skirts as she stood. The clattering of the horses' hooves grew louder against the cobbles, beating a tattoo in her skull. Like the final bells of midnight on the clock that seemed to grow louder and more resonant with each strike.

"I apologize, Lilly," she said as she bent and picked up the cup, placing it back on the table with the saucer. Her hands shook, and the teacup fell to the side, the leaves spilling to the linen of the tablecloth. The horses stopped, leaving nothing but the metallic sound of their tackle, their uncomfortable shifting on the cobbles, their restless huffing against the bridles. The man on the box jumped down and spoke with the butler, who disappeared into the house. A moment later, he emerged with a line of footmen, and they started unloading her things.

Celeste walked to the entry of Perry's home as the men carried her belongings past her to the rooms she had occupied since they had arrived at Westcreek. Her trunks, her cases, her dressing table, her favorite chair, her failed attempts at knitting, her books. She did nothing as they carried the entirety of her life—to this point—up the stairs and down the hallway out of sight.

"Celeste," Quinn said. His voice was calm and steady. His hand came to her shoulder and rested there carefully, not disturbing her, but letting her know he was there. He stood behind her, watching her as she watched her life go past. The last case disappeared, and the footsteps and noise of the delivery with them.

She waited for a moment, expecting to see the footmen return. They didn't, and silence fell like a heavy blanket around them. The men must have gone back out through the servants' entrance. Quietly and unseen, as servants should, as her life with her family seemed to have done. That parade was the most noise her life had made since she'd been born.

She turned to Quinn. Perry stood behind him. "Your things will be perfectly safe here until you return from Paris," Perry said. She nodded in response.

"Did you send for them?" she asked as her gaze fell to the floor.

"I did not," Quinn answered. "My mother must have let them know…" He didn't finish the sentence. He didn't need to.

That one small part of her that had hoped her family would come to her, congratulate her, accept her now that she had married—and married well… it sucked into her belly like a rock in a drain, then broke, flooding her veins and forcing her to action. She turned and went to the stairs. When she heard Quinn follow, she paused on the stairs and waved him off. She raised her chin and followed what constituted the whole of her life down that silent hallway.

Calder

The mouth on his cock wasn't as impressive as the Mary-Ann had promised, and Calder pushed him off and tucked himself away. He complained, but Calder cut a look at him, and he got off his knees and left him on the deck. Calder wasn't sure why he'd thought that a good idea. He hadn't come up here to find a bit of scarlet. He'd come up to the deck to watch the stars pass above the clouds made by the steamer. To attempt to clear his head and consider the things Rakshan had said.

To think about Quinn. Something he'd been quite actively avoiding. Or perhaps he'd come up to this deck knowing he could find some rough trade to take his mind from Quinn. Because he did miss him.

Calder sat forward in the chair and dropped his head into his hands, disrupting every hair on his head. He wanted to go home to Quinn. He didn't want to be on this boat bound for India. He didn't give a whit about what these men were doing there. That wasn't true. He did care. He simply cared more about the fact that he'd left Quinn badly. He'd shoved him at Celeste and left him to deal with the wreckage on his own. Because he was frightened.

And there it was.

So many people looked up to him, so many men in the peerage and in service, and Calder didn't want any one of them to know that he would prefer a good buggering over the fairer sex any day of the week. Because that's exactly what they would think. It wouldn't be about his relationship with Quinn, even if peers married their cousins quite openly to tie up family fortunes—those cousins were still women. Nothing about that was illegal, but everything he and Quinn did together was.

And Celeste… Quinn had said Calder could trust her, and Calder wasn't sure what bothered him more, that Quinn might be right, or that Quinn was close enough to Celeste to know that it was true. He'd always known Quinn would jump a fence when he wasn't around, but something about him jumping the fence with this woman simply ate at him. He didn't want to like her, but he did. Not in the sense that perhaps Quinn did, but certainly in the sense that he thought they would get on fairly well. Except that Quinn was his. And he didn't want Quinn to want to fuck her.

Right now, though, Quinn wasn't his. He was hers, because Calder had left him in England with her and run off to India to chase a ghost.

This was a disaster. His life was a disaster. There wasn't much he could do, though, not from this ship in the middle of the sea. He had at least another week before he would receive word from Warrick when they came to land in Alexandria. Another week of nothing but berating himself and wishing he'd done everything differently that night.

Calder closed his eyes to the stars and brought Quinn's face before him. That beautiful face, the deep eyes that bored through him, that pleading gaze—oh God, but when it turned and Quinn took him, there was nothing for it. Those were some of the best moments of his life. Giving up and giving in to whatever Quinn wanted to do.

He wanted to feel his tongue in his arse now, his hand on his purse, boiling the mettle from his balls until they ruptured and the hot splash soothed his skin. His blood rushed his groin, and Calder rolled to his side, tried to avoid thinking of Quinn, the want was so deep. The depth of it equal to the pain of his own betrayal. The look on Quinn's face when he walked from the room.

"Skulking about on the upper decks of the ship is more likely to get you slit and tossed over than to fix whatever it is that troubles you."

"Rakshan, how long have you been here?" Calder asked as he watched him walk from the shadows of the deck toward him.

"Long enough to know you're avoiding me as a method of avoiding the truth," Rakshan replied.

"Yes, well." Calder stood from the chaise longue and shook out his pant legs, which had twisted on his thighs. "We can return to the cabin now."

Rakshan walked beside him as he strolled the deck, cabin as a destination, but in no hurry to actually be there.

"You have known Quinn all your life?" Rakshan asked.

"Yes, my first conscious moments of my childhood involve him in some way or another."

"Did you love him then?"

"Did I? Not beyond what I was supposed to feel for any of my family, that inbred emotion that families promote to guard their own."

"And love came—"

"Much later." He tapped his fists together as he considered it, trying to pinpoint a single moment in time when his thoughts of Quinn turned from family to something more. He couldn't. Perhaps his want of him now colored all of his memories retroactively.

"Our family—you must be aware by now—is rather close. Quinn and I grew up together, nearly as brothers, because of our similar age. All the cousins tended to band together by age, if not sex, and we still do. Though the fact that Calder's family and mine were in London more than at any country estates kept us even closer."

"Did you fight it?" Rakshan asked, and Calder stopped, turned toward the rail, and leaned his arms on it, his gaze far at sea.

"I did, yes. It's funny, that, because of the two of us, Quinn is passable in society. He could take a wife without much distress to himself, but I—I've no interest in women, more of an aversion, to be honest. I think that frightened me as a child. When we were young, before our experiments with each other's bodies had become something more serious, Quinn had been the one to pursue me, and so I fought it, and when Quinn began to want something more from me, I refused him for as long as I could. As it happened, that wasn't very long."

"And now?"

"Now I wonder if we'd been apart for long enough, if he'd moved on, if we'd let each other be…"

"That doesn't appear to have worked in the past. What leads you to believe it would work at this point?"

"The hope that one of us could have a normal life in society."

"Your objections to what you want are all based on what society wants, what your family wants. They are not based on what you want or what Quinn wants."

"Of course they are. We cannot possibly live without restriction."

"You cannot? Or you are afraid of that possibility? Are you afraid Quinn would become bored with you and leave you?"

"I've always been afraid of that. He has possibility, and I do not. His parents are much more strict with him than mine are with me. If he refuses to tell his family what he wants from life, how can I trust him?"

"You do not understand what trust is, my lord. Trust is the fall before the net appears. You expect Quinn to hang the net before you even deign to approach the edge. How must that feel for him? What have you given him?"

"I've given him everything."

"Have you?"

No, of course he hadn't. Calder forced Quinn to bend to his will. He wouldn't allow him to move to his house, even though Quinn had suggested it many times. He had refused to make any sort of statement, regardless that it could have been passed off as making use of the massive town house, which he had mostly to himself. There were things that could have been done. He had refused all of them, constantly asking Quinn to first make that ultimate sacrifice.

"I'm a horrible person," he said.

"I very much doubt that to be true, my lord. What I believe to be true is the fear you hold of being discovered and your life as you enjoy it being destroyed. I know of your fear of Warrick. I know he held his discovery over you in threat to keep you from disclosing his whereabouts. I know many things about this life you've created next to the cliff. Your life should be in the flight, my lord, not in the safety. If you never take flight, what kind of life do you lead?"

"A safe one," he replied.

"Is it safe? You're on a ship bound for India, my lord, looking for a man who should be dead. Attempting to stop the trafficking of women and children into England on behalf of Her Royal Highness. How much of what you do for the Crown is safe?"

Calder looked over at Rakshan, who stood next to him with his hands behind his back. He expected his expression to be smug. Of course, it wasn't. The thing about Rakshan was that he never behaved in that way. He wasn't British and would never reprimand or accost anyone. Rakshan spoke from a deep and true place, not from some superficial position of judgment.

"My lord," he said.

"Yes, Rakshan?"

"We can turn back at Alexandria."

Calder considered that for a moment. If it was simply Exeter and Soundringham and the rest, he would have agreed to it. "I can't leave this to Warrick," he said. "I won't do that to him. He was honorable and true to me. I will do the same for him."

Rakshan nodded. "You have a few days yet to decide what to send."

"Send?"

"A telegram, my lord."

Calder turned back to the dark at the side of the ship. What could he say to Quinn? Rakshan was right. He did have a few days to consider it, and now, of course, that was about all he would be considering.

Quinn

uinn's chest felt tight and uncomfortable as he watched Celeste walk up those stairs to her room. He didn't follow. He would accede to her wishes. The day after the wedding, she'd retreated to the room she'd been in during their stay and had not returned to his bed. Not that he expected her to, or wanted her to, or needed her to…

It really would help the situation if he would stop lying to himself. It wasn't even that he wanted her as a husband should want a wife. It was that he wanted to be close to her again. Just to hold her, to commiserate with her, to know that he wasn't alone in this, and to be sure she knew that same thing.

He turned to Perry. "You've been so welcoming, and I cannot thank you enough for everything you've done. For opening your home and your life to Celeste, I will forever be in your debt."

"You would do the same, so I have no hesitation in doing so. You both have a home here for as long as you have need," Perry said.

Quinn nodded and followed Celeste up the stairs. He paused at the landing, tapping his thumb on the stair rail as he considered. He turned and walked the opposite hall to his own suite. He needed to find her a home so she had someplace to call her own when they returned from Paris. He had planned the trip for a month, which gave him that much time. He couldn't believe how her family had handled her, but he didn't have time to deal with her parents, or his.

He thought he could purchase land with a house, and they could build a life there much like Perry's—away from London society and judgment—

and Celeste could be happy there. He would look into estates that had fallen from entailments and were in disrepair due to lack of funds. He would call in favors and use all of his resources to search England for the perfect home.

He sat at his desk and pulled out the sheaf of paper he kept for letters. He needed to write to Mr. Shaw, the architect who had helped both Roxleigh and Perry with their estates. He'd done brilliant work on Eildon Hill when Rox had taken over, and he wanted to be sure Mr. Shaw could refurbish, rebuild, or do whatever necessary to Celeste's home when he found it. He remembered seeing the duchess's room at Eildon Hill. He wanted something like that for her, but he had some ideas of how to make it even more. He needed to let Mr. Shaw know exactly what to look for in the search.

Q

Quinn opened the carriage door and helped Celeste out to the docks to board the steam ship for Calais. They would continue on to Paris from there by rail. She gained her feet and tipped her head back to look up to the steamer, and Quinn held his breath. Her gaze traveled the side of the vessel. He was certain it was the first time she'd seen such a large ship in person. When her gaze reached the bow, her fingers tightened on his, and she dropped her gaze. She looked back up to him.

"Perry mentioned you had money," she said.

"Did he?" Quinn asked.

"He did." She looked back to the steamer, and he knew she was inspecting the newly painted letters at the bow. *The Lady Celeste.* "Would it be too forward for me to ask just how you came to your…situation?"

"My situation?" he asked with a smile. She nodded. "No, not forward at all since it is now *our* situation. My father funded my first foray into speculative trading. I happened to be quite good at it. My company grew to include private ships for that purpose, and eventually I was offered an opportunity to fund a project to build a groundbreaking vessel. That which you see here. She is a steamship propelled by screws instead of paddles, and the sails have been removed entirely. She is also lit by an electric dynamo instead of gas. It was originally designed by Edison for the *SS Columbia*. We combined all of these things into the ship you see here, the first of her kind. Steam-powered with screws for speed and no sails to cut a clean path and aid in stability against the wind in the crossing. Electric lights, which remove the gas lamps and inherent danger therein."

She stared at the name on the bow. "I would like to know more about everything you just said, but I'm still—"

"She'd been named *The Lady Adeleine*. I had them change it, Celeste. She carries your name as she will carry you, my most precious cargo. Now, would you like to see your rooms?"

She nodded, but didn't say anything more as they boarded the ship via the private gangway near the quarterdeck. He had a private suite on this ship, which he would let to special guests and family as needed. He swung the door to the cabin wide and waved Celeste forward. She walked to the windows, which stretched about a third the width of the stern and wrapped around the port side.

She ran her fingers over the backs of chairs as she walked to the windows and looked out over the long, crowded dock. So many families stood below, wishing their loved ones off on their voyages. Waving and throwing kisses. There was no one on that dock throwing her kisses, though. The whole of her family was here on the boat, really.

"It's a handsome room," she said, and it was a handsome room, Quinn agreed. He would need to have it decorated more to her tastes. Later.

"The bedroom is just here," he said, opening the door toward the center of the suite as she approached and walked through. "There is a small switch here for the lights. Simply turn it. The main cabin lights are next to the entry."

"How many trips have you taken aboard the ship?" she asked.

"This is the maiden voyage. She was completed recently. Just in time, it seems," he said with a smile.

"She's a lovely boat, but this room was not designed to entertain a woman," Celeste said.

"Ship," he replied, avoiding the rest of what she'd said. She nodded once and reached up to unpin her hat. "Let me help you," he said, and she turned her back to him, tilting her head to the side so he could see the pin. He pulled it out, the devil of a thing at nearly six inches, and lifted the hat and handed them both to her.

"I'm going to see the captain, briefly. Would you like to accompany me, or—"

"I'll stay here," she said.

Quinn nodded and left her in the cabin, pulling the main door closed behind him. The trip across the channel was rather short, but the ship was scheduled on from Calais to Le Havre, parts of Spain, and through the Strait of Gibraltar, landing finally at Marseilles before going on to Alexandria and Bombay, after which she would return the way she came.

The Lady Celeste was outfitted with the most exquisite decoration and design possible. She was meant to be a crown jewel, a ship on which the passengers could enjoy the ride as much as the destination, and this first sailing had sold out in no time, proving once again that Quinn knew where to invest his money to make the most of it.

Celeste had been correct in the assessment of the decorations in his cabin. It wasn't designed for a lady. He'd designed it with Calder in mind, the furnishings dark and sturdy and simple of color. No frills. No fancy wall fabrics. White enameled walls in the main cabin and dark paneled wood in the bedroom. Blue. *His* favorite color.

When Quinn had embarked on this plan years ago, he'd imagined the maiden voyage would be made with someone else. He'd imagined himself a voyage of nothing but pleasure and carnal pursuits, in a place where nobody could touch them.

He had greatly misjudged the future. That sort of speculation escaped him.

Celeste sat in the chair and watched from the windows as the steamer pulled away from the docks, from Dover, from everything she'd ever known. In her wildest of dreams, she hadn't thought that she would ever be taking a trip to the City of Light. Nothing about her life at this moment had been expected.

The door to the cabin opened, and Celeste turned to find Quinn. "Are you enjoying the launch?" he asked.

"I—" She shrugged. She wasn't enjoying much of anything at the moment. He came and sat in the chair next to her.

"One day, if you like, we can take the voyage to Marseilles, perhaps all the way to India. For now, we will be in Calais shortly and then on to Paris."

Celeste nodded. "She goes all the way to India?"

"She does, yes," Quinn said. "That's the most financially rewarding route at the moment."

"So it's all about the money, is it?" she asked.

"Not entirely, but my company was built to make money, that part is true enough."

Celeste thought about everything Francine had said about the women she knew to be from another time. How they were all drawn to someone specific. Irrevocably. It nudged something lose in her memory, something she hadn't thought of, but was always there. It was a memory of day she came here. The first face she remembered belonged to a boy whose name she would never forget—*Quinn*. A second face stood just behind him as he crouched down to see if he could help her. The face was haloed with gold hair.

"Calder," she whispered before she realized then looked to see if he'd heard her but he gazed somewhere far beyond the ship out into the world and she imagined his mind had followed.

She considered telling Quinn about her past, but then decided against it for now because they had enough to manage without trying to figure out that bit. Certainly Quinn had enough on his mind without having to come to terms with this. She nodded again, watching as the Cliffs of Dover disappeared into the horizon.

❦

They finally arrived at the Grand Hôtel du Louvre that evening and were taken directly to a massive suite that overlooked the Place du Palais-Royal. Celeste had been entirely overwhelmed by the day, the ship, the private train car, and now this incredibly majestic hotel. She wanted to close her eyes to all of the beauty and sleep because she was simply exhausted.

She allowed Quinn to help her remove her clothes, and she crawled into the massive bed that also looked out over the Palais-Royal, and she was asleep before she even registered the soft down pillow beneath her cheek.

❦

At some point in the night, she opened her eyes to find Quinn standing at the windows looking down on the Place. The city was lit, even in the dead of night, and she could clearly see his form against the soft glow from outside the room. He stood with his hands pressed against the glass, his shoulders broad and defined as they swept down to his narrow waist, his naked hips, his strong thighs and legs.

Once again, Celeste marveled at the beauty of him, unable to turn away, for the pleasure of looking at every curve and dip of his structure was simply so great. For the first time, she noted the long valley of his spine

bordered by the two great muscles of his back. Below those muscles she could see the dip toward his hips, two dimples on either side of his spine, the perfect shape of his arse, the moonlight and gaslight from outside limning his curves as though he'd been painted by a master.

This man was her husband. It saddened her that the thought brought no joy with it.

He shifted, bringing his hands to his hips, his gaze dropping from the window to the floor, and Celeste pulled the sheet up to her nose as though she could hide from him.

"You're awake," he whispered over his shoulder.

She inhaled deeply, savoring the light, flowery scent of the room, lavender and lemony.

"We should try to be friends again, Celeste. If we remain as we are, my mother—your parents—they all win. You and I have the power to find some semblance of happiness in our lives. It may be a difficult road to find it, but why don't you simply be you, and let me be me, as we were before the world came between us and forced us together, into two people who can't sit quietly in the same room."

Celeste pushed the sheets down and tossed her feet over the edge of the bed to the floor. The nightgown she wore tangled at her feet because it was too long, and she lifted it as she walked across the floor to stand behind him. "I thought we agreed that it's very difficult for me to have any sort of conversation with you while you're naked," she said.

He looked back over his shoulder at her, and the edge of his mouth kicked up in a smile. The first genuine one she'd seen from him in quite some time. As he turned toward her, she dropped her skirt and brought her hands to her chest, weaving them together to keep from touching him.

"Did we actually agree on that, or did you simply command it and expect it to be?" he asked.

"I fail to understand a difference, Quinn."

He laughed, just a quick burst that raised his chest and let it fall. He crossed his arms there, and they stood gazing at each other. She memorized the shape of his face, the new lines that seemed to drag his features down. "It seems we are at an impasse," he said.

"Is that so? You realize your nudity puts you at a great disadvantage."

"How is that?" he asked. "You seem to be the one unable to function when you see my cock."

"Now you're just baiting me," she said as she closed her eyes. "What if someone broke into our room? What would you do? Protect me with no clothing on?"

"Who do you imagine is going to break into our room?"

"I don't know…some nefarious sort of ruffian who wants something from you."

"I know no such ruffians," he replied.

Celeste started to smile, but it turned into a yawn so great that her eyes closed and her jaw popped by her ear as she covered her mouth with both hands.

"Come on," he said. He took her hand and pulled her toward the bed as she tripped over her hem. He tucked her in and went around to the other side, where he lay facing her. "You'll have to become familiar with my nakedness, wife, as I don't ever wear clothes abed."

"Wife," she said, and it sent a chill down her spine.

"Merely stating a fact, Celeste, nothing more."

"Are we to pretend our way through this entire marriage?" she asked. Marriage, sex, babies…

"Pretend, no. There's nothing to pretend. We are married, you and I. What we do within our marriage is entirely up to us. I wasn't strong enough to stand up to my family where my love for Devil was concerned—until it was too late and that choice was taken from me. I'll be damned if I'll let that destroy your life as well. This is you and I, Celeste. What happens—or doesn't happen—between us is up to us and nobody else. Understood?"

"Your family expects—"

"My family's interest in my life ended when they—when my mother worked to destroy your life to save her own arse. Don't forget that. I'm telling you now, this is between us and no other."

Quinn reached out and smoothed his hand up her cheek, swept his thumb across her eyebrow until she was unable to keep her eyes open any longer. "I believe in you, Quinn…"

Calder

Calder closed his eyes and allowed the dream to wash over him. It had been the first restful night's sleep he'd had in weeks, and he wanted to savor it and the residual feel of Quinn's hands on his body and his mouth on his cock. God, but that night had been incredible. They'd grown so much more bold in exploration, eventually convincing his parents that they needed a camp set up in the woods so they could pretend they had a British camp in India.

Perhaps that's where his interest in the country had begun. He and Quinn had looked at the images that came back from India, the ceremony, finally the crowning of Victoria as empress. London had been thoroughly obsessed with India when they were children. Quinn's interest waned when his parents refused to buy him a commission because they wanted him to do something other than serve as a soldier, which was all he would have been.

Some days, Calder wished they could go back in time and avoid all of this. Everything they'd become, everything they were to each other. Because attempting to rid himself of it now was the worst sort of agony.

Quinn

She'd fallen asleep with his name on her lips, and it was the sweetest thing he'd ever heard. He watched her sleep for a time before he also drifted off, and when he woke with the dawn, he was ready to take action. He had so much to do. He felt hopeful that the distraction would keep his mind from Calder and whatever it was he was doing.

He went down to the lobby to send off a few telegrams and speak with the concierge before returning to the room to find Celeste dressed and finishing her breakfast.

"Was I away that long?" he asked.

"More than an hour," she said.

He looked at the mantel clock. "We should be going soon. Lots of things to do today."

"Is that so?"

"It is." He walked to the table and picked up a pastry and walked to the windows overlooking the Place. It was a beautiful day. He finished his pastry, drank a quick cup of coffee, and took her hand. "Shall we?"

She stood. "You didn't even pause enough to enjoy that," she said.

"You're quite correct. Was it delicious?"

"It certainly was. You would know if you hadn't rushed."

He led her to the elevators, and they walked out to the Place. Quinn took her hand and placed it on his arm, leading her to Avenue de l'Opéra, where he stopped and pointed to the far end.

"Celeste, there is the Paris Opera," he said as he pointed to the building at the far end of the avenue. Her fingers tightened on his sleeve, and they started walking toward it.

"Are we…can we…"

"Not at this moment, no, but we will. Right now, we have an appointment to attend."

She relaxed her hold on him, but her gaze never left the opera house, staying with it until they turned on Rue des Petits Champs, and it disappeared behind the buildings. He led her down a narrow street for a couple of blocks and turned her down the Rue de la Paix. About halfway down the street toward the opera house, he stopped in front of a large building. It must have been seven stories at least.

"We're here," he said.

"Where's here?" She looked at the window of the shop, where a long curtain covered the interior, and scanned the façade. Above the door was a single word. WORTH. She released his arm. "The House of Worth. Quinn."

"They're expecting you." He pointed toward the main door, and a liveried man opened it for her, and she stepped inside. She was greeted by a lovely woman in black who led her through the main-floor salon to one of the upper-floor salons. There, she was greeted by women dressed in the most beautiful gowns, and Quinn couldn't take his eyes from her as she felt the fabrics, ran her hands over the velvets, satins, and watered silks, touching the brass buttons and skimming the feathers in the hats. She turned back to him.

"It's all so lovely, Quinn."

He bent at the waist. "At your service, my lady," he said.

A man, smaller than Quinn by a few inches, came into the salon. "She's a vision," he said quietly.

"I agree," Quinn said as he turned to him.

"Charles Worth," he said.

"Quintin Wyntor. It is my honor to meet you, sir," Quinn said.

"I believe the honor shall be mine," he replied as his eyes studied Celeste.

His scrutiny would have been quite unsettling had it been from any other man, but Quinn was aware of who this was and what he was about, so it seemed rather required.

"Lord Wyntor, there's a chair in the corner, there, for you. If you have any questions, please do ask."

And with that, Mr. Worth walked straight for Celeste and introduced himself, and Quinn was all but forgotten for the next three hours.

He treated her like royalty, having his men bring a settee to the center of the room for clients to sit on while he talked about the silhouettes he thought would suit her. He had his ladies change their dresses to show her examples, had men bring bolts of fabric for her to touch. He told her that with her complexion she could wear nearly any color, but he thought the softer colors suited her best. The purple and lavender would bring out the subtle pink in her cheeks and the green of her eyes.

She did nothing but smile and nod and follow his direction. After an hour, the door to the salon opened again, and a taller man with a beard and moustache entered. Quinn stood. "Mr. Sargent," he said as he extended his hand.

The man nodded and shook Quinn's hand with a warm smile. Quinn motioned to Celeste. "My wife, sir. She saw the portrait you did of my mother and fell in love with it. So I thought a wedding portrait of her…" He trailed off as he watched yet another man appreciate Celeste in a way that was unnerving. "Well, I'll let you…" he said and nodded, going back to the chair in the corner as Sargent approached the settee and introduced himself.

The three of them spoke at length about silhouette and color and setting, and what felt like hours passed as Quinn watched from the corner, unneeded. Finally, decisions were made, dates were set, and Celeste remembered he existed.

eleste stood from the settee and looked around the room, finally finding Quinn in the far corner. Mr. Worth took both her hands and bussed her cheeks, and she turned to Mr. Sargent, who kissed the back of one hand and one cheek with a smile hardly visible for his moustache. She gave them both a parting curtsey and went to Quinn, who stood as she approached.

"Well?" he asked.

She had no words. Beyond Quinn and most of his family, she'd never been treated so well by men—by anyone of stature—in her life. The dressmakers in London had been disappointed, at best, when having to make her society dresses, and never had her mother wanted a portrait of any kind done, photographic or painted. She took Quinn's hands in both of hers and squeezed them tight to her breast. She didn't have the words to express what this experience meant for her at the moment.

He pulled her close and kissed her temple, then pulled one hand free and smoothed her hair behind her ear. "Would you like to have some tea, or are you hungry?" he asked.

"Both," she answered quietly. He took her hand and placed it on his arm, leading her from the salon and back to the street.

"We can walk toward the opera house if you'd like to see it closer. There are several cafés on the avenue where we can stop on the way back to the hotel."

She nodded.

"When do we return?" he asked.

"Five days," she said. In five days, she would have a fitting for several bespoke gowns by Charles Worth. In eight days, she would have a final fitting for the dress she would wear to sit for Mr. Sargent. Quinn had kept those promises to her, but what had she done for him? What could she do for him?

They walked together as if they were more than just friends. As if their marriage was true in name and in deed. As if she had everything in the world she'd ever wanted, when the truth was so very different. Quinn was doing everything he could to see her happy in this marriage. The problem was that, while he did that, Calder got farther and farther away.

She stopped and turned him toward her. "Quinn, you need to leave. You need to get on a boat and go after Calder. You can't wait any longer. This is it."

Quinn stared at her. "I can't possibly leave you here in Paris. That's… absolutely not…it's out of the question," he replied.

Celeste twisted her fingers as she considered ways to get him to go. "Lilly. Ask Lilly and Perry to come. Francine and Roxleigh have returned to Eildon and taken the girls with them. They're in that big house all alone—"

"Which is probably how they like it," he cut in.

"Oh, but who doesn't want a trip to Paris?" she squealed and immediately dropped her gaze as people turned in the street to look.

"I don't…"

She looked back up and could see him considering it.

He shook his head. "What about you? I can't abandon you. I can't. We're married."

"We are married, yes, but it isn't like you can marry him," she said as quietly as possible. "So what exactly is standing in your way? It's not me. I won't let it be."

"But—"

"No, Quinn!" She took his hand and pulled him up the street and around the corner.

"What are you doing, woman?"

"We're going to the hotel. You're going to send a telegram to Perry. They can be here tomorrow or the next day. I'll stay in my room until they arrive, I promise. I don't have to go anywhere. I'll spend your money on room service and books and wait for them to arrive. You are leaving. You're leaving." She turned to him, and he bumped into her, catching her before she fell. She hadn't been so excited in a very long time. She couldn't even remember how long. "Quinn, you're leaving. You're going to go get Calder back, do you hear me?"

She watched his face run the gauntlet of expressions, from confusion to frustration to fear, but finally his muscles relaxed, and his eyes brightened. She saw the realization sink in, and his grip tightened on her arms. "You mean it?"

"I mean it."

"We can be happy. You would be happy to—"

"I couldn't possibly be happier, Quinn. This is what I want. I want the two of you to be together. I want your friendship and love, I want my small cottage in the north, and I want Calder by your side every day," Celeste said, and she knew in that moment that it was true. "That is what I want. Don't you see? It's perfect. We're perfect. It was meant to be." Celeste felt her skin prick in the awareness that her future could be with them, that they could be a family, if only Quinn could get to Calder. He had to get to Calder.

Quinn smiled and took her hand and pulled her toward the hotel as she held on and tried to keep up with him, giggling the entire way.

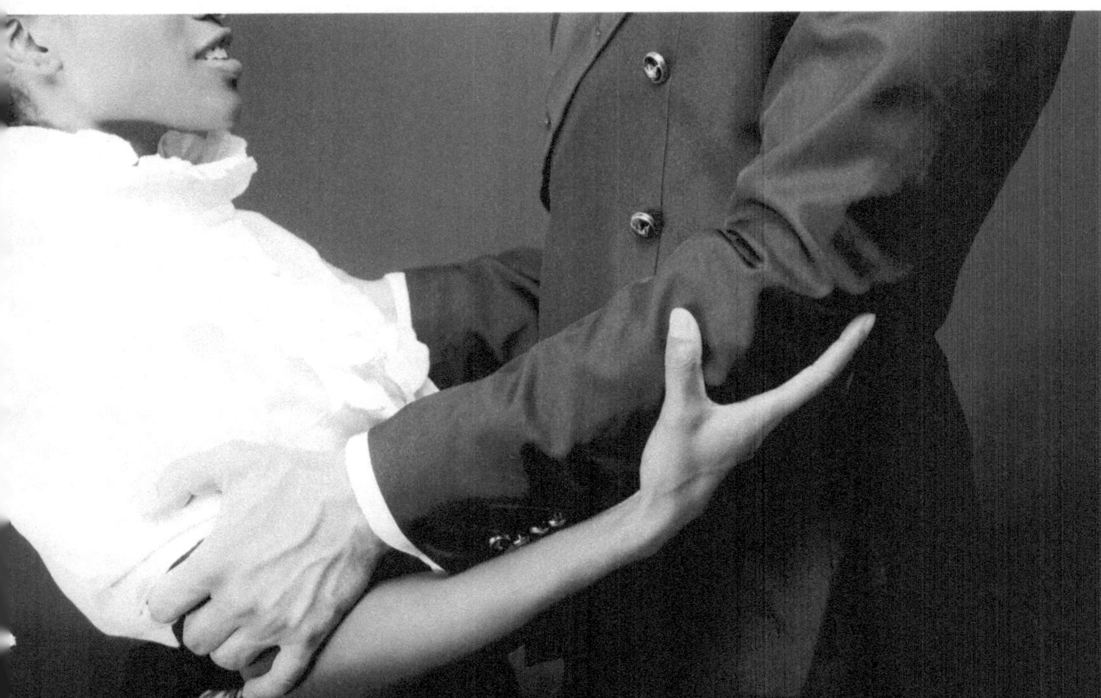

Celeste

Perry and Lilly were on their way to Paris, and Celeste insisted Quinn leave straightaway so he could intercept *The Lady Celeste* instead of finding a berth on some other steamship. There were things that needed doing before he left, though. He had several business matters to handle before he was out of range of communication for two weeks.

Quinn took the train from Paris to Marseilles and took the time on the journey to compose several important telegrams. The first was to his father.

> *I love Calder*
>
> *I am going after him*
>
> *Celeste is safe*
>
> *I am sorry for everything*
>
> *Quintin*

As short as it was, it was the most difficult of them. He sent a separate telegram to his mother because he refused to lay that at his father's feet.

> *I'm in love with a man*
>
> *Celeste is helping me find him*
>
> *No further communication is necessary*
>
> *Q*

The third was to Warrick because Quinn had no way of knowing how to contact Calder in Alexandria without knowing which steamship he was on or when he would arrive.

> *I am for Alexandria*
>
> *Send word to Calder to wait*
>
> *We can continue aboard The Lady Celeste*
>
> *Please update via the same*
>
> *Quinn*

He had them sent as soon as he arrived in Marseilles and managed to catch *The Lady Celeste* before she moved on. If he failed to find Calder in Alexandria, he would have to continue on through the Suez Canal and, ultimately, to Bombay. From there, he wasn't entirely sure what he would do. He hoped Warrick would at least point him in the right direction and have word once he reached Alexandria. They would remain at dock for two days to allow for communications before continuing on for the rest of the voyage.

Calder wouldn't receive anything until he was in Alexandria, and Quinn didn't have time to wait in Marseilles for a response. He left on *The Lady Celeste* and hoped that Warrick would get the message to him and Calder would wait.

Quinn had never planned to take such a long tour on his own. Thankfully, the ship provided a great deal of diversion, from the large library to the exercise facilities and the gaming deck with skittles, table tennis, and shuffleboard. There was no end to the things he could do aboard *The Lady Celeste*. Quinn, though, all he did was stay in his cabin and stare out the windows as the sea was left behind, and he prayed that Calder would listen.

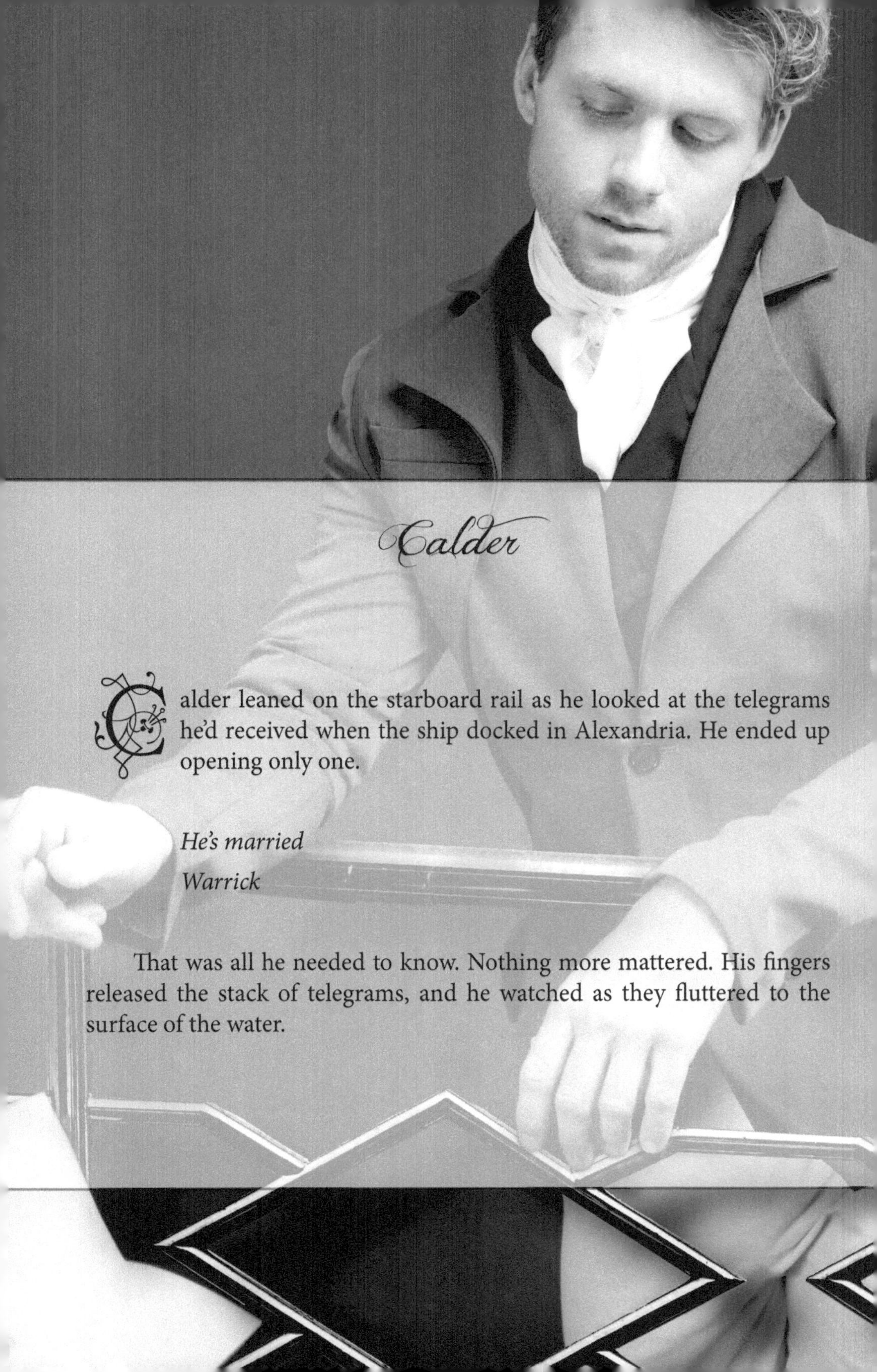

Calder

alder leaned on the starboard rail as he looked at the telegrams he'd received when the ship docked in Alexandria. He ended up opening only one.

He's married

Warrick

That was all he needed to know. Nothing more mattered. His fingers released the stack of telegrams, and he watched as they fluttered to the surface of the water.

Celeste

eleste had promised Quinn that she wouldn't leave the hotel on her own, but she didn't keep that promise. She had tried, but the first two hours of the day had been so very miserable and boring, she simply had to go somewhere. Perry and Lilly wouldn't arrive for a couple of days, Quinn was on a train for Marseilles, she had nowhere to be, and she was in Paris.

She dressed in the simplest dress she had so she wouldn't call attention to herself and let the concierge know she was going out and that she would return shortly in case there were any messages. Then she walked out into the beautiful sun that bathed the city.

Celeste hadn't been entirely sure where she would go, but her feet took her without hesitation down the Avenue de l'Opéra. She felt her heartbeat pick up with every step, not once looking away from the opera house at the end of the street. It was so incredibly beautiful, the large green-domed roof, the striking façade with the gold statues at the upper corners. By the time Celeste stood on the walk in front of the building, her heart was racing.

A small set of stairs led from the small square in front of the building to several entry ports with locked heavy black gates—but the far right gate was open just a bit, and she walked to it.

Act like you belong here and nobody will think twice, Celeste.

She did so, walking straight up the stairs, through the gate and the door it protected and into the main building.

The lights were dim, as there were no public hours, and lighting the vast entry of the Paris Opera House was certainly unnecessary, but Celeste could feel the size of the entry with every step she took. Even as carefully as she walked, she could hear her footsteps echo, telling her of the vastness of the room she'd entered. She crept forward carefully until she came to the grand staircase, which was lit somberly by the few skylights at the roof. Even so, it was dramatic. Even so, it was the most grand staircase she'd ever seen in her life.

She looked around, listening carefully for any hint of another person, then she picked up her skirts and ran through the wash of light and up the stairs to the very top before turning and continuing up as high as she could get in the building. She found herself in a small hallway leading off in both directions, doors along the wall in front of her.

She put her hand to the wall and followed it as far as she dared into the darkness before choosing one of the doors. When she paused to calm her racing heart, she could hear the soft strains of a violin, the notes from a piano, the undertones of the supporting cello, and a few reed instruments, and tears pricked at her eyes. She placed one hand on the seam of the double doors, the other on the handle, and she clicked the latch and pulled it open just enough to slide through. The music washed over her, and she waited, pressed herself to the closed door, and just allowed the sound of it to calm her heart and steady her nerves.

"Attend!" someone said, and Celeste turned, but the voice had come to her from below. The sound carried throughout the auditorium so perfectly it had felt as though the person was just behind her. She couldn't quite see over the balcony rail, so she took two steps forward, and then another, and another. The lights from the stage came into view slowly, and Celeste ducked as she walked to keep them from her. She pulled one of the chairs to the very edge of the box, just behind one of the curtains, and she sat down.

The man who she assumed had spoken was leaning against the edge of the stage, speaking with both the orchestra and the dancers, but she couldn't hear what was being said. She saw him nod, then back up a pace, and everyone went back to their respective places.

Oh God.

The conductor tapped his music stand.

Oh God.

The chin on the lead ballerina came up as she took her place and turned to stone, her pose so perfected that she seemed immovable.

Oh God.

The slow strain of the cello was first, sweet and deep. Long and passionate.

Oh God.

And then the dancer moved, and Celeste's heart soared. She moved across the stage as though she didn't even touch the surface, as though she were a bird in flight, the movement of her arms and legs so smooth and soft that Celeste's bones ached with the want to be just as free as she was.

Before she knew it, Celeste was on her feet and leaning over the rail just to get closer, to watch, to take it in, to feel the wind of the music against her face. It was glorious.

Celeste spent the rest of the day hiding out in the box, listening to the music, and watching the rehearsals. Occasionally, she stood and tried to do some small movement that she'd seen, as if to cast it to her memory for her muscles to recall later. Mostly, she did her best to stay hidden so she wouldn't be thrown out. At the end of the rehearsal, when the dancers looked as exhausted as she was exhilarated, Celeste stood and quietly left the way she'd come, as if she'd never been there, just another phantom in the opera house.

As she returned down Avenue de l'Opéra, she considered the past months, where she had been to where she was now. Her entire life had been upended in a way that she honestly couldn't account for. If she had to draw a map in order to end up in exactly the same place again, she wouldn't know how to do it. She didn't know if she would be brave enough to try.

While Quinn still didn't quite understand her, the important part was that she understood herself in a way she never had before. She'd always questioned herself and her body because she simply didn't feel the things that those around her felt. She didn't experience the same feelings that those around her did. She couldn't fathom the emotions they referred to.

Now, though, she could. She understood that she wasn't like most of the others she'd met. She understood that, for her, being aroused wasn't so much physical as it was mental, and even the mental wasn't truly the same, as she would have thought, because though she didn't want to be touched, she did want to watch Quinn and Calder.

It was their relationship that mattered to her own awakening. It was seeing them together that unlocked whatever it was in her that simply hadn't been interested in passion. It was them, specifically, who gave her the ability to explore her own needs. Certainly there was a modicum of fear associated with the future, but at least Celeste knew she could face it. She knew that whatever came of it, she wasn't alone, which was what she thought she would be.

She'd never thought she would marry a man who would allow her to be herself even if that self didn't conform to the norm. She'd never thought she would find love and passion. She'd never thought she could be happy.

She stopped at the small park a block from the hotel. She was happy. She sat on a bench and considered it, because…this feeling was as unfamiliar to her as lust and passion had been only weeks ago. Her heart felt full and heavy, her chest warm, and she simply could not stop smiling. She covered her mouth with her gloved hand and looked up to the clouds as a flock of pigeons rose to the sky and took off, their wings beating a tattoo as they sent a soft breeze toward her.

She was happy, and she was in love. Perhaps not in the traditional sense. Perhaps not in a sense that made sense. Perhaps not in any sense that had even existed before now. But she was. She knew it like she knew her true name, Grace. She loved Quinn for who he was, for what he'd done for her, for how he cared for her, for the things he did for her, for how he made her feel every day since they met. She loved him. She would tell Quinn once he returned, because she wanted to be sure he understood her, and he had the worst habit of not understanding her.

She stood and hurried back to the hotel, even though there was no true rush, as the telegram she was to send wouldn't be received for a couple of weeks. But she didn't want to change her mind.

> *Keep Going*
>
> *I love you*
>
> *Celeste*

Apparently Celeste was going to tell him she loved him in the telegram. She handed it back to the man with the direction and turned to go to her room. Lilly and Perry would arrive tomorrow, and there was so much in the city to do and see. She needed to rest and be ready for their arrival.

Until then, it was just Celeste in her room with her memories of Calder and Quinn, the giant smile that simply refused to fade, and the ability to take care of herself.

eleste opened the last trunk and pulled out the silk satin ball gown, handing it to the lady's maid.

"Oh, Celeste, this one is beautiful," Lilly said, stopping the girl and reaching out to the layers of fabric that made up the bustle. "The color—it's simply delicious!"

Celeste walked over and ran a finger down the shoulder, fluffed the soft pink skirts. "It's my favorite of them. I can't wait to wear it for Quinn. I know he'll love it."

"Have you heard from him?" Lilly asked.

"No, not since he arrived in Bombay, but I imagine it difficult for him to send anything. I'm sure he will when he can," she said.

"You miss him," Lilly said as she nodded at the girl, who took the dress and left the bedroom to press it and hang it. Lilly turned back to Celeste.

"I do. I miss him terribly. Is that strange to you?"

"No, I know there are many different sorts of love. That of a parent for a child, that of a husband for a wife, love between sisters"—Lilly reached out and took Celeste's hand and squeezed it—"and between friends. I could see the two of you care for each other. That much was plain, but I also know there's more to it than that, or else he wouldn't be off chasing Calder, would he?"

"We are married, Quinn and I, but it was born of necessity."

"And yet, I can see how much he loves you."

"You were at the wedding. You saw—"

"Of course I was, and what I saw was two people who loved each other giving up everything to save one another. I thought it beautiful."

"It was easily one of the worst days of my life—seeing Quinn give up everything he loved to protect me."

"Is that what you think? No, Celeste, he gave up nothing to save you. Your perception is skewed. The two of you were headed toward an agreement as it was…weren't you?"

"Before that night, perhaps, but—"

"But what?"

"But Quinn was going to leave the farce behind. He intended to go after Calder then."

"Celeste." Lilly turned her to look straight at her, held her shoulders. "The day you were married…that was just the beginning of your possibility."

"But Calder won't understand."

"He will, probably more than most. Give him some credit. He knows how this works when one holds a title—or four. He and Quinn cannot marry. He's perfectly aware of that fact."

"But I came between them. It was more than just—"

"Celeste, move forward. You're married. Let the past go."

"I can't, not until Calder comes back. Not until he understands."

"You sent Quinn after him. What more can you do?"

"I don't know, but I have yet to return the favor Quinn bestowed when he married me. Sending him after Calder…"

"That was your apology."

"Yes, of sorts. But it was more than that. It was correcting a wrong. It was making amends, but it was also fixing a rift I'd made long before that. More than anything else, I owe Calder. I cannot make amends to him unless he returns with Quinn and allows me to do that."

"I hope you get that chance," Lilly said. "Because the love I saw between you and Quinn is worth fighting for. I know Calder better than I know most of the family. He's strong and honorable and lovely. He'll understand. He may be hurt right now, but he'll understand." Lilly pulled Celeste close and hugged her.

"I've never felt this for anyone. It's all terribly foreign to me. So is the friendship I've found with you and with Francine. I don't know how to thank you both."

"Don't give it a second thought. You're just as important to me. It's odd, but I've always felt a bit removed from the peerage and a little overwhelmed by the titles. Even though they're family. It's just…I wasn't raised in it, you understand?"

"I do. I understand the feeling of being on the outside, even as the daughter of a marquess."

"Because of your skin."

Celeste nodded, sweeping her hands up and down her forearms. She looked at her hands. "Yes, I was never accepted by my family because of my skin. I was never quite accepted by society because of that lack of support from my family. I was never quite accepted by men and women of color, even those in the gentry, because of my status. I had no one. Until I met Quinn. Meeting him…it was like coming home."

"That I understand entirely," Lilly said. "I couldn't possibly live without Perry. Listen, I'll leave you to settle in. We'll have supper early, in a couple hours."

"Thank you, Lilly."

They hugged again, and Lilly kissed her cheek. "See you soon."

The door shut behind her, and Celeste turned back to the chest, pulled out a photograph of Quinn from Paris. She missed him, that much was true. She missed him very much. She missed Calder as well, even if she hardly knew the man. His presence in Quinn's life was a tangible thing. Quinn was a better man when they walked together. Quinn was a different man when Calder was missing from his life. He was a shell, he wasn't whole. It was painful to see, and they had to figure this out, and Celeste believed, somehow, that they would. Quinn would bring Calder home and then… what then?

She didn't know.

But she could imagine things.

Like seeing Calder touching Quinn again.

Like watching as Quinn brought Calder off with only his mouth, maybe his hands.

Like being a witness to their passion.

Calder would never trust her enough to allow her that close to them again. But she would have them forever where she needed them—in her mind. She didn't even have to actually be there to see Calder shove Quinn over, see him push his fingers in Quinn's arse, see him slide—*Oh God*, she should stop.

She turned to the cheval mirror, her face flushed. She waved her hands in front of it to cool off. Watched how her chest rose and fell heavily, her breasts pushing against the edge of the corset behind her shirtwaist. She lifted her arms, undoing all the buttons on her shirtwaist, her skirts, untying her petticoats, letting all the fabric fall to the floor around her feet.

With her left hand, she held one of the four heavy posts on her bed. With her right, she lifted her breasts out of the corset until her nipples rested at the edge, the pressure from the boning enough to send strings of excitement surging through her blood. She skimmed her hand down the corset, the skin of her abdomen such a soft, sweet contrast to the brocade silk.

She let her hand hover there, over her pussy, feeling the heat, letting it warm her, and she closed her eyes.

Calder pushed his fingers into Quinn, readying him for the full force of his cock entering his body. The look on Quinn's face—the tension mixed with pure, unadulterated pleasure—stole her breath. It was an expression she was familiar with now. An expression she yearned to see again. Her breath picked up again.

Calder shifted, lined up behind Quinn. He took his cock in hand as he held on to Quinn's hip, steadying him, and Celeste's hand met her pussy. Her middle finger teased her softly, slipping between the folds of her skin. Calder thrust, and so did she. That first push made Quinn's hand clench on the doorframe, and hers clenched on the bed post as she felt for the spot—the one just there that made her blood heavy, made it pulse against her finger.

Calder grabbed Quinn's shoulders as he thrust. She grabbed her mons as her fingers worked, and her body clenched and Quinn cried out. Calder released him, letting him slide to the floor. Celeste let go and turned, pulling the chair from the secretary over to the cheval. She stood next to it, her hand running along the furled wooden back above the inlaid cushion. This chair had no arms to rest on, though.

She looked at the seat and remembered how Quinn's fingers had pressed to the seat of another chair, how he'd tasted the wetness that had pooled between her legs. Her knees buckled. She turned the back of the chair to face the cheval, gripped the wood, put one knee on the seat, and leaned forward, pressing her breasts against the wood, watching her expression in the mirror, searching.

Quinn. *Calder*.

Calder sitting in the chair, Quinn hovering over him, Calder's hands on his arse. She smoothed one hand back, over her own arse, and slid it between her legs from behind as Calder pulled Quinn down over his cock. Two fingers slid into her vagina as another teased her clitoris, and a chill rushed her skin as her body heat soared.

Quinn stood and walked to the bed as Calder watched, then scooted back into the pillows and took himself in hand. He slid his other hand around his leg and pushed one finger in his own arse, and Celeste…she circled that tight ring of hypersensitive flesh with one finger, slick with her own fluid.

She teased herself, remembering how Quinn had done it. He pulled at his cock with one hand, and she pushed past that tight ring with her other, and she lifted up, straddling the chair as she ground her pussy into one hand and the other moved slowly—so slowly—until her body jerked, shook, shuddered, then collapsed against the soft velvet back of the chair, the furled wood biting her cheek.

That inimitable peace washed over her, and Celeste relaxed into it for a moment. Savoring it. Then she stood and dragged her body to the bathroom and ran a bath. She came off again, then soaked for a while.

As she crawled into bed, she vowed—once again—that no matter what happened next, she would be certain that Calder and Quinn were together, and were happy, no matter what she had to do to see to it. Quinn had done for her what no one ever had. He'd cared for her without reservation. He'd allowed her rein to discover herself and use him to whatever end she needed. He loved her unconditionally.

Loved her for who she was even if that meant he could never have what he thought it was he wanted from her. Loved her enough to want to give her the world and let her be.

As Celeste drifted off on these thoughts, she realized she was happier than she ever had been, happier than she had ever hoped to be, happier than anyone had any right to be.

Celeste had found herself. Now she had to work to find her place in his world.

Celeste is autochorissexual.

Autochorissexuality is a subset of asexuality. Celeste would probably identify as gray asexual in the 21st century.

She is also a woman of color. Her grandmother is from Capri, her family most likely immigrants.

Her hero, Quinn, is bisexual—the spare.

His hero, Calder, is gay—the heir to a duke.

This book is Celeste's story, it's her sexual awakening, her HFN. The next book is Calder and Quinn's HEA.

So, when I say Quinn's her hero, it's not in the traditional romance genre sense.

Except it also is.

The reason I'm labeling them here is because I refuse to marginalize or participate in any sort of erasure by not stating exactly how Celeste, Calder, and Quinn each identify. Or how they would most likely identify in the 21st century.

"And what is the use of a book, "
thought Alice,
"without pictures or conversations? "

Alice's Adventures in Wonderland
-Lewis Carroll

find me:

If you loved this book you can join my newsletter to be notified of releases before they come out, and to participate in fun giveaways.

JennLeBlanc.com

@JennLeBlanc

IllustratedRomance.com

Facebook.com/IllustratedRomance

9 781944 567170